THE ANCIENT NEMESIS

ERIC WILKINS

ISBN:
978-1-952874-26-0 (paperback)
978-1-952874-27-7 (hardback)
978-1-952874-28-4 (ebook)

Printed in New York by:

OMNIBOOK CO.
99 Wall Street, Suite 118
New York, NY 10005
USA
+1-866-216-9965
www.omnibookcompany.com

For e-book purchase: Kindle on Amazon, Barnes and Noble
Book purchase: Amazon.com, Barnes & Noble, and
www.omnibookcompany.com

Omnibook titles may be purchased in bulk for educational, business,
fund-raising, or sales promotional use. For more information please
e-mail info@omnibookcompany.com

DEDICATION

To my sister Teresa Washburn, her husband Spencer and all the Washburn family for allowing this entity to enjoy a little bit of heaven's beauty, under the starry Marion, N.C. mountain skies. Thanks for allowing me camping privileges on your private beautiful mountain.

Thanks to all the brave astronauts of space exploring nations who have the bravest, and most dangerous jobs out of this world. I envy them so. But most of all! Thanks to the best Mama from planet Earth, Ruth Anstead Wilkins, who passed away, July 7th 2002. I miss her so. She believed in me. Now I do too.

CONTENTS

PROLOGUE

For the first time in many years, humans from Earth set out from Mars base, to explore the unknowns of the outer solar system. After the Mars base had been completed, funds were depleted and it took more time than originally estimated, for the mining operations to pay off the massive debts. Now, with the profits begging to roll in, the I.S.D.C or International Space Development Corporation, had begun to demand budgeting for new exploration and research.

A crew of four were chosen, based upon their specialized education, experience, and ability to work together in a long term isolation from other humans. The human need for companionship was not overlooked, and after some debate two couples were decided upon.

The crew of four were awakened from cryogenic suspended animation, as the explorer ship Nova silently approached the small worlds, barely projecting in the forward monitor screen.

Mission commander Johnny Adam Wilkins, First officer Eric Paul Alley along with Operations specialist Joanna Elizabeth Wright and Mission specialist Christy Armstrong Alley readied Nova for the exploration into the unknown territory of the Pluto Charon system.

Twentieth century knowledge and facts of theses mysterious worlds predicted that Pluto and Charon were merely small cold Kuiper belt objects that always presented the same face toward each other. Knowledge was soon to be assimilated to the contrary of what anyone imagined.

Inward burned a bright yellow star that sustained all known life in this solar system. One astronomical unit away was planet Earth, the most beautiful planet known at the time. That is until this adventure to the Pluto Charon system began.

The year now, twenty-one eighty-seven, and humankind had explored much of the inner planet systems but never before had any humans from Earth traveled this far out toward the edge of our solar system.

The story begins.

CHAPTER ONE

THE ARRIVAL

Nova and crew approached the Pluto Charon system, at a speed of thirty kilometers per second. Nova's engines fired sporadic bursts gradually slowing for rendezvous with this mysterious double world system and its five known moons. Even now at two days distance, these worlds seemed so small in the forward viewpoint with the large moon Charon eclipsing Pluto approximately every five hours.

These small worlds orbited each other like no other worlds known. None of the crew knew what mysteries lay ahead or what they might discover. Visual and radar were uncertain on exactly what these two heavenly bodies were made of and very little was known about their surface features and composition of atmospheres. These were certainly four brave souls that were prepared and qualified for exploration.

CONVERSATION ON THE COMMAND DECK.

"Telemetry confirmed," Johnny read the data out loud that was obtained from the forward long range scanner satellite probe. "This is unreal. He exclaimed, his eyes opening wide as he studied the printout from the ship's main computer.

The crew listened with amazement as he began to read this fascinating data. "Pluto's appears to be just a little larger than Charon but has only one tenth the mass and gravity of Charon. Pluto's data reads to be approximately one thousand four-hundred eighty-five miles in diameter. That's smaller than the Earth's Moon with one-tenth Earth gravity, while Charon's diameter is approximately one thousand miles but with gravity ten times that of Pluto," he finished "How could that be?", Eric, the first officer exclaimed. "That moon has gravity equal to Earth. It also has an atmosphere but long range scanners can't discern what it consists of yet. We're still too far away." Joanna spoke up. "Nothing in the solar system has a mass that dense. That just can't be. I've never seen anything like this before. It would seem that instead of Charon orbiting Pluto, Pluto's orbiting Charon."

"Yeah," Eric agreed. "The fact is that Pluto's got one tenth gravity while Charon's reading gravity equal almost to Earth's but the center point of gravity is very close to Charon." "OK.",Johnny sighed, then ordered "Joanna, You and Christy check out both Landers and keep in constant radio contact. I'm going to put Nova into a three second per revolution spin. That will give us about one tenth gravity aboard the ship. Eric and I are going to see what other data we can configure on Pluto and Charon and contact Mars base to inform them of our current status."

The crew immediately went about their duties as Nova was forty two hours away from rendezvous with the two mysterious dancing worlds. Silently but swiftly the four brave astronauts and Nova crossed the final dark void toward unknown discoveries. The message would take five and a half hours to reach the fourth planet, which was now on the same side of the sun as the expedition. The vast distance between planets was so immense that even at the speed of light the digital light beam message would take hours to traverse the huge span of dark void between worlds.

"Mars base will be delighted when they received all of this fantastic data we've transmitted," Eric said, as he finished sending the broadcast on the high frequency transmitter. Every two hundred and twenty eighty Earth years the Pluto Charon system became the eighth planet from the sun, as they crossed above Neptune's orbit and remained there for about twenty years until they again crossed above Neptune's orbit headed outward on their long, seventeen degrees off plain, elliptical journey. The mysterious pair of planets and their moons were now well above Neptune's orbit, heading inward, as Nova and its explorers gradually slowed their approach to the orbiting group of small dark penlight worlds. Nova the exploration ship was a remarkable piece of twenty-third century technology. Total length of the ship was two hundred and thirty-six meters. Nova was assembled in Mars orbit, taking more than two years to construct before Nova and crew were launched on March third, twenty-one eighty-six. Now January sixth, 2187. Nova and crew silently sailed closer to their intended destination.

U.S.S. Nova was a beautiful vessel that was essentially three ships. The forward command module that sustained the crew and two landers in case of the necessity of a rescue mission. Every contingency had been equipped and all systems had at least one backup for safety. There was no chance of a speedy rescue from Mars Base. All they could depend on in this far away journey were themselves, and this good ship Nova.

So far, all had progressed well as the crew gathered for their final main briefing, before rendezvous with the approaching pair of, never explored, never directly viewed worlds. Then following awakening, the conversation begins.

Johnny's voice broke the silence, "Listen up crew! Here's where we stand. We're twenty four hours away and this will be the last major briefing before we arrive. Eric and I have examined our options and decided on a figure eight orbit around Pluto and Charon. That orbit will bring us to an approximate altitude of one hundred sixty-one kilometers above the surface of Charon. We'll then fire full retro and pass behind Charon and on toward an orbit, a little less than ninety-two kilometers above Pluto's surface. Therefore, we'll be making one complete figure eight orbit of both worlds every five hours. This should allow us ample time to scan each planet before making a decision on which to explore first. Once we've unanimously made that decision, this exploration orbit will allow us to commit to an elliptical orbit of either Pluto or Charon.

He nodded toward Eric as he ended his brief. Eric, give us your latest update on the forward scanner information." "Right!", Eric followed. "We've decelerated to approximately twenty-five kilometers per second and are on a perfect intercept course. Ships overall status is one hundred percent and all systems on the forward command ship are in excellent shape. Nova's main nuclear hydrogen engines are working perfectly. Remaining fuel level at ninety-three percent including the extra fifty thousand gallon hydrogen oxygen reserve fuel tanks strapped between the two landers."

"The long range forward scanners can't tell us much more than we've already learned. There is a very curious anomaly that shows Charon's temperature and atmospheric pressure to be warmer and denser than anyone had imagined. Temperature estimate not exact, but reading approximately a thousand degrees Fahrenheit. Atmospheric pressure reading at surface is .875 millibars," he continued.

"We're still too far away to tell exactly what the atmosphere consists of yet. But there's no way this moon should be that warm. If these readings are correct, there must be an inner heating source inside this amazing small moon. We're too far out for it to receive very much radiation from the sun. This truly is remarkable. Charon defies all logic and explanations of physics. But that's why we're here, to learn what's out here. We're on our own out here. We have each other to depend on and good old Nova is our only lifeline," Eric finished solemnly.

"How did the two Landers check out?", Johnny asked

"Christy and I checked out both Landers eight hours ago and they both checked out one hundred percent perfect. Explorer one and two are ready to go. No problems detected anywhere."

"O.K.," Johnny captained. "I know we're all excited but we're only twenty-three hours away from trans-insertion orbit burn. We'll need some rest before we arrive. Eric, Joanna and Christy, I recommend that the three you should get a few hours rest while I stand first watch. As soon as you've all rested six hours, I'll catch a few hours sleep before we arrive. That's my direct order." Johnny's voice echoed throughout the ship. The three astronauts retired to their adequate quarters to ponder possibilities and induce temporary rest. They'd been on duty for hours and soon they were induced to sleep in programmed separate cryogenic chambers

CHAPTER TWO
THE INCIDENT

The grand ship Nova and crew sped silently swiftly ahead with Johnny sitting studiously at the controls while the others slept. Four hours had passed as he'd watched and studied the monitor readouts of the forward radar screen. The system was growing gradually larger by the hour. Johnny's mind was deep in thought when abruptly he was startled to reality by an alarm sounding from the forward radar. An explosion in the aft lander shook Nova violently. Eyes wide-open Johnny restrained himself in one tenth gravity attempting to bring Nova out of it's induced gravity spin. Nova shook and rumbled in the shockwave of an invisible swift object knocking Johnny unconscious to the floor. Johnny awoke staring into the faces of two beautiful girls and one rugged, bearded older male face. "

"What the heck happened, boy?", Eric asked, looking extremely concerned.

Eric helped Johnny to his feet and he began rubbing his head while mumbling. "I'm not sure," while struggling to gather his thoughts and composure.

Eric spoke again, "You must have bumped your head on the forward console. We were awakened by the mini-bot and found you in the floor unconscious." Joanna and Christy injected you with a stimulate and put a patch on your head.

Johnny then suddenly realizing the throbbing pain in his head reached up to touch his bandaged bump. "Man!", he exclaimed. "That sucker really hurts."

The girls helped him further to his control chair. "Sit down," Joanna ordered, "Get your head together." They all then headed to their own stations strapping themselves into their chairs.

Eric spoke, "The ship is stabilized. You've been out about an hour. The minibots reacted to the collision and stabilized the ship before awakening us from our sleep."

"Sheesh," Johnny mumbled.

Eric continued, "We're about ten hours away from orbit insertion burn and we seem to have sustained some damage to Lander One. I don't know what the heck happened. I haven't even had the chance yet to go back and check out all of the damage. When you get your thoughts together, try to remember any thing about what actually happened."

Johnny, still groggy, but thinking back to the moments before the explosion, sat up now in his chair, rubbing his head. "It's coming back now!", he exclaimed. "I remember. It came out from behind Charon." He looked over at Eric's concerned face.

"What came out? What are you saying?", Eric's look was incredulous.

"Radar tracking picked up an incoming target that came from behind Charon," Johnny insisted. "I know what I saw," he said, "and the evidence is here in the recorder. Some kind of a dark thing approached us fast from behind Charon, then looped behind and then the explosion happened," he insisted adamantly. "Then the radar records it returning back toward Pluto as quickly as it appeared. That's the last thing I remember before I hit my head." Johnny finished while gently rubbing on his throbbing head wound.

Eric, Christy, and Joanna now looked at him even more concerned than before.

"You've got to be kidding," Eric said. "There are no aliens way out here. I think you must have a concussion. Are you sure it was real?"

"Yes it was totally real, and I didn't say aliens." ,Johnny snapped back. "I said something dark came from behind that moon and then there was an explosion. It moved way too fast to track accurately. I don't know what it was. It certainly scared the mess out of me though. I've never seen anything like it. It just suddenly appeared out of nowhere.

Then the explosion and I awoke staring up at the three of your faces. I know what I saw, dang it! It was real. Something sure put a hole in number two Lander. Didn't It? We'd better go back and check it out ASAP and attempt to repair the damage."

"Okay then," Eric shook his head. "You and Joanna stay and monitor the console. Christy and I will go back to check out the Lander and attempt to make repairs."

"Stay in radio contact," Johnny ordered. "We're nine and a half hours from orbit entry. Call me as soon as you've analyzed the damage."

"Right!", Eric agreed getting to his feet and steadying himself in the light gravity.

Christy was already ahead of Eric, saying, "we'd better suit up. The damaged Lander's showing a rupture and zero pressure and a small amount of radiation."

"Right!", Eric replied. "We'll have to make an e.v.a outside to weld a plate over the rupture. I'll need to haul up the welder from the center cargo bay. I'll meet you back at the lander entry hatch in about fifteen minutes." Christy made her way back toward the rear of Nova's cargo storage bay. She approached the hatch to the disabled Lander.

"I'd better wait for Eric," she thought while checking out her suit pressure and air status. Thinking back to her last exit of this same hatch when she and Joanna had sealed it upon their final check. "What could have happened?" She pondered. "The lander was fine then."

Just as her thoughts ended. Eric approached hauling the repair equipment on a floating cargo buggy with his helmet dangling from his right hand.

"Give me a minute. I've got to finish suiting up. I've got to check my gauges." ,Eric insisted snapping his helmet lock with a click, then pressurizing his suit.

Christy hadn't heard a word that he'd said until now when his radio suddenly crackled into her helmet.

"Am I transmitting?"

"Loud and clear," Christy answered back. "Lets get the utility cart into the depressurization bay."

They glided the tool cart in together with just enough room left for the two suited astronauts. The hatch sealed as they tripped the beam of light and Christy entered the command that controlled the decompression pump. A bright red light illuminated above as the cabin air supply evaporated the remaining air into the void of space. The pressure dropped and the temperature became 459 below zero or absolute zero.

Eric reached for the latch and the remaining air escaped from the small cabin as the hatch slid open revealing the inside dark shadow of the cylinder hall that was thirty meters in length. The cold vacuum of space instantly kissed their suits as Christy and Eric stepped inside the airless Lander.

Christy was the first to notice the fragments of debris in the isle half way up the long tube that led to the main deck of the Lander.

CHAPTER THREE
MYSTERY ROCK

"It looks like a small dense meteorite rock," she ascertained, approaching the eerie fragment in the barely lit center of the chamber.

"Be careful. Don't touch that stuff.", Eric said as they both focused their helmet lights down at the pulsating black matter.

"Let's get up to the main controls and get some light in here." They both stared up at the puncture hole ten feet above them. "Looks to be about ten inches." ,Christy noted as they quickly moved on toward the blinking console and the four empty cabin seats ahead.

They glided into the forward chairs and strapped themselves momentarily in.

"I'm bringing up the lights." Eric engaged the breaker on the console in front of him and to the left.

The ship was suddenly full of light and their eyes began adjusting to the sudden change.

"The lander appears to be normal," Eric spoke up. "That is as far as power and fuel supply status is concerned."

His left glove began clearing moisture frost from the gauges that showed the smaller ship's status. He flipped the switch that brought the ships pulse engines on line and the Lander hummed to life in the cold environment of space. He then tested the ships smaller thrusters gently tugging at the controls.

Johnny's voice crackled into their helmet. 'What's the status?'

"The Lander appears to be in apparent good shape." Christy replied.

"That is except for a ten inch hole in the corridor ceiling." Eric spoke up. "It's going to take us a few hours to repair that hole. We'll have to go outside to weld a plate."

"O.K. then." Johnny returned. "I'm temporarily shutting down the braking engines and gravity rotation while you guys are outside the ship. We don't want to take any chances."

"How's your head?" Eric asked.

"Oh! I'm alright now," Johnny replied. "Headache's almost gone. I'll be fine. We haven't had any more activity from the planets. Everything's quiet now. You'd better hurry up. We're only eight hours away from orbit entry."

"Oh!" Christy spoke up. "We also need to do something about that dark matter in the bay floor. It appears to be a strange dark pulsating black rock about six by two inches. We'll stow the intrusion rock in a containment module for later analysis."

"Okay then," Johnny's voice crackled again. "Get that hole sealed and get back up here as soon as possible. We're going to need that back up Lander."

"Roger that then." Eric ended his message and floated toward the outside air lock.

CHAPTER FOUR

OUTSIDE EXCURSION

They rode the magnetic excursion platform that floated freely through the hatch that opened to the blackness of space. They moved cautiously along the outside hull of the Lander and came to a halt a meter below the damaged area of the ship. Christy provisionally attached the platform magnetically to the ships hull just below the rupture hole. Eric activated the welder as Christy held a meter diameter, round metal panel up against the hull. Eric braced himself into the foot restraints and started working to weld the plate.

The torch acted as a small retro rocket engine and it was all Eric could do to resist the backward force. Once the plate was tack welded, Christy seeing his difficulty let go of the plate and fastened herself in the foot restraints directly behind Eric to stabilize the backward force from the torch and Eric was then better able to weld a perfect bead around the patch.

"There! I think that's about got it." Eric exclaimed upon completion.

"We've been out here about one hour eleven minutes." Christy informed.

"Not bad. That weld looks like it will hold just fine. Lets get back inside and pressurize the Lander and check it out for leaks." They disengaged from the hull and floated gracefully back toward the awaiting open hatch and the inner safety of the ship. The platform slowly glided through the cargo lock and the hatch sealed behind them.

"I'll fill her up with atmosphere while you get that strange rock or what ever it is under containment," Eric suggested. "You'd better be careful. We don't know anything about that stuff. You should engage the mini-bot to handle it. It'll be a lot safer."

"O.K.," Christy agreed. She floated away in the zero gravity toward the cargo storage of the mini robot station.

The small metallic half meter being hummed to life as she activated the artificial intelligent robotic device. She typed her command code into the odd looking creatures keyboard. (R.A 2) Robot assistant two.

They felt the return of one tenth gravity as Johnny reengaged the ships rotation.

"Execute task." She typed the detailed job description into its tiny keyboard. The robot followed her exit and then hovered toward the awaiting mysterious dark rock.

She stood five meters back and watched as the little creature attempted to pick up the dark rock and placed it in the awaiting containment box. The small robot strained as it lifted the six inch rock into a quick analysis position directly over it's head.

Even though the ship was now back under light gravity it was a strenuous task for the little robot to move the rock into the containment box.

CHAPTER FIVE
FORBIDDEN DARK MATTER

"This certainly is strange dense matter." Christy thought. "That little six by two inch rock fragment weighs eighty pounds in one tenth gravity. That's amazing." She exclaimed silently to herself. "This jagged dark rock is like nothing anyone had ever encountered."

Never had any human laid eyes on such a mysterious object. It was blacker than any black known. The rock radiated heat as it pulsated in the containment box.

She commanded R.A.2 to seal and store the box and went forward to report her mysterious initial findings to the rest of the crew over the radio.

Eric brought the cabin pressure back to normal as she approached him removing her helmet.

"Seven hours to insertion burn." Johnny injected over the speaker. "You guys need to get on back up here and help get ready." he insisted. "We'll worry about that rock later when there's more time."

"O.K.", Eric replied. "As soon as I power down the lander we're on our way. We'll be there shortly."

After stowing the gear and exiting the lander they made their way back through the long center of the main ship to where Joanna and Johnny sat in their console chairs on the main deck.

"Orbit insertion burn in twelve hours and ten minutes." Johnny informed. "Is everything all right with the Lander?" "Perfect now'" Eric replied. "That is with the exception of that weird rock stored in the main center cargo bay." "That sure is some exceptional weird matter."

Christy reported. "A quick analysis by the mini robot shows a super dense material unlike anything yet known."

"O.K. Well done. I hear you all." Johnny said. "Lets get our minds off that rock and onto those two big rocks approaching in the forward view screen."

The view of the approaching worlds was growing by the hour as the ships engines again braked gradually toward the Plutonian system.

Joanna radioed the present status of the situation back toward Mars base and the crew diligently prepared for the important retro burn that would put them into orbit around the dancing worlds.

The drama and suspense had begun to take serious effect on the crew. The crew had very little sleep especially Johnny the one who knew this ship best inside and out.

Nova and crew sailed to within one hour away from insertion burn. "Let's all get to our stations and strap in Johnny commanded."

Johnny sat high in the forward chair while Joanna sat in the right forward chair. She monitored the radar telemetry. Christy sat the chair directly behind Johnny. It was her duty to monitor the distance and along with Joanna supply Johnny and Eric with essential data as they approached toward their destination that loomed ahead.

It was Eric's job to monitor the entire over all status of Nova and the Landers.

The clock ticks away seconds and Nova falls toward the two dark, eerie worlds and Johnny takes full command.

"I'm bringing us out of our gravity spin"

The ship strained against the resistance of rotation as Johnny fired the side thrusters.

He brought the ship to zero rotation and they became weightless as Christy called out telemetry.

"Charon's downrange nine thousand kilometers and we're approaching at eleven point six kilometers per second." "We're quickly picking up speed as we get closer to the high gravity moon." Joanna reported.

"OK." Johnny Captained . "We've got to slow down to eight point eight kilometers per second to achieve figure eight proper orbit."

"Charon, six thousand kilometers down range speed now twelve point three k.p.s." Christy reported.

"Two minutes until engine burn." Johnny brought the ships mighty engines on line as he skillfully rolled the ship around to face it's engines toward the leading edge of the dark light moon that now grew in size by the second.

"Ten seconds!" he spoke anxiously. The four chairs turned opposite just before Johnny pushed the red breaker to fire the nuclear hydrogen main engines to slow them down for orbit insertion. The engine roared to life like mighty thunder as the trio of crafts fought the resistance of the small high gravity world that pulled them more and more by the second. Nova shook and rattled as the engines slowed them from the heavy pull of Charon's gravity.

"We're down to nine point two k.p.s and slowing," Christy yelled, over the engine roar. "Let them burn!" she exclaimed excitedly." Charon's two thousand four hundred nineteen kilometers downrange."

"Ships total status looks good." Eric reported.

"Thirty seconds until engine shutdown!" Johnny screamed above the thunderous roar. "How's our speed?"

"Nine point three k.p.s and slowing." Christy shouted back.

"Ten seconds," Johnny readied his right hand on the breaker.

"Eight by eight k.p.s", Christy shouted.

Johnny threw the breaker, the engines fell silent and the dark light eerie moon rolled by beneath Nova.

For the first time they had a view of a mysterious round dark body with a thin hazy purplish radiating infrared atmosphere. Radar telemetry read one hundred sixty one kilometers above the surface. The swirling purple hazy clouds above Charon rolled by beneath. Suddenly as they fell around Charon a beautiful Pluto popped into spectacular view.

"Oh my!" Joanna shrieked. "Look at Pluto. It's got a giant heart, It's so beautiful!" she exclaimed. "It's a small marbled purple blue world with pink purplish clouds." And, It's got a land mass that is almost heart shaped.

" And look over there." Christy exclaimed excitedly. "What in the blue blazes universe is that? It appears Pluto has another tiny moon orbiting very close to it. It's too far away to make out yet. That makes a total of six tiny moons encircling this pair of worlds. That's a total of eight bodies in this system including Pluto and Charon."

"Man oh man!" Johnny beamed. "Nobody's ever going to believe this."

" There is very little solar radiation out here but Charon seems to be giving off heat from within. Pluto has a light atmosphere thirty five kilometers thick and Charon's atmosphere is forty nine kilometers thick. Charon's atmospheric pressure data reads, eight hundred and seventy five millibars and Pluto's reading three hundred and four millibars. That's incredible." Eric thought out loud.

"We expected these worlds to be frozen dead bodies but would you look at that!" Johnny boasted. "The two worlds orbit each other approximately twelve thousand, two hundred miles apart."

"It appears that Pluto orbits Charon once every five hours and Pluto also rotates once on it's axis every ten Days. The moon Charon is emitting infrared dark light radiation in the form of dark body heat. It's much hotter than we expected. It also is heating the immediate area of Pluto's orbit." Christy reported, after a bit of computing.

" OK crew!" Johnny brought order back to the excited clan. "Lets get ready this is not over yet. What's our position?"

"We're approximately seventeen thousand kilometers from Pluto and our speed is nine point five K.P.S. We're scheduled for the next engine burn in one half hour." Joanna reported.

Eric spoke up. "What's the information on the small moon orbiting close to Pluto? What can you tell us about it?"

" It appears to orbit Pluto approximately once every ten days approximately four hundred eighty seven kilometers above the surface. It always remains on the dark side in a gyrosyncronous orbit. It's a tiny circular moon approximately sixteen kilometers in diameter. All these worlds are perfectly round and the most fascinating fact is that Charon is rotating on its axis extremely fast once every fifty eight seconds." Joanna reported.

"This whole area of space is bathed in ultraviolet dark light emanating from Charon. Unbelievable Beauty," she added. "Everything's glowing in black ultraviolet light."

For the first time they noticed the purple glow of their white space suits and the total cabin of Nova aglow with eerie dark light. The approaching world Pluto ahead was also lit on one half of its circumference with purple blue hazy light while the tiny moon always on Pluto's far side reflecting it's pale beam of dark light toward Pluto's night. A remarkable sight to behold indeed. And to top it all off, the purple pink hazy clouds in the stratosphere of Pluto's dayside made a scene that any artist would aspire to paint on canvas.

"Seven thousand kilometers downrange and closing fast." Christy's voice brought the crew back from their trance in the mist of the beauty of this all.

" Roger that!" Johnny replied.

"Speed now, ten point six k.p.s and increasing velocity. Prepare for second burn in nine minutes and thirty seconds from my mark. Mark!"

Eric programmed the digits into the computer. "Trajectory looks perfect." Joanna reported. "We're right on course."

Johnny readied the powerful engines again vectoring them toward the purple lit Pluto ahead.

"This will be a big burn." Eric reported. "We'll need to slow down to five point six k.p.s. That will put us on parallel figure eight loop course back toward Charon with a final minor trajectory burst required as we loop around Charon. Remaining fuel status will then be at eighty six percent hydrogen remaining with oxygen cylinders at ninety one percent."

"Buckle in!" Johnny ordered.

The four recliner chairs flipped around again one hundred eighty degree's with their backs toward Pluto. The mighty nuclear hydrogen engines again ignited in the eerie strange dark light of this far away system. Nova shook and vibrated this time more intensely than before. The thunder of its engines braking more furiously as they were forced further back into their seats by the tremendous gravity forces. The furry grew even more intense when Johnny brought the engines up to eighty percent power.

"We're down to eight by six k.p.s and slowing!" Christy shouted above the engine roar.

"Burn Nova burn!" Johnny screamed above the rumble almost laughing with excitement as the crew rode the three ship rocket that brought them so far from home.

"Six point nine k.p.s." Christy reported loudly.

"Engine shutdown in ten seconds." Eric's voice cracked. "Five by eight." Christy's voice echoed after the fury fire ended. Then there was total silence.

Nova fell around the dark side of the purple blue, pink marble world. Billions of miles from life on Earth and on the outer edge of this solar system, no one could have possibly dreamed this beauty existed this far out from Sol.

Pluto until this moment had never been seen close up directly by human eyes. Pluto was so far away from Earth that telescopes could only see two small specks surrounded by tinier specks. Now this. A nine hundred mile diameter infrared light mini star, that exists on the edge of the solar system nurturing and sustaining Pluto.

As the ship rolled behind the dark side of Pluto they were startled by the abrupt loss of the purple black light that lit half of Pluto and its three smaller moons.

Into total darkness the craft sailed a blacker blackness than any had ever experienced. The details of the surface on Pluto's night were invisible to the eye. Radar revealed areas of water and mineral ore content in several locations. The only light anywhere came from the tiny moons dull glow. No one spoke as the ships analyzers gathered continuous information and data. The CPU recorder clicked steadily away while the dark side of Pluto rolled beneath their ship.

Johnny gave an order that broke the silence. "We're rotating slightly. Engage lateral thrusters."

Joanna complied. The mini thrusters barely could be heard as they fired short burst to stabilize the slightly spinning ship.

"Stable figure eight orbit achieved." Eric read his data out loud. "Speed five by seven k.p.s, altitude sixty three kilometers above Pluto."

Laughter broke among the crew when the ships mini robot chanted the words, "Condition Nominal. Ship status Normal. Figure eight orbit achieved!" It repeated the phrase again while the crew laughed and clasped hands in celebration of the whimsical robots report on status.

"Well done indeed!" Johnny congratulated the crew while polishing the minibots dome with a few quick rubs and then the crew of four slapped hands again in success.

The ships inside lights seemed dull in the darkness of Pluto's shadow. The celebration ended as quickly as it began when suddenly Nova and crew emerged from darkness into beautiful ultraviolet purple black radiation.

" Wow!" Joanna spoke first.

"It's absolutely beautiful!" Christy exclaimed.

For the very first time they viewed the entire system as a unit. Fabulous Pluto and its tiny moons passing behind them as they coasted silently again toward the dark light emitting Charon ahead.

Far past Charon shone a brilliant distant yellow star. Sol the brightest star to be seen was over fifty astronomical units away. The Majestically imposed Charon lit the immediate area with its dark warm light. The crews heads bobbed back in forth between the visual of the two major worlds in total awe of the beauty of the entire scene.

Nova was now safely in a figure eight orbit that brought it to each world every two and a half hours or one completion of the figure eight orbit every five hours and six minutes.

Johnny designated command of the ship to the lead mini-bot. The little mechanical entity was well able to sail Nova between the two worlds.

R.A.1. studiously armed the mini thruster's and stabilized the exploration orbit to a precision status.

CHAPTER SIX
THE EUREKA MESSAGE

"Nova Commander's log, Star date January thirteenth, Twenty one eighty-seven. The crew of Nova expedition radioed Mars base the news and data pictures of the successful deorbit around Pluto and Charon. End log."

At this distance from Earth at the speed of light, it would take their data message well over five hours to reach Mars base. They will have orbited the bodies again before Mars base and all on Earth received the Message of EUREKA. And several more times before they received a reply. It was absolutely imperative that Mars base be the first contact point. Earth at present in a straight line was behind Jupiter's orbital plane and direct communication wasn't possible because of Jupiter's radiation interference with radio data streams.

This journey by humans is merely beginning. How could the robotics Voyager and Horizon crafts of the twenty first century have ever discovered this? Even if the Horizon mission did pass within a few thousand kilometers their twentieth century sensors could not have recorded the rare beauty of the dark ultraviolet mini planetary system.

This exploration journey was destined for human eyes and intellect only. Only human words could describe the Awe and humbleness of being here in this hidden far system of dark light worlds.

The onboard processors clicked away recording the mysterious scientific facts of Pluto and Charon and Thimbus the moon, newly named by Johnny, was sixteen kilometers in diameter orbiting very close to Pluto.

The crew were exhausted. Many hours had passed since anyone had rested and fatigue was very evident among them. The past few days since awakening had been strenuous and the crew agreed to get some sleep while the mini robot monitored and fine tuned the status of the sling shot figure eight orbit.

While they rested the data continued to be processed by the computers aboard Nova. The cryogenic sleep suspenders were also capable of controlled hourly sleep rates to let the astronauts rest well in challenging situations. The four humans dreamed away of discoveries and exploration.

CHAPTER SEVEN
LIFE ! INTELLIGENT LIFE

Nova had coasted around the system two more times before they gathered around the galley ten hours later. Their minds were fresh and alert after being induced into a much needed rest. The ship was back in a spin to simulate one tenth gravity. They ate their meals and discussed the awesome data the computer had collected while they slept.

Suddenly, Eric's eyes lit up as he read in astonishment the data fact sheet beside his cup of coffee. The pastry in his right hand fell continuously as if it were in slow motion floating down to the table with perfect processional grace then bouncing slightly several times before settling.

Eric grabbed up the sheet of paper from the table and commanded attention instantly by saying,

"Listen to this!" as he stood up. "Pluto's atmosphere consist of oxygen 21 percent, nitrogen 63 percent and carbon dioxide 15 percent, and one percent various other lighter gasses. The atmosphere is approximately one third Earth's pressure and extends approximately 18 miles or 30 kilometers above the surface. And guess what else?" He paused looking at the three in shock while he stroked his bearded jaw. "Theirs Life down there. Life!"

"What do you mean?" Joanna spoke first.

"L.I.F.E.", he retorted. "This data fact sheet says there is plant and animal life on Pluto's surface.

" That's impossible Joanna insisted. How could that possibly be true? We're so far from the sun."

"Not as far as you might think," Johnny then stood up while reading his own data sheet.

"What do you mean by that?" Eric questioned.

"Just what I said." Johnny boasted grinning at the sheet of data facts.

"Come on" Christy teased. "What is it?"

"You ain't gonna believe this!" he spoke as if he were an ancient western cowboy star.

"That Moon we call Charon is a mini sun of sorts." He paused again keeping them in further suspense. "Even Einstein couldn't have imagined this!" Johnny rubbed his chin as he pondered the strange facts further.

"Charon's upper atmosphere is emanating a thousand degrees Fahrenheit temperature and it drops to near eight hundred degrees Fahrenheit at a thousand kilometers altitude and the temperature gradually recedes as it bathes this whole area of space that encompasses Pluto and its moons in approximate ninety five degrees to the upper atmosphere of Pluto.

The temperature on Pluto's surface lit side is a comfortable seventy-eight degrees Fahrenheit. Charon's not a moon!" he exclaimed to the others. "It's a friggen small black light infrared sun that's more unique than anyone could have possibly imagined."

"How can you call it a Sun?" Christy questioned further. "It's a Cold fusion Sun." Johnny Insisted.

"Explain further." Eric requested.

"Well you see. Sol is huge and burns hydrogen converting it to helium intensely at thousands and thousand's of degrees. The sun is radiating its heat many million's of miles into space while burning hydrogen intensely with super hot nuclear fusion."

" This amazing small world that we've been calling Charon, works kind of in reverse of that. Except on a much smaller scale. Charon's only nine hundred miles in diameter but its core is super cold very dense matter. Its center is so super compressed and burns not with heat at its center but it burns with Cold Fusion. Cold fire burning from it's center is radiating upward until it reaches the surface and through friction with the upper mantle it becomes ignited at the surface and changed to infrared heat light giving off ultraviolet black light radiation."

"To be even more specific. If you took a planet the size of Earth approximately 12,500 kilometers or 8000 miles in diameter. Squash it under extreme pressure down to the size of Charon. You've got what you call black matter at its center. Black matter is so dense and compressed together so tightly that its atom's are repelling each other furiously and violently under extreme cold pressure."

"The center of Charon is vibrating violently over a billion trillion times per second, producing ultrasonic cold sound waves that radiate outward and ignite the Cold Fusion process kilometers below the surface."

"Charon's upper atmosphere is approximately forty six kilometers or twenty eight mile's high and is made up of Argon gasses. Helium three near the surface is held down by the combined mixture of Nitrogen, Oxygen, Carbon dioxide above creating a light plasma at the surface that ignites when impacted by the exiting inner changing frequency sound waves. We've now discovered the most important find of the century."

"Make that the twenty two centuries." Joanna said excitedly.

Johnny seemed somewhat winded from his condensed long speech but his face beamed with joy of this utopian discovery.

The others were stunned by the fact's and on that January day in 2187, Nova Ship was full of celebration as it sailed a figure eight orbit between fascinating new world's awaiting their exploration.

Lt. Comm. FIRST OFFICER LOG LT. Eric Paul ALLEY U.S.S NOVA EXPLORER . All things are created from atoms. Created by all things of condensed matter, many new things are yet to be discovered upon an alien sunrise. End log.

Nova and crew had settled down from the new discoveries. They began an extensive two week analysts of all the new data constantly being received by onboard sensors and probes dropped to the surface by parachute. During this exploration orbit time, extensive analysis was done on the rock that had pierced the hull of number two lander. It was a very strange piece of matter weighing eighty six earth pounds in the one tenth ship gravity. It was an unusually unique black piece of matter that on Earth would weigh approximately eight hundred sixty pounds. Its atoms were made up mostly of condensed Beryllium. This super compressed small rock was so black it almost seemed to suck in the lighting of the center analysts lab in the stasis chamber it now occupied.

Two weeks after arrival to Pluto, Charon systems the crew gathered around as Johnny began the meeting.

"O.K. People! I've made my decision. Tomorrow we land on Pluto. We've learned all we can from this exploration orbit. In about twenty two hours when we loop around the back of Pluto, we'll fire the engines putting us into a hundred kilometer by sixty kilometer orbit over Pluto's Equator. If all goes well and both of the landers check out, Joanna and I will detach Lander one from Nova and descend down to the surface. You and Christy will remain aboard Nova command ship and monitor our descent and status. If something should go wrong I want you two to be ready to rescue us. If everything's all right after twenty four hours, You guys can descend to the surface in Lander two and join up with us on the surface. Tomorrows a big day. Lets get some sleep he said ending the briefing of tomorrow's agenda."

That conventional rest period Johnny fell asleep in Joanna's arms. Eric and Christy made love that night with the stars for their blanket and the black sun for their light. They all were soon sound asleep.

The mini-bot R.A.1. was alone at the controls. Its CPU processor clicking mathematically in time with Nova's main computer. Only time would divulge the mysteries.

Star date January twenty eight, 2187, 0815 a.m.

The crew gathered around the galley and chattered happily about the days awaiting adventure. Joanna and Christy ate muffins and drank milk while Johnny and Eric gorged on their ham and simulated eggs, which they had offered to share.

Eric whispered conspiratorially to Johnny, "One tenth gravity and they're still watching their weight."

Both girls turned to look at Johnny with concern as he choked on his eggs.

By 0900 hours they occupied their assigned stations and Johnny relieved the little robot from its duty of automatic pilot. They sat strapped in as Johnny brought Nova from its artificial gravity spin to a near zero rate. The mini thrusters could be heard slightly through the hull as the little maneuver engines brought Nova ship to a zero gravity state. Nova was half way to Pluto and the awaiting planet appeared in their forward view screen.

"No more figure eight's" Johnny laughed. "This time we orbit Pluto."

The crew were busy programming the computers for the Pluto's orbit insertion burn. That task accomplished they were less than five minutes from engine burn.

"What's our status?" Johnny questioned

"Pluto's Five Thousand kilometers and approaching at eight point three k.p.s. Two minutes." Christy reported. "Speed now 8 by 4 k.p.s"

Again Nova pointed its engines and the astronauts Chairs reversed for the slowing down of the exploration ship. "Fifteen seconds" Johnny Reported.

Then there was a short silence until the main engines roared to life again. The three bolted together ships worked in unison slowing Nova down to three point five k.p.s required for orbit insertion.

The mighty engines fell silent and they now coasted silently ninety six kilometers behind Planet Pluto. From the dark side of Pluto they coasted until suddenly they were again bathed in the ultraviolet light from the dark radiating Charon.

Sparkling reflections glistened below as they rolled around toward the dayside of Pluto. The beauty was beyond words. Pluto's heart shaped surface rolled below slowly now as the magnificent planet revealed its beauty bathed in the light of the ultraviolet mini star. The planet beckoned for exploration. The hazy purple atmosphere filled with pink purple clouds whisked around the globe in the direction of Pluto's rotation.

The darker brown land mass was surrounded by a greenish liquid ocean on Pluto that was three parts oxygen and four parts hydrogen. Pluto was surrounded by an atmosphere eighteen miles thick and compressed down to three hundred seventy five millibars.

Here on the edge of the solar system was this magnificent beautiful world teaming with unknown plant life. Only the hours ahead would reveal the secrets of the newly discovered Pluto and its tiny moons around its black ultraviolet mini-star.

Then Suddenly The Drama Changes and the situation intensifies.

CHAPTER EIGHT
CONTACT

A low frequency sound to the tone of a chiming bell suddenly began paralyzing the four explorers aboard U.S.S Nova.

Eric later remembered being conscious but no matter how hard he tried to move he could only stand still and think of the message that he was beginning to hear over the ships radio speakers.

The others were in the same state of hypnosis. The message began as a low frequency pleasant non threatening English feminine voice tone. The inside of Nova lit up with beautiful multi spectral ultraviolet light. Then a vision of suddenly imposed presence appeared before them. The four explorers stood bravely but concerned and unable to move as the message from Planet Pluto began.

(We are the Plutons) Unless you show aggression your craft is in no danger the message questioned. State your purpose for being in orbit around our territory. We are Plutons.]

Johnny stood there frozen and stuttered before he was finally able to respond with speech.

"We're four of humankind from the Planet Earth the third planet from the sun. We are explorers who have traveled a vast distance to explore this region of space. We did not know that there was intelligent life anywhere in our own solar system other than our own species. We call our race humans from Earth. There are two females and two males aboard our ship and we are here as explorers and certainly meant no harm to your race. We do, I assure you, come in peace!" Johnny ended his response to the surprised sudden close encounter of the fourth kind.

In the eerie light it seemed like minutes had passed in slow motion before there was another response.

The ship was filled with silence as the Plutons waited another long three minutes before responding. The crew remained frozen in a suspended animation trance while still waiting for a reply from the Plutons.

Suddenly the musical strange voice began again.

(Greetings Four Earthlings. You will be welcomed to our planet as long as your intentions remain peaceful.)

Suddenly the beautiful Planet Pluto lit up below them as the planets cloaking defense system stood down from the concealed alert of their arrival to this alien far away land.

The brown land masses lit up more with ultraviolet lights as the crew suddenly realized they'd passed to the dark side of Pluto's circumference.

The pleasant voice continued. (It is agreeable, that you four from Earth are allowed to land your craft at the transmitted position in approximately two of your earth hours. We the Plutons, will await your arrival and greet you accordingly at that time.)

The communication abruptly ended with the interior of Nova returning back to normal blackness while shock and jubilant celebration preceded the following conversation.

CHAPTER NINE
THE RECEPTION

"We've been in orbit two weeks. How could they have completely hidden their civilization from us so well?", Johnny questioned.

Eric was the first to respond, "I don't know Johnny but it's quite evident that we're certainly dealing with a highly sophisticated race of beings here."

"I wonder what they look like?" Christy chimed in. "Are they humanoid? Or maybe like spiders?" she joked. "Do they have space ships? Can we breath the air on Pluto? Are their intentions really peaceful?"

Johnny listened intensely to his comrades queries. Eric spoke up. "If I didn't know this was absolutely real, then I could fathom that it was almost a perfect dream. I sure never would have believed any of this before this very moment. Never in a billion years."

"According to their atmosphere content we should be able to breathe the air at surface pressure but until we land and check it from that perspective we can't be sure. Its thin but with oxygen supplements it should be all right and the temperature and pressure seem acceptable for short period durations." Joanna reported.

"Do you think they are big or little? That voice seemed very feminine indeed. I wonder if they all are females?" Christy looked over at Eric and winked with a smile. "I do wonder if they have rules and laws in their society? I wonder if our appearance will be frightening to them?" Christy continued her wondering until interrupted by Johnny's leadership.

"Readings from the computer printout of the aliens communication. These co-ordinance from the Plutonian's are on a small continent mass just above the equator. Lets get busy and prepare Lander one for the descent to our reception. Activate two robots he ordered Eric. One to pilot Nova main ship and the other to man Lander two in case we should need rescuing." He laughed as he winked at Joanna. " What say ye all? Do You think we should break orbit and run for our lives or are we here to explore regardless of the consequences?" He certainly left no doubt by the command in the tone of his voice that his vote was for exploration.

The vote was four for landing and zero for retreat.

"So be it then." Johnny commanded on with expert ease. "The plan is that all four of us will descend to the surface in lander one. Let's make the lander ready then and we'll deploy informational beacons back toward mars base with the news and our intentions and status. Let's just assume the Plutonian's won't destroy the probes and we'll deploy two message beacons directly toward mars intercept orbit just before detachment from Nova."

So many questions filled the minds of the four crew members but their priority now turned to preparing lander one for descent.

The time had dwindled to forty five minutes when Johnny at the controls bellowed out. "Take us to their leader! We're on our last orbit before undocking from Nova for descent."

" We're as ready as we're going to get. Eric replied. Permission to fire the probes, coordinates locked in."

"Permission granted." Johnny commanded. "I hope we're doing the right thing here!" he chuckled showing reservation and wiggling spider fingers at Joanna while grinning with his pearly whites. "Get ready for the spiders." Johnny joked. The girls laughed but you could tell they really didn't think that the spider comment was funny anymore.

"I can think of uglier things than spiders. Doesn't really matter how ugly they are. They could still eat humans." She jested. "Come on down we'd like to have you for dinner! Literally!"

"Alright crew!" Johnny's demeanor suddenly changed to a more serious tone. "Lets all get sharp here. I haven't landed a ship on a planet lately. I just might be a little out of practice. I'm going to need some help. Every body get strapped in. We're going down there."

The suspense grew as they approached separation from mother ship Nova. She was the life line that sustains them and their only means of returning home to Earth.

"Ten seconds to breakaway." Eric reported.

" Roger that." Johnny quipped. "Here we go. Two, One. The jolt startled the crew as Lander One catapulted away from the mother ship."

Johnny took control of the lander and oriented it for the approach and proper vector for atmospheric entry.

The Landers hull began glowing with ultraviolet heat as the friction of Pluto's atmosphere heated the Landers underside shield. The main boosters reverse fired slowing the Lander until it pitched over and began the final descent mode. Johnny gradually slowed the lander to ten meters per second. Altitude fifty thousand feet and closing nine meters per second. Conditions nominal Eric reported. Twenty two thousand feet closing six meters per second. Christy noticed the hazy purple pink clouds as they rolled pass the upward forward window.

Five thousand feet and closing three meters per second. The tension mounted as Johnny increased the power to the main descent engines.

The atmosphere intensified and the glow of purple florescence became more prominent as the lander now hovered two hundred feet above the surface.

Johnny guided lander down slowly past a half meter per second and in twenty seconds the lander softly touched the surface as the purple dust settled and the engines fell silent.

A gentle whistling whisper of Pluto winds blew the remaining dust toward the high rising pink snowcapped mountains toward the black star that had just began rising in the east.

Outside the forward porthole the crew viewed in astonishment a sparkling emerald city. The crew could see in the distance hexagon metallic shiny dwellings and their rooftops absorbing the early morning light. Exotic trees along the edge of the landing pad expatiated the purple tip sparkling mountain range along the eastern horizon. Toward the city hovering vehicles buzzed the busy roadways that went between the structures. The vehicles floated just above the ground and moved around swiftly with mathematical precision. As the crew watched a brigade of vehicles began approaching the fifty meter tall alien ship from Planet Earth.

The reality of one tenth gravity and the round horizon had settled into the crew as they idled and checked the status of the Landers systems. They immediately began preparing to exit the craft. The Nova crew stepped into the elevator and descended from the top of the winged vertical rocket that towered above the surrounding alien city on Pluto.

The elevator slowed in the last part of the descent until it gently rested on the surface. The atmospheric pressure equalizes and the doors slide open. Christy then Joanna descended the ramp to the last steps off the ladder followed by Johnny and Eric onto the smooth Pluto soil. Christy was the first to make her small boot print in the fine powdered Pluto soil.

The air was sweet and thin. The smell of exotic flowers filled their nostrils when they first breathed the thin pleasant but adequate atmosphere. They all stood shoulder to shoulder in front of the Lander while many of the Plutonian vehicles approached.

As the alien vehicles came closer their appearance became more distinct and a better description was available. The lead craft was arrowhead shaped with a green tinted dome that was approximately one third of it's total four meter height.

A brigade of fourteen oval arrow followers were double in size compared to the first but mathematically spaced to form a perfect v with the smaller vehicle at the very point making a total of fifteen.

An armada of fourteen Pluton vehicles paused and hovered eighty meters away as the smaller point vessel began moving silently forward until it was approximately ten meters away from the four astronauts. The craft abruptly stopped and sank softly to the surface without a sound or stir of dust in the soil.

The green dome from the rim to it's top became opaque as a small solitary gray skinned tear drop slanted eyed Pluton sat at the control. The opaque dome ascended into the frame and the Pluton smoothly floated from his vehicle and settled to the surface on delicate knobby limbs about three meters in front of the four explorers.

Johnny's first impression was to think that somehow, this alien being and himself had met somewhere before in the past of his subconscious existence. Whether it was a dream or ancient Earth data about gray's, Johnny knew he was destined to be here at this precise moment in time.

Eric's eyes focused upon the cold dark stare of the large black tear drop eyes of this one meter tall gray being. It's huge proportioned head with tiny lips and small nose and a hairless rippled budging cranium sat atop a frail thin neck with short four fingered arms attached to the shoulders of a frail delicate ribbed knobby kneed body.

Joanna and Christy stood between the two human men and flinched not a muscle as the creature slid toward the center a meter away directly in front of the two female astronauts.

It seemed they were either in a trance or were somehow already communicating telepathically with the Pluton. The longest moment passed before the Pluton spoke to the visitors.

The two pearl black teardrop eyes continuously blinked and starred upon the Earthlings. It's tiny nostrils twitched as the Pluton spoke and its voice resonated in the sweet air of Pluto. The crew listened intensely to these words.

"You are a most curious species. Your appearance to us is as startling as ours must be to you. Humans from the yellow sun, We the Plutonian's welcome Ye of Earth to our world of the black light sun."

"My designation as leader of the planet you call Pluto is Rominus. We are a peaceful frugal society. Our planet exist in harmony with the star you call Charon. We have existed here for many thousands of your Earth years."

"We have known of humans since their enlightenment many eons ago. Our ancestors were there when Earth and Mars were almost destroyed by the Nemesis that came into the solar system and caused great catastrophe among the planets. Rominus paused for a moment to allow a response from the Earthlings."

The four astronauts stood under an ultra violet sunrise while a purple sky and pink clouds whisked by overhead as Johnny began first response. They were surrounded by more Plutonians now as the others began exiting their vehicles in the same floating manner as Rominus. Johnny spoke his response to Rominus and the crowd of gathering Plutonians.

"My total designation is Johnny Adam Wilkins he paused briefly. I am assigned commander for this mission. This female on my right is Joanna Wright my true love and soul mate in life. To my left is Christy Armstrong Alley and the hairy ugly older male beside her on the end whose about to pee in his britches is Eric Paul Alley."

The Plutonians broke out in what sounded like reversed alien laughter. Joanna poked Johnny on the shoulder for his brazenness and took a step up to Rominus and squatted down on a more personal level and spoke these intelligent words.

"Please be patient with us. We are extremely overwhelmed with all this new knowledge we've accumulated in the past two weeks. We have so many questions that we really don't know where to begin."

Rominus seemed quite pleased that the pretty female was at his eye level. He seemingly curled his tiny lips, smiled and spoke with affection.

"Come now! Oh welcomed visitors from Earth and visit our city called Ultropolis. There are many questions from both cultures. Let us now depart to a more suitable location where we Plutonians may bid you a more hospitable welcome." Christy walked up and patted Rominus on his wrinkled gray head and the other three Earthlings laughed as the Plutonian purred and seemed pleased at the two females affection.

They stood up and followed as Rominus abruptly turned and led the way. The brigade of Plutonians glided silently just above the colored streets toward the beautiful emerald city Ultropolis and was followed by the four humans. A very strange sight indeed to see four humans towering above and behind the Plutonian Rulers brigade on the sidewalks followed by many more of the Plutonian creatures.

Their pedestrian system was as refined as the vehicle system was with moving mathematical sidewalks. The brigade entered the center main boulevard of the alien city they named Ultropolis.

The ancient shiny structures surrounded by exotic plants and alien trees of fruit flourished under oxygen canopies in the ultraviolet warmth. Pluto was a paradise. A place of serene beauty. Sidewalks were mathematically perfect as the crew progressed behind the Plutonians on silent gliding pathways.

At the very end of a royal blue flowered avenue existed a grand palace of ruby red aurora. Earthly descriptions revealed it to appear as a peaceful mountain castle scene on Earths ancient Ireland. A beautiful Palace Indeed.

This grand structure was surrounded by an emerald green flowing river moat whose heavy water source was being fed from a large lake that was being spanned as far as the eye could see by numerous equal spaced, silver immaculate bridges that glistened from the blacklight sun.

The sweet smell of the rich oxygenated water filled the air as they crossed the silver moat to the awaiting crowd of Plutonians that lined the walk to the door that was rolling up for the parade of royalty.

Rominus and his cabinet glided inside the palace followed by the Earth guests. Inside the palace they were led to a large room with four chairs that had evidently been hurriedly prepared for the visiting representatives of humanity. The aliens stood as they gathered around the sitting humans. Rominus began speaking.

"We do not require food as humans do. Our bodies get energy through the radiation from the black star light. However! We do require and ingest a small amount of vegetable matter and liquid sustenance on a regular schedule. So we do understand the requirements of humans and have prepared a great feast of exotic Plutonian vegetables and meats. We assure you that it is completely safe for your consumption."

The others spoke not a word as Eric leaned forward and tried the food that tasted quite appealing and he then sipped the delightful nectar that the Plutonians supplied. Eric questioned licking his lips from the sweet nectar. "You spoke before of a Nemesis. What is this thing you call Nemesis?"

Rominus hovered closer as he began a long explanation of the question Eric had been first to ask.

CHAPTER TEN

THE NEMESIS EXPLANATION

"Many Earth years ago when the giant reptiles roamed your planet. Our race of beings came to this system of planets fleeing a dying world and a star that exploded and went super nova. Our original ancestors are from a star system four hundred and twenty seven light years away that you call the Orion system. Betelgeuse was our dying star and our original planet that was destroyed was once called Ultropolis, the same as our city here on this world."

"When our ancestors retreated to this system they first settled on Mars. Many eons ago Mars was a hospitable environment for our species. Mars was a much different world then. Its atmosphere was much thicker than now and its low gravity was ideal for our species." He paused briefly. "That was before the Nemesis.

"Define Nemesis?" Johnny questioned.

Rominus continued the lengthily description.

"For nearly a thousand of your Earth years, our species lived and thrived successfully on Mars. Mars was a watery world then much warmer than now. The waters once flowed freely near its equator."

"Our main settlement on Mars was near the area you call Cydonia. Many thousands of years ago when the dinosaurs roamed the Earth, our ancestors lived successfully on Mars until the day the great havoc came. When the great Nemesis entered the solar system the perfect harmony of the worlds were no more. The black planet was strongly attracted by the Jovian planet Jupiter and propelled inward toward the sun creating great destruction in its wake."

"Before the Nemesis there was once a fifth planet between Mars and Jupiter with a moon half the size of this world. That planet is now the Moon that your culture named Charon. The Nemesis passed close to Jupiter and was slung inward colliding with the moon of the then fifth planet. The dark heavy small star accelerated greatly by Jupiter's gravity collided and destroyed that moon and pulled this once fifth planet Pluto from its orbit as it passed. Both worlds tumbled inward toward Mars and Earth causing their axis to wobble and then further inward passing even closer behind Venus causing its poles to flip and rotate slowly in a reverse direction than the rest of the planets in this system."

"The duo Nemesis pair then passed close behind your yellow sun and was slung furiously toward the edge of the solar system.

In the outer system the pair of flung rogue worlds were almost captured by Uranus and Neptune's gravity causing its present day almost one hundred eighty degree procession wobble. This final grab of Neptune's gravity settled the Nemesis and its newly acquired planet Pluto into the erratic seventeen degree out of plane orbit they it has today."

The long winded and detailed answer to Eric's question ended as the aliens curiously watched their reaction to the Plutons answer.

Johnny spoke up next asking. "You say your ancestors lived on Mars. How did you get way out here on Pluto?"

"I'll answer your question." Rominus replied. "But When I do. It will be our time to ask you Earthlings a question." O.K. then Johnny agreed. The Plutonian began again.

"At the time of the approaching Nemesis our ancestors original base was at Cydonia Mars. Our scientist and astronomers detected the Nemesis dark body way before it first entered the solar system. We had three years to prepare for the fast approaching black mini star."

"Many of our race died when the Nemesis collided with the then fifth planets moon. Twelve percent of our ancestors fled the colony and survived in spaceships for years after the cataclysm of events.

The Mars colonies were doomed and some of our survivors escaped total destruction by retreating to Earth before the Nemesis collided with the then fifth planets moon."

"Our species could not function well in the heavy air and gravity of Earth but we had no choice. Our ancestors had to survive any way they could. They first settled inconspicuously in the desert lands that you call Egypt and devised a plan to build protection structures with the help of the primitive but strong back humans of the era. When the devastating Nemesis had passed, Earth went through a hundred year freeze that killed the survivors of many of the reptiles and exotic animals that once roamed the hot moist {EBN] Earth before Nemesis."

"Primitive humans of the time were trained in great numbers to help with the huge structures that would shelter our survivors and as many humans as could possibly be saved from the approaching doom of the Nemesis."

"The giant structures you call pyramids protected the few of my race and yours from the passing stars furious destruction. With the help of the strong backs of the much larger upright hybrid humans, our ancestors and yours worked together to prepare sufficient large heavy structures that would protect us from the terrible winds and falling fire and ice rocks being thrust at Earth and all the inner worlds when the chaotic Nemesis passed their way."

"Uranus and Neptune's gravity were the finale saving grace that grabbed the small black star and trailing moons and debris and slung the entire mass into its present day out of plane erratic orbit."

His long answer continued." Our ancestors and Yours survived protected from devastation and the later extreme cold until the Earth's atmosphere settled back down. Since the beginning of what you know as Pangaea it took another century for the dust to settle and the thawing of the now flowing continents and the new Earth was born again."

"The waters thawed and flowed again but huge earthquakes and floods ensued on Earth. It took centuries for Earth to again become prosperous for surviving Humans."

"The humans helped save our ancestors and they in gratitude saved as many humans and animals as was possible at the time. There was such short time to prepare for the then great dreaded Nemesis black star."

"Earth was not well suited for our race. The heavy gravity and thick air was slowly killing off the fragile generations of our survivors. Our species had dwindled to less than five hundred, six centuries after the Nemesis had passed."

"Our surviving ancestor's eventually had to make preparations to leave Earth and search for a better suited home for our race. Our remaining scientist with the help of improved Earthlings built ships similar to yours."

"They left the Earth to explore the solar system. Finding no immediate planets suitable for our species my ancestors decided to investigate the dark Nemesis on the edge of the solar system that had caused all of this great Havoc."

"They soon discovered that the once fifth planet had survived and settled into a stable orbit close to the dark Nemesis. This small planet Pluto was suitable for our species to modify and perfect for teraforming into its present day state. My ancestors soon learned to harness the radiation of the dark Nemesis star and engineered our DNA structure to survive and adapt to the ultraviolet black sunlight. We whom have occupied and modified Pluto since humankind were able to survive without our assistance have procreated here and steadily increased in population for over five thousand Earth years since the passing. Our population is approximately one billion Plutonians on this planet that you Earthlings call Pluto."

"The Ancient Nemesis Chronicles foretold that one day humankind would develop technology and travel to surrounding planets. That day has serendipitously arrived. We have anticipated the coming of humankind for many centuries. Now here you have arrived. The four of Earth whom are great explorers. You stand on the once fifth planet from the sun that now circles around the dark Nemesis star that once almost destroyed the inner solar system."

"Our ancestors and yours survived because they worked together to overcome great devastation. We are here because you are here. Our people are both survivors."

The explanation abruptly ended with, "Are you ready now to answer our first question?"

"yes! We'll do our best." Christy answered for the group.

The great room of Plutonians grew quieter as Rominus paused a moment while the murmuring of the gathered crowd died completely down. He began his question first with a brief statement.

CHAPTER ELEVEN
THE PLUTONS QUESTION

"Ultropolis is a leadership world of the remains of the galaxy star Betelgeuse in the constellation Orion. While Earth's Columbus, Magellan, Erickson explored the circumference of your oceans. We the Plutonians were hard at work teraforming Pluto. We sent large cargo ships to Neptune to harvest gases for our atmosphere. We toiled for centuries to make this a hospitable world."

"We the Plutonians have secretly visited Earth many times since that time. As you may have noticed we are a frail species. Our bodies can not survive high gravity or radiation like humans. The four of you were able to get within one hundred miles of the black star in your two week exploration orbit without any ill effects. The question We ask is this. Will you now help us?"

"Help you how? Johnny asked suspiciously.

Rominus continued. "It is true that our species has traveled the galaxy. We have encountered many of these dark matter bodies in our journeys. None of my species has ever been able to explore a dark sun. A strong dose of the near Nemesis radiation would harm us very quickly."

"It is known by our scientist that these small stars do contain hidden secrets that could unlock much knowledge. If the four of you Earthlings will help us explore the dark star, We shall both reap the secrets and technology of the mini-stars matter. Neither of our species can do it alone but together we could make a formidable exploration team."

"Your ship and your space suits with a little modifications will allow humans to remain on the surface for twenty eight earth hours before the black radiation would cause damage to you. Five Plutonium scientist would go along with you and remain in the orbiter while the four of you descend to the surface for twenty hours of exploration."

"Our five scientist will be in contact with you from orbit and with video we will be explorers too. There is great danger involved Rominus stated. If something goes wrong on the surface they cannot withstand the high radiation for more than an hour. But they should surely try and die as they undertake this risk together with you. What will be your answer?" Rominus ended with, "Can we explore this Nemesis together?"

Johnny paused briefly rubbing his chin in thought. "We'll need a few moments in private to discuss this proposal between the four of us."

Rominus agreed with a nod of his alien gray head. He directed the four to a private chamber off from the main room to discuss the proposition in private. His last words ringing in the minds of the four. "Take all the time you need to discuss the proposition. We will still remain friends even if your answer is no. Although we would be disappointed, we shall surely honor your decision."

The four closed the peculiar hexagon door to the small chamber that allowed them privacy. The days adventure had lead to the beginning of startling new opportunity of discovery. The assimilation of the fact of the existence of a race of alien gray beings was only one of the situations they had to contend with. The four in private just looked at each other for the longest time in awe of all that was happening to them. Finally Eric spoke up first shaking his head in disbelief of the dilemma they faced.

"You know what guys? I know this is a little hard to believe but I kind of like those creatures out there. They seem sincere about exploring that dark star but it's our butts that are on the line here. If we land on that tiny dark star it may kill us too. Anything, hostile or friendly could exist on the Nemesis." He looked over toward Johnny and the girls to see their reaction to his statement.

"Shucks," Johnny spoke out. "I know You're right man. But it is in our mission plan if possible to land and explore both worlds. We were planning on exploring Charon regardless of the existence of Plutonians. Seems logical then, if the plan is approved with Earth officials first, we should explore Nemesis with their help. We can definitely use some quality orbital back up. Heck! We don't even know what to look for down there. Their science and technology is more advanced than ours. The possibility of sharing their advanced technology and all the new discoveries on the dark sun awaits also. I do think we should trust them. I say we go." He stated emphatically. "What do you think girls?" Johnny delegated the discussion over to them. "Are you game?"

"Are we sure the Plutonians can be trusted?" Joanna asked. "Yeah! Christy followed. Suppose, after we get what ever it is they want from the Nemesis, they then capture us all and refuse to let us contact Earth?"

"I know you've got a valid point there." Johnny spoke next. "This matter definitely requires that we contact home base first. We will need to delay our response until we can get back to the Lander and talk it over with officials on Mars base and Earth. They need to know the situation about what is going on before we can give the Plutonians an answer to their Question."

"That Message will take considerable time with our radios. It'll take over five hours each way for us to even communicate all this happenstance and this fantastic proposition. I say we get back to the ship and discuss this whole matter with Mars base and Earth." Eric broke in.

" Yeah! I agree."

"Then it's a unanimous decision." Joanna stated. "I do think we need some help from home too. Lets see what they think about all this."

Christy and Eric both nodded in agreement.

"So be it then!" Johnny ordered.

The crew informed Rominus of their cautious position and after a feast and long discussions of the mission plans the four explorers were graciously allowed to leave Ultropolis and return back to the safety of Lander One.

CHAPTER TWELVE
AGREEMENT BETWEEN WORLDS

They were all exhausted by the time they glided out of the alien city. It had been many long work hours for the humans since they'd rested. They'd landed on Pluto more than twenty four hours ago and Pluto's Nemesis was only one fifth of the way across the zenith of the eastern mountain ridge ultraviolet sky. Pluto's revolution was once every ten days, making its daytime five earth days long.

Though twenty first century technology had discerned that Pluto and Charon were tidally locked to always face each other, this was not the factual case at all. Until now, The Plutons cloaking device technology presented the pair of worlds different than they actuality are. The Horizon robotic probe that was launched from Earth in two thousand six and others since had only recorded what the Plutonians wanted to reveal about the system. The Plutonians surely knew of the probes arrival in 2015 and allowed it to pass while they were in the same cloaking mode as they were in when the explorers arrived here now.

The four were astonished at the thousands of Plutonians traveling the road and glide ways. All this beauty to behold under the blacklight shining star through the purple atmosphere beautified by the green heavy waters and pink fluffy clouds. The Lander grew closer as they rode the walkway out of Ultropolis toward the safety of their ship. They were alone now. All the curious aliens had disappeared as they rode the elevator taking them up to the cabin on top of the Lander. The crew were exhausted from the long hours of amazing happenings.

The long interplanetary briefings to Mars base took many more hours as they locked into the overhead main ships radio and transmitted the fantastic data of the existence of Plutonians and their history and the courageous joint expedition that the Plutonians had envisioned on this historic venture.

The first response from Mars base would take well over ten hours to return to the awaiting crew. Joanna and Johnny slept in each others arms while the Eureka message traveled through the void and Eric also had snuggled up in Christy's arms and they all slept soundly with out any aid from the cryogenics chambers.

The Eureka message traveled the long light journey home toward Mars base. The news was then transferred across space inward toward the beautiful blue green brown white water planet Earth.

It took several Pluto days to set up the continuous communication between Ultropolis and Mars base. Many messages crossed the vast distance between the politicians on three worlds. Setting up the treaty and the ratified an agreement to share knowledge was eventually agreed to and the plans were laid out for the first ever joint human alien expedition to a dark mini star.

Upon issuing the proper commands the mini-bot had detached Lander two from Nova and landed near Lander one. Progress was being made and the crew found themselves continuously hard at work with the Plutonians modifying both of Nova's Landers with new alien technology. The crew assisted in installing many improvements to Landers One and Two. After twenty one earth day periods had passed they prepared to rejoin the improved ships up to the mother Nova ship in orbit.

The plans were that the Earth astronauts would launch from Pluto in Lander one and the Five Plutonians would launch in Lander two immediately afterwards. Both ships would then dock with Nova's main stage in orbit.

Both new extremely modified ships were docked to the Nova and the Crew of four humans and five gray alien scientist were ready to depart on the ultimate short journey to the Nemesis that was only twelve thousand two hundred miles away.

March third, twenty-one, eighty-seven. The crew of nine were strapped into the new exploration ships as Johnny approached the moment of firing the modified engines on Nova to take them out of orbit and head for the black star.

With the aliens help the new ship could now communicate with Mars base at ten times light speed and new technology made it possible to maintain one tenth gravity aboard without spinning the ships. The improved sensors and powered up energy shield made the new Nova a formidable exploration vessel.

For centuries the Plutonians had lived so close to the infrared dark star. They'd learned how to change their d.n.a. structure to harness and nourished the life giving ultraviolet rays. Regardless, Until this very moment in the space continuum timeline, neither race would have ever been able to undertake this historic dangerous mission alone and survive.

CHAPTER THIRTEEN
THE NEMESIS LANDING

Johnny's voice crackled "Five seconds crew."

The tension grew as he fired the main engines that the Plutonians had helped re-engineer. The crew was expecting the roar of burning hydrogen that they were so accustom to but this time things were a bit different. The new more efficient engines no longer roared but purred steadily as the new Nova left Pluto's orbit and fell gently inward toward their new world to explore. This time with a crew of four Earthlings and five Plutonians and three mini robots.

The dark small star ahead in the view screen grew closer as the new version of Nova and its two culture astronaut team fell swiftly behind the dark star that had for eons withheld its mysterious secrets from all.

The five new astronauts were two females named Latilia, and Serdia, two of Plutonians best astrological scientists and three males Plutonians named Qwerto head of all Plutonian science and his two physics advisors named Zxico and Pertravio. It was a little hard for the Earthlings to get use to the Plutonian names but these five crew members had worked closely with the Earthling to modify Nova into the super explorer ship that it had evolved into.

The scientists of Pluto had also modified Nova's three mini robots so they could better assist the astronauts while on the surface.

New Nova in a high orbit around the dark sun now took on a detailed two day surface mapping study of the Nemesis that once almost destroyed both civilizations.

Two days after orbit entry the entire crew gathered on the main deck of Nova to discuss the findings and agenda for the planned surface descent. New technology enabled detailed analysis of the dark star. Improved sensors drew their attention to unusual anomalous readings near the equatorial region. The difficulty with obtaining exact locations was made more difficult by the excessive high rate of spin on its axis once every fifty eight seconds. This was going to be an extremely difficult world to land on. The Nova lander and the Earth crew were going to have to match the Nemesis stars exact rotation rate in an upper atmosphere that was extremely hostile with winds blowing several hundred miles per hour at times. This would take a remarkable pilot to land a rocket ship in what would have been considered a great hurricane on Earth.

At the end of the briefing the landing coordinates were finalized and Johnny assured the crew that he would be able to land on the stormy Nemesis. The new Landers had extreme new stability baffles that would allow the ship while landing to be somewhat impervious to the high winds of Nemesis.

The four Earthlings boarded Lander one and prepared the lander for undocking. This would certainly be a dangerous landing attempt. The five Plutonians would remain aboard Nova's lander two in a five hundred kilometer high orbit.

The crew expressed their salutations and the four Earth astronauts with two of the improved robots undocked Lander one and catapulted away from Mother ship Nova.

Lander one chased the spinning black star in the attempt to match up with its fast rotational speed. Nova lander spiraled inward while the engines hummed efficiently and the ship entered the very top of the Nemesphere . Slowly but surely the Lander spiral forward and eventually matched the rotation speed of the spinning dark star. Lander one turned main engines downward firing blue flames toward the dark ultraviolet sun.

Johnny's voice came through as they started the descent, "Lets all stay super sharp. Everybody do their jobs and we'll get down safely."

"Descent speed 30 meters per second, altitude fifteen kilometers engines nominal." Eric announced

"I'm staying on those baffles we've got wind speed out there that are already eighty miles per hour and rising." Joanna reported.

"Roger that." Johnny Returned

Christy's voice followed "Switching view screen to reverse radar."

A blurred glowing cloudy picture popped up on the view screen showing the engines flaming purple blue flame and beyond that a misty darker purple that trailed off to ultraviolet darkness.

"Temperature outside is reading 800 degrees Fahrenheit, present altitude is six point two kilometers." Eric reported. "entrance begins!"

"All right now crew and machines." Johnny coaxed

The ship suddenly lunged sideways as the baffles momentarily lost its lock of stability when struck by a three hundred mile per hour gust of the Nemesis atmosphere. Bring the new shields on line Johnny bellowed above the roar of the Nemicanes atmospheric furry.

A red aurora surrounded the sinking ship and the ship stabilized to an acceptable level.

"That's better." Johnny yelled out. "Can't see a dang thing on that fuzzy visual. We'll have to depend totally on radar to tell what's below us."

Joanna tuned the radars signal response tighter as they almost hovered momentarily at two kilometers. Johnny again began lowering the ship through the swirling mist below.

The radar projection flashed and changed the viewer revealing a jagged smoky mountain range about three kilometers downrange. A large field of what appeared to be black moving boulders below the Lander blipped across the radar screen. The Plutonian Qwerto by proxy satellite focused a laser projector beam down toward their exact landing coordinates and the ship descended from a kilometer above the surface tracking the beam.

Through the mist on visual showed a mountain range with dark purple lava flowing cones that were constantly firing ultraviolet black lightning bolts at the bottom of the Lander as it crossed over several more ranges of black mountains. The Lander shields absorbed most of the super conducting electricity bolts but it managed to momentarily knocked out all the systems aboard as the ship went totally dark for four seconds and began to move sideways until the back up computers came on line.

The back up computers took control and stabilized while the craft descended down to five hundred meters above the surface.

They'd temporally lost contact with the Plutonians in orbit and one more major strike from the Nemesis lightning and the lander would have to abort. Johnny's nerves of steel took hold as he took the controls and eased the lander down lower into the dark valley toward a smooth clearing area two kilometers down range.

The winds were calmer in the valley as the ship sank lower between two mountains with red fiery caps of boiling liquid on top.

"Fuel status, 60% fuel remaining. Back up systems looking good. Altitude fifty meters and moving forward ten meters per second." Eric's voice broke in.

Johnny, realizing he was approaching too fast, instantly fired the forward thrusters, slowing Nova Lander, as they sank to within ten meters above the dark stars surface. Another lightning bolt lit up the valley floor as Johnny eased down to within three meters hovering momentarily to eye the surface below. One meter above the surface the contact light came on and Johnny cut the engines. The lander fell to the surface with slight bounce before coming to a silent stop.

"Dang." Eric exclaimed. "You dropped this thing like a rock those last few feet. Didn't you?"

Busting out laughing at the beads of sweat on Johnny's forehead

Johnny retorted with, "That's all right old man. That wet spot on your britches will dry in about an hour. We're not dead. Are We?" He laughed, as Eric looked down.

Neither girl had spoken past the last fifty meters of the descent but they came alive now while chastising Johnny and Eric to get serious and check the ship's status out.

The laughter died down as the reality of the heavy gravity applied itself to the Nova lander and its crew. It had been more than three years since any of these explorers had experienced gravity as strong as Earth's. The sudden assertion of force weakened their knees, as they gradually became accustomed to the dark world's heavy grip.

The storm outside howled, as the ship suddenly shifted a little while settling down and attempting to screw its anchors into the thick surface of the star.

"I'll be working on getting the main computer back up and running." Christy sighed, "We definitely will need it working."

"Yeah, let's get this ship repaired and checked out. The clocks ticking crew. We've got twenty four hours before we must leave this world and nobody is leaving this planet without me." Johnny laughed a little, as the crew diligently went to work bringing all of Nova's systems computer programs back up and running.

"The Landers status seems to be O.K. now." Christy reported. "The lightning bolt caused some circuits to melt in the main CPU. We'll have that repaired in an hour. The anchor screw motors shut down shortly after they attempted deployment. You guys will have to check on the anchor status on your e.v.a. outside the ship."

"Roger that." Eric replied.

"What's our remaining lift off fuel status?" Johnny questioned.

"We're down to about 55% fuel remaining. We're fine on fuel status but one of the mini robots took a good jolt of lightning. I'll work on that. Don't worry though. I'll soon make the little floating bugger operational again." Eric laughed.

"O.K." Johnny replied. "I'm going on down to the cargo bay and get the surface gear and suits ready. Christy can repair the main computer. We'll all meet at the elevator in one hour. The Crew quickly repaired Nova's minor flaws and the ship seemed in good status on the mysterious black world Nemesis."

CHAPTER FOURTEEN

FOOTPRINTS ON NEMESIS

At the elevator chamber, Johnny and Eric, along with two of the small robots stood ready to explore. In full space suits they closed the hatch pumping out the air in the chamber and the elevator touched the ground. The remaining pressure equalized and the elevator door slid open revealing a misty, hot, steamy, hard, and shiny surface. Johnny stepped out into the ultra darkness first. Their suits hissed expelling used carbon dioxide into the air as the temperature and pressure equalized.

Johnny stepped from the one meter rung to a black glowing surface smooth in texture. "Surface temperatures two hundred fifty degrees." He reported. "We certainly don't want to punch any holes in our suits."

Johnny walked over examining closer the screw anchors from the bottom of Nova.

"Look at this!" he beckoned to Eric to come closer. "The drill bits on the end of the ship's anchor screws are all chewed up and broken."

"The surface compaction is reading over 42." Eric reported holding his tricorder near the surface. "Compared with Earths 5.2 compaction this surface soil is eight times harder than earth is at the surface. It sure trashed those diamond drill bits on the anchors. There's no way to repair those. Even if we did, the bits would only break again."

"We're just going to have to deal with the anchor status as is." Johnny stated. "The ship appears to be stable enough. Let's get busy and lower the surface access utility ramp and get the ground rover operational."

Twenty minutes later the crew had the scientific instrument unpacked and activated and the land rover deployed onto the surface.

The two astronauts and two robots boarded and departed on the E.V.A. excursion toward the direction that the Plutonians had specified.

The immediate landing area was a smooth dark glasslike valley floor near the foot of two dark luminous mountains that towered over the surrounding scene. The outside lander lights seemed swallowed by the darkness all around. The headlights of the land rover would only project to about ten meters ahead as the cautious moving vehicle drove ahead losing visual of the lander with Joanna and Christy still aboard.

The radio crackled and spat static as the atmospheric lightning broke up their voices when communication was attempted. Eric was at the joystick of the rover driving cautiously toward the specified computer co-ordinance.

The winds howled around the rover as they drove past several large boulders. Zig-Zag patterns of ultraviolet electricity lit up the darkness ahead revealing the base of a tall dark mountain about a kilometer away.

Eric drove on around a boiling crater of alien goo that gave off a crackling sound and shot bubbles of molten fire into the Nemesis atmosphere. Both astronauts and robots were strapped into the mobile machine that made its way closer to the frightful sight that came into view out of the forward rover window.

CHAPTER FIFTEEN
THE GIANT REPTILE EVENT

"What the heck is that? Awe shucks. Look over there!" Eric quickly ducked the rover in behind a huge boulder. The two were at first frightened by the two giant ghostly reptiles fighting tooth and nail five hundred meters ahead. Huge creatures of mass destruction threw each other to the ground quaking the surface with violent thunderous vibrations.

Eric quickly cut the lights to the rover and hoped the creatures hadn't noticed their arrival. Violent lightning bolts lit the surrounding scene as the creatures continued their furious battle.

"Awe shucks man." Eric whispered. "I never thought I'd ever see anything like this. How can there be life down here? How can those things breathe this hot poisonous atmosphere? They must be a hundred meters tall."

"Dang if I know." Johnny replied back, in a husky whisper. "Look at the feet on those things. They've got six elephant type legs and one foot could easily squash this rover." "You've got that right." Eric said. "They're so busy fighting let's hope they don't see us."

They'd been on the surface for nearly three hours and two more hours at the lander before departure. Johnny and Eric remained as calm as possible as the two Nemesis giants battled on for almost another hour, while the astronauts waited for the conclusion of the fierce battle. Finally one of the creatures stumbled away into the darkness and the other disappeared behind the tall mountain that was intended to be their destination.

The two sat quietly in the rover for a few moments before discussing their equipment status and air reserves remaining.

"Eric, I think we're in good shape but I hope we don't see anymore of those creatures."

"Yeah, me too. We only have about a half kilometer to go." "Must I remind you that its right in the area that one of the creatures retreated to?"

"What do you think? Should we take a chance and go on?" "Heck Yes!" Johnny said. "We didn't come this far to quit now. Besides, If one of those things appears while we're on the surface. You won't have to outrun the creature."

"Meaning what?" Eric Replied.

"It's me, that you're going to have to outrun!" Johnny teased.

They both laughed in the tension of the moment inside the rover.

"Shoot." Johnny stated. "Let me drive this thing a little."

He turned the headlights back on and took control of the joystick.

"Well alright, but go slow." Eric said. "I already have one wet spot," he grinned back at Johnny.

The rover toiled on across the surface heading for the spot where one of the creatures had vanished. Johnny drove ahead a little faster ducking left and right around two craters of boiling exploding luminous liquid. The rover continuously dropped sounding buoys on the surface every sixty seconds to mark their path for the return journey. The two little improved robots were steadily clicking as they recorded the surrounding environment and the vehicle's status

For fifteen more minutes Johnny drove the dark Nemesis path that led them to the fast approaching foot of the mountain. The thunder rumbled against the hills as he drove up to a huge cave opening in the side of the mountain. "Well!" he said, braking the rover to a stop. "This must be it. Inside that cave entrance are the exact coordinates that the Plutons wanted us to investigate. They do have some mysterious energy readings." Eric replied, pointing his tricorder toward the dark entrance.

Just then the radio crackled with static and Joanna's voice came through to their speakers.

"Are you guys alright? We've been trying desperately for hours to find a frequency to break through this interference."

Qwerto's voice came through as soon as Joanna's broadcast had finished. "We have first visual now and we and can see what you see." His peculiar alien voice sounded extremely excited.

"Ok Qwerto." Johnny replied. "I was beginning to think you Plutons weren't going to make it for a while. Anyway, We've made it to the coordinates that you've specified. We're approximately five kilometers north east of the lander. We had to wait out a dinosaur fight to get here. We weren't informed that there was huge creature life down here, much less huge creatures like that. We seem to be adequate for the moment. We're just getting ready for the cave e.v.a excursion."

They finished their briefing and got into the small decompression chamber leading to outside. The two explorers were suited up in full space suits and checked each others suit status.

Johnny pushed the green breaker letting the remainder of the cooler air out of the small chamber. The hatch slid open to a hot steamy surface and after a pause the two stepped together to the hard surface of the dark Nemesis Star.

CHAPTER SIXTEEN
INTO THE ALIEN CAVES

They'd been on the Nemesis now for more than six hours as Eric followed Johnny through the dark path to the cave. The Nemesis wind howled furiously against their backs leading them away from the safety of the blinking strobe light barely visible from the mouth of the humongous cave entrance.

The powerful beam of light from their helmets barely pierced the enveloping darkness as they stood and peered into the mystery hole.

"After You." Eric's static voice crackled in Johnny's helmet.

"Boogie Boogie dude. Follow me if you dare." Johnny quipped back and stepped quickly into the darkest darkness he'd ever experienced.

Eric had trouble keeping up with the bouncing beam off the walls from Johnny's helmet light. The team ventured cautiously forward as the darkness totally encompassed them. The eerie wind howl had ceased as they entered the cave and now all they heard was the low frequency hum of their suit's life support system and a mysterious crackling sound.

Suddenly Johnny stopped in his tracks as he noticed something odd way ahead in the darkness. Eric was about fifteen seconds behind and caught up as Johnny pointed his energy detector tricorder toward the anomaly. The energy meter read off scale as Johnny showed the scanner to Eric. Down the long path of the dark cave they could see an orbed glowing light of indiscernible constant changing colors.

Two brave astronauts ventured further toward the colored beckoning light. The cave suddenly opened up into a huge chamber as the source of the lights came into view.

A golden emerald luminous light filled the chamber emanating from behind a huge purple gold row of boulders and thousands of dark matter nuggets were strewn randomly across the chamber floor.

Johnny reached down to pick up a one inch rock of the purple gold matter. Caught by surprise he lost balance and fell to the ground on his knees as the little rock extremely resisted his pull. Eric rushed over as Johnny staggered back to his feet brushing the dark soil from the kneepads of his spacesuit.

"What the heck is that stuff?" Johnny Questioned. "It sure is dense and heavy. That little one inch tiny nugget must weigh two hundred kilograms. I wasn't ready for that much gravity resistance."

"I think possibly, we may have found what we came looking for. Whatever that stuff is we can't lift it. We need the robots and a super boosted gravity dolly in order to get any of this heavy matter back to the ship. Maybe, between the four of us, we can get some little stones loaded onto the dolly. I'll head back to the rover, get the robots and gravity dolly and be back here in a half hour."

" Alright then." Johnny replied. "You be careful. I'll be right here when you get back. I might do a little exploring until you return but I won't go very far. I'll meet you back here at this spot in exactly one half hour."

Eric walked back into the darkness following the beaconed signal path they'd left while entering the cave.

Johnny was alone in the cavern and couldn't resist the urge to prod a little further toward the back of the glowing chamber. Mysterious golden blue heavy rocks were everywhere. Small ones, large ones, and almost everywhere that Johnny looked there were glowing black gold heavy matter tiny stones. He'd made his way past a large boulder when suddenly he halted in his tracks at the vision he saw of a protruding blue wall. He couldn't believe what he was seeing. The wall was in motion. Johnny checked his suit status to see if he'd developed a leak and possibly inhaled some of the poisonous atmosphere that filled the cavern. His suit's status was eighty five percent remaining air and portable life support was functioning perfectly. The temperature in this area of the cavern had dropped to a cool sixty-eight degrees Fahrenheit.

CHAPTER SEVENTEEN
THE DEITY IN THE -*FLOWING WALL

He cautiously approached while his suit expelled the carbon dioxide he breathed out and dissipated into the cooler atmosphere around him. He stepped closer toward the mysterious wall of flowing multi spectral colors. When he was two meters away from the anomaly, he stared intensely into the hypnotizing vision that appeared floating inside an alien entity's doorway.

He couldn't make out distinctive characteristics of the aberration but he realized that he was in the presence of a supremely knowledgeable deity. Johnny's mind became intertwined with an awesome being of unlimited knowledge that beckoned Johnny inward toward its enlightened domain.

He extended his right arm forward and suddenly his body dissipated into the midst of the Nemesis anomaly. Knowledge that he was completely safe and wouldn't be harmed was imposed into his thoughts waves by the entity. The being's identity at first remained anonymous but Johnny found himself engrossed with a deep discussion of planetary bodies and physics. Knowledge of new galaxies and a total universal physics were explained in detail in Nemeseconds.

Reality as Johnny had known was suddenly passed away and replaced with the comprehension of a unique nature of all science's. It was as if his mind had expanded a thousand-fold in an instant. A blue vapor surrounded Johnny while visions of extreme futuristic knowledge about love and of all living organisms enveloped him. He was suddenly made aware that the Supreme Deity admired his courage but began providing him with a warning premonition that he and his comrades could be in extreme danger if they remained on Nemesis for much longer.

Johnny suddenly was returned outside the entrance of the aberration doorway. When he turned and looked behind him there was only a rock silver solid face boulder. His light beam penetrated upward around the stalactites into the darkness searching for any evidence of the portal he'd returned from.

He made his way back to rendezvous point with Eric and he was amused that only two minutes had passed since he'd entered the portal. He walked around the big dark boulders to the open cavern and saw Eric and the two robots arriving riding the gravity dolly.

"It seems as though you'd just left." He radioed Eric. "What do you mean man?" Eric retorted. "I've been gone about twenty-five minutes. It took me ten minutes to get the gear and activate the robots and the robots don't need a headlight to find their way through the dark like I do." Johnny laughed, and began commanding the topic. "You are not going to believe what I've discovered."

Eric came closer to Johnny realizing that something had changed. Johnny had an aurora around him that gave off an amber glow in the boulder-filled cavern. Eric was astonished at the look on Johnny's face as he stood helmet to helmet with his fellow astronaut.

"Come with me," Johnny ordered. "That heavy matter is a mild discovery compared to what I'm about to show you. I'll introduce you the real reason we came here." Johnny turned and headed back toward the far northern wall toward the Deity that awaited his partners enlightenment.

They walked away, leaving the mini robots idle as they crossed the cavern of Nemesis matter strewn randomly on the cavern floor.

Eric was as stunned as Johnny was at the anomaly wall that had reappeared. He immediately stopped short when he saw the flowing entity ahead.

"Come on," Johnny insisted. "You won't regret this."

Eric followed cautiously behind as they approached closer to the flowing anomaly. Johnny grabbed Eric by the arm and pulled him into the dimension and they both stood in the enlightenment of super intelligence and knowledge.

Eric was immediately enlightened as Johnny had been about many worlds and beings of all kinds and the many cultures that inhabited the universes.

Suddenly they realized that the universe was not a place created by accident with a single big bang but instead the multi-verse is a huge never-ending creation much larger than the biggest possibility humanly imaginable. That life and intelligence not only existed in humanoid terms but on the molecular and stellar scale as well. Stars had sex and gave birth. It was inside dark matter mini stars like Nemesis that many a Deity lived with their existence in harmony with the universe and truth of scientific nature.

They now realized that the universe was teeming with life in many forms and dimensions. Everything that is, was created by everything that once existed in a different state of physics. The Deities of the dark stars were not gods themselves but definitely powerful angels of unquestionable power.

Johnny and Eric were instantly transported back to the golden cavern where the two mini robots rested patiently awaiting their return. They both glowed with the mystical aurora that once enveloped only Johnny. Now they glared at each other with new eyes and understood the potential powers inside the golden rocks that decorated the cavern. Johnny laughed at the dilemma he'd faced earlier with the super heavy stone. He knew now that they possessed super ordinary strength and powers.

Johnny bent over to the ground and picked up a small golden nugget of the Nemesis matter that weighed eight hundred fifty kilograms or 1900 earth pounds and placed it gently on the souped up portable dolly that the robots stood behind ready to tow back to the rover. Eric grimaced at the little carts structure and power source as it strained to support the immense weight of the three inch by one inch Nemesis stone. Their new knowledge and expanded mind grasped the theory of displacement of gravitons. Eric turned grinning at Johnny and said, Johnny if we work together, I know that we can accomplish the stone retrieval task the easy way.

Johnny's new enlightenment allowed him to know exactly what Eric was thinking and they both channeled their brain waves toward a collection of super heavy stones causing the Nemesis stones to silently levitate a meter above the floor.

It all seemed so elementary to know how to channel their thoughts to the bottom of the stones interfering with the pull of the Nemesis gravity.

It had been thirteen hours since arrival on Nemesis and there they stood floating the stones and laughing at the two little robots straining while trying to pull the gravity cart with a single small stone toward the exit.

The robots pulled and jerked causing the tiny heavy rock to roll toward the back of the floating cart. The cart abruptly tipped over and the stone fell to the ground with a thud and the little creatures were thrown backwards and fell at the loss of its extreme weight.

Johnny and Eric laughed so hard at the mini-bots that they momentarily lost their concentration on the floating stones and the stones came crashing to the ground with a big thud that shook the ground violently and made the robots fall over again. The two laughed again at the two kicking clicking toy like computer creatures and eventually gently sat them upon their fat little wheeled feet then again levitated the floating stones above the cavern floor.

They took one last look around and departed back down the long dark beacon path that led back toward the waiting rover. The two mini-bots pulled the empty cart and the floating stones followed hovering behind them.

Back into the flashing Nemesis storm they exited the cave and headed toward the strobe lights of the waiting surface rover. They floated the stones down gently inside the rover and loaded the robots and dolly back aboard.

Johnny looking at his watch then said. "We've been on Nemesis for fourteen hours. Its only a two hour sprint back to the lander. What do you say we possibly do a little more exploring?" He gestured off toward a different direction than they had yet traversed.

"We're only going to be here once. We'd better do it while we're here." Eric agreed. They both started walking toward the corner of the dark mountain that had been the battle ground of the humongous Dinosaurs.

CHAPTER EIGHTEEN
TAMING THE SIX LEGGED BEAST AND THE PEGASUS COLONY

LEGEND OF PEGASUS

Pegasus is a winged horse in Greek Mythology. The majestically winged horse was born from the trickling blood of the Gorgon Medusa. Pegasus flew up to join the Gods and was caught by the Goddess Athena. Athena tamed the horse with a golden bridle. At this time it's said that Athena gave the golden bridle to Bellophron before he started out to fight the Chimaera. Bellophron also tamed Pegasus with it but he soon became too proud. Pegasus threw him off and flew into the sky where Zeus made him into a constellation.

PEGASUS WITH POETRY

Another legend of Pegasus is that the Muses were holding a contest of song. The music charmed the streams and made Mount Helicon grow toward the heavens. The god Poseidon ordered Pegasus to make it stop growing by striking it with his hoof. Pegasus did and the fountain Hippocrene sprang forth. Its waters inspired people to write poetry. Two other fountains of inspiration, Aganippe and Pirene were also made by the hoof of Pegasus. In this way Pegasus is connected with poetry. A poet is said to mount his Pegasus when he begins to write.

PEGASUS AS A CONSTELLATION

Pegasus is a constellation of the Northern Celestial Hemisphere, found well up in the evening sky of autumn. A large square called the Great Square of Pegasus marks it in the sky.

Showing no fear the two trod off onto the misty, steamy surface with lightning flashing all around while the rover disappeared behind them in the howling atmosphere of Nemesis.

They'd lost all contact with the lander and the Plutonians but they focused their new enlightenment power back toward the lander and made the girls aware that they were all right.

Eric followed Johnny into the Nemesis void being able to see much better in the dark since his enlightenment. They walked for almost an hour while their remaining air supply dwindled down to sixty-five percent.

Soon they came to the edge of the mountain that the monstrous reptiles had disappeared behind. A long path to the left went steeply downhill and then again to the right ending in an abrupt halt as the two stood perched on the very edge of a steep cliff. Staring over into the dark abyss they could see a giant reptile below on the valley floor. The creature bellowed out hot gasses that turned to fire dissipating into the Nemesis air. Suddenly the hairy giant beast spotted their helmet light beams and bolted toward them as the ground thundered beneath its six humongous three claw toed feet.

The creature spit fire as it charged ahead toward the two astronauts but Johnny and Eric stood their ground while the monster thundered closer. For an instant they where a little scared but then Johnny laughed, and spoke to Eric.

"Hey man! How's your wet spot?"

Then He laughed again and the two turned and focused their enlightened mind power on the charging fire spitting beast. The monster floated from the ground as they levitated the beast two hundred meters skyward.

The creature grew even madder as it kicked and fanned the misty air and shot another ball of fire down toward the amused explorers. Eric turned the approaching fireball around in mid air and hurled it back toward the pissed beast. The fireball spinning now struck the beast in the under belly and it fell to the ground creating a Nemesis quake that caused the astronauts to fall down while laughing.

Johnny got up first brushing the dirt from his butt and reached his hand down to boost Eric up. They looked over at the unconscious beast and decided they'd better explore onward before it awoke.

They climbed back up the curved path reaching the summit turning left into the darkness. The creature awoke and howled furiously in the Nemesis dark but Johnny had disappeared around the corner. Johnny ventured ahead into the night looking here and there for a new mystery to explore. He heard a crackle in his radio and turned around discovering that Eric had disappeared. The radio crackles again and he caught a couple of garbled words. He walked back downhill and saw Eric in the valley below standing beneath the creatures left foot.

It was like a scene from the Barnum and Bailey's twentieth century circus except instead this took place on a dark Nemesis world on the edge of the solar system. Eric stood beneath the beast left front foot showing no fear while levitating the beast with one foot extended and examining the big three toenail tusk growing from the Nemesaurus monster.

"Dang Johnny!" The radio crackled again. "You've got to come and check out the foot on this thing." The Nemesaurus was standing docile and calm now with five legs on the ground and one levitated in the air just above Eric's head. "You must be crazy," Johnny protested and then laughed saying. "Awe shucks, what the Heck!"

Johnny floated down the steep cliff where Eric and the creature were. The radio crackled and Qwerto had reestablished the communication link that the Plutonians had earlier in the mission.

The link was garbled and distorted but Johnny got in a short briefing before the ragging storm on Nemesis made it impossible to communicate with the Plutonians anymore.

Eric further examined the Nemesaurus anatomy while Johnny walked to the hairy gray long scaly tail, jumped on and began climbing up its scales like they were steps. He climbed on up further until he'd reached the summit and crest of the beasts ugly head.

The creature stood docile as Johnny in his pumped up space suit took up such a little spot on its broad green wrinkled cranium.

"You must be crazy too," Eric said.

Johnny stood balanced on its crown and the Nemasaurus's three nostrils spat fire into the winds. The beast upon obeying Johnny's command lowered his long neck and head toward the surface and the astronaut casually slid down and around his three smoking nostrils and stood in front of a huge center eyeball.

Immediately Johnny placed his space helmet against the creatures one huge blood shot eye and mumbled commands to the creature. It snorted smoke thrice as if it understood a truce and when Johnny jumped to the surface it stretched its neck and head skyward to the position it had occupied when Johnny stood on its cranium.

The Nemesaurus acknowledged the humans induced truce then bellowed a piercing screech of fire. The two astronauts walked a hundred yards away from the Nemesaurus and stood and watched while it casually stumbled out of sight in the howling misty atmosphere.

The Nemesis lightning flashed intensely in the vague distance making the whole scene appear to be something out of an old twentieth century Godzilla movie. Instead, this was actually occurring on a dark sun that once threatened all life in this solar system that uniquely occupies a specific quadrant in the spiral arm of the Milky Way Galaxy.

The momentary excitement was over when the two realized that their air supply had dwindled to fifty-five percent while they'd toyed with the giant Nemesaurus.

"OK," Johnny spoke. "We'd better get back to the rover and head toward the lander."

"Yeah," Eric replied. "We definitely wouldn't want to run out of air out here."

"You've got that right," Johnny retorted. The two walked in amazement through the Nemesis night following the homing beacons they'd left on the trail earlier.

Johnny and Eric walked past a boiling pit of molten Nemesis hot matter. It gurgled and spat slow motion blobs and then quickly fell backwards into ponds of molten molasses goop.

Eric thought to himself after observing the gurgling lava pond. "I'll dispatch a mini-bot over the pond to get a small sample of that gooey matter." Johnny heard his thoughts and agreed that was a wise decision. Johnny was thinking how heavy all this matter would be if the Nemesis didn't rotate so rapidly. If the Nemesis rotated once every twenty four hours as planet Earth does and as heavy as this matter already is, it would be heavier on Earth due to less centrifugal force at surface level.

After stowing the samples the astronauts began working around the rover setting up data stations to be left on the surface after their departure. They set up the seismometer which required drilling a hole five meters down to extract a soil sample and allow a hole for a dangling probe.

Johnny struggled with the powerful drill machine for a few minutes falling to the ground several times when the drill would catch a chunk of super hard rock and propel him sideways from the strain and then spinning to a stop when the trigger was released. He was getting tired.

Johnny had worked so hard trying to dig the hole that he'd momentarily forgot about his newly acquired powers.

"Hey Eric!", He called out. "Come over here a second and give me a hand."

Johnny rested a moment while Eric finished lining up the laser reflector and adjusting it to precisely track the magnificent Pluto that was crossing the sky every twenty nine seconds.

The two paused a few minutes to admire the purple planet that rose over their head taking twenty nine seconds to cross the horizon disappearing past the mountains then appearing again after a half nemetar.

"Man! That's some view," Eric exclaimed.

"Yeah, it sure is. We won't ever get to do any of this again any time soon," Johnny quipped back.

"Well I wouldn't worry too much," Eric spoke up. "We still are a heck of a long way from Earth."

"Yeah you're right." Johnny said. "Pluto's pretty all right but it'll never be as beautiful as Earth."

They reflected on their journey a moment and with their new powers, they then went back to work installing the seismometer and getting core samples.

"That's about got it," Johnny remarked. "It's getting late. We'd better finish loading the tools and get back toward Lander One. The girls are probably getting really worried by now. We've been out of radio contact for quite a while."

It took fifteen minutes to store the core samples and tools then they climbed aboard the rover and pressurized the cabin with Earth air. They unlocked their space helmets and breathed in the fresh air while vacuuming the dirty Nemesis soil from each other's suits and discarding the dust to the outside environment.

"Man! that stuff has a funny smell. Don't you think?"

" Yeah," Eric replied. "It sort of smells like manure candy. Don't it? Smells like we both stepped in something." "Yeah, I hope the alien dirt residue isn't hazardous to humans." Johnny reached out for his tricorder and analyzed the residue on the floor inside the decompression chamber.

"I'm getting some fairly strange readings but it seems to be harmless enough to us."

"OK." Eric replied. "I'm going to plug up our surface e.v.a. packs so they'll be recharging on our drive back to the lander."

"You've got that right," Johnny replied. "My air supply had dwindled down to thirty-five percent. I only had a few hours life support left."

"Yep me also." Eric returned. "We will need fresh air by the time we make it back to the lander."

Eric stored their pressure suits on the charger and Johnny slid in his seat behind the control stick of the rover.

The weight of the heavy gravity was taking its toll on the pair of explorers. They took a few moments to review their fantastic exploration on the surface and discussed their present status.

"Looks like the rover's down to fifty-three percent power remaining. By the time we reach the Lander, power will be approximately twenty percent. It appears everything else checks out nominal."

"OK," Johnny replied. He eased the joystick forward a little testing the controls and then stopped. "All right We're ready to go except for one thing."

"Yeah the heavy rock matter," Eric replied. "We wouldn't want their heavy weight to damage the rover motors."

"O K then! I'll drive while you levitate the rocks in the cargo bay behind us so they want interfere with the rovers power."

"OK," Eric answered. "I'm just taking the amount of rock mass weight that can safely be loaded on the lander and still be able to lift off."

Eric levitated the rocks a meter in the air behind his seat in the cargo bay. Johnny drove off into the misty steamy dark Nemesis toward the direction of the lander beacons.

They rode on past more boiling pits of molten matter and through the boulder strewn landscape. The pair were almost half way home when Johnny suddenly stopped the rover.

"Did you see that?" Johnny asked excitedly.

"I saw something," Eric answered.

Some sort of creature glided across the sky. Johnny stood up trying to see past the corner of the windshield.

"I had my back turned but I saw something out of the corner of my eye as I was turning around," Eric replied. "I couldn't quite make out what it was though. What ever it is landed past that mountain and I could swear I saw a horn in the middle of its forehead."

"Well! I can't see it anymore," Johnny stated as he engaged the rovers forward drive.

Abruptly as he swerved around a large boulder and past a clearing, a steaming lake came into view surrounded by exotic plant life. Contentedly grazing on the far side, stood a herd of fifteen mystical unicorns that were eating vegetation shrubs in the middle of a hillside valley of plant clovers.

The rovers forward wide band halogens fell on a herd of fabulous golden winged tiped Pegasus's that suddenly looked up as the rover slid to a stop. The entire herd bolted and huge feathered wings appeared from each unicorn as they momentarily hovered in flight then swiftly sailed across the lake toward the rover.

"They're absolutely amazing," Johnny sighed. It soon became apparent that the Pegasus creatures were both male and female as they hovered in formation directly overhead. Each four legged winged horned unicorn was approximately two thirds as tall as the rover. They now hovered directly above the rover's clear canopy in a flying v defensive formation.

All golden wings flapped precisely in unison and they alternated positions precisely with the speed and accuracy of a flock of hummingbirds. The followers continuously and abruptly changed positions back and forth lining up directly above and in front of the stunned astronauts inside the stationary rover.

Johnny and Eric's eyes made contact with the forward Pegasus and appropriately their new enlightenment allowed them the ability to verbally communicate with the entire herd simultaneously. Super fast data flowed through the astronauts minds and into the robots recorders. In moments they had deciphered the code to the unicorn's mathematical clicking musical tone language.

The conversation began with acknowledgment, greetings and wishes of well being, from the entire flock of fifteen in the Pegasus Colony all at once. In a Nemetar (nemesis revolution or approx. one earth minute) of their time the communicated dwindled down to one beautiful toned clicking musical voice of the point leader.

"We are but a single colony of remaining Pegasus of this Nemesis world. In a recorded past Nemetar of ancient Earth history the legends of Pegasus are very much true about our ancient existence among early Earth human species. Each Pegasi Muse of our tribe are two billion of your Earth years old. I hear, see and speak for all in this purpose of our communication with encountered species of Earths present Nemetar. The prod began."

"Have thy natives of Earth given consideration of thought as to what your female and male species have accomplished in a Nemebillion years since our ancient acquaintance? Is thy survival of species destined to be abolished here on this forbidden Nemesis world or shall thy kind survive the ultimate tragedy that awaits the near future of your joint expedition of braveness?"

"Do you stand to the character of progressed human kind experiences? Shall you or your frail Grey humanoid accomplices acquire the courage of ultimate sacrifice?"

The lead Pegasi had golden feathered wing tips and was fur white, silver hooves, silver mane with golden streaks and wore a sparkling Nemesis blue emerald Mulet around its jeweled gold bridal adorned neck. Pegasus's voice paused for the humans response to their prod.

Johnny and Eric suddenly became aware that the Pegasus had opened a visual link to Joanna and Christy and also the Plutonians in orbit overhead.

Johnny replied in human voice which was immediately translated into the Pegasus musical clicking tones

"Yes Pegasus. We four of Earth and our five Plutonian comrades in orbit represent the best of a cumulative ability of our two joined humanoid cultures. Our collaboration is the single reason we were able to explore here on the Nemesis."

Johnny and Eric, having suited up, exited the rover, and stepped into the howling Nemesis environment. The flock of fifteen Pegasus's descended to the surface and alighted in a V formation then spread out into a perfect circle. Simultaneously the Pegasus's touched horns to the surface and gracefully sank into a curled-up relaxed position upon the ground.

The lead Pegasus spoke again.

"Please come forward into our protective circle. Allow us a closer inspection of the humanoid species that you represent."

The two astronauts walked toward the lead Pegasus that once flew the point position and when they were within five meters of the circle their suits suddenly vanished as they stepped into the protective influence of the Pegasus circle.

A sparkling aurora field tightly encased the astronaut's skin as they stood there naked in the center of the Pegasus's. Their visible bodies were as human translucent skeletons with all their organs and main arteries exposed in the purple Nemesis x ray light.

The Pegasus's were also half translucent in appearance while inside the circle.

Johnny and Eric were so infatuated by the reality of the Pegasus's inner and outer structure. Their fascinating organs and the precision melodic rhythm of their two palpitating ruby red hearts encased by their outer winged beauty was beyond human word description. Their horns are the essence of their perfect existence that's directly linked to their brains ability to perceive while transforming and controlling the very nature and properties of matter itself.

Eric's hand touched the horn of a Pegasus and caressed the brow of its head. He felt a unique tingling velvetiness when he brushed the mane of soft fur on the neck of the Pegasus. While the Pegasus were in a lying down position, Eric, Johnny and all the Pegasus's were on an eye to eye level and instantly communicating cultural facts between the entire group simultaneously.

Suddenly the fifteen Pegasus's condensed down into two separate gold wing tip unicorns as the two from Earth sat straddling each their own crimson red velvet saddle.

The two humans leaned tight to their manes while both Pegasus gracefully bolted skyward. The cosmonauts leaned forward and lay in close between the folds of their graceful velvet fur winged Pegasus.

At first they sailed high up into a huge climbing spiral circle, then gracefully gliding north and still higher toward an omnibus huge dark mountain in the extreme distance that the cone lingered just above a surrounding billow of ultraviolet Nemesis clouds.

Bursting through to the top of the Pluto lit reflected clouds they soared on just above the jagged sharp ridges of the highest mountains on Nemesis then softly settled downward and lit left of center of an amazing cone valley they called Paradise.

The Pegasus Paradise.

Here, high up among a dreaded dark Nemesis mountain, existed the entrance to a land where fifteen Pegasus's dwell.

Like John Wayne and Gene Autry, the two slid and dismounted while the bowed neck water drinking Pegasus's lopped sparkling water from the stream. One Pegasi rose its head and spoke.

"It is extremely necessary for you humans to immediately drink a quantity of this water." Two goblets instantly materialized and they were induced to partake.

Here was a Paradise in the middle of exotic mountain peak on a far away world. A fantasy land of flowers, fountains and gardens along with the trickling liquid of the golden waterfalls in every lateral direction. Feathered foul of numerous species inhabited the alien treetops and the pair now followed the Pegasus on foot downhill along a cobble stone path that led around the inner rim toward a crystal lake far below and in the center of everything.

The two asked the Pegasus. "Why not sail down there in flight? Wouldn't it be quicker?"

"Oh No!", replied the Pegasus sternly but politely. "We mustn't ever do that. For if we do! The crystal gate below will never allow us to pass."

"Pass where?" The two Earthlings queried.

"Patience is like science, some things have to be shown and you'll both will be very soon," Pegasus replied. "This journey downward along the inner cobble stone road is a decontamination process that systematically cleanses us all of the Nemesis particle contamination.

The process allows your human blood and ours to adapt to the pressure modulation slowly. It is forbidden to ever fly inside the Epitomic Cone. The matter inside these cobble path walls increases in density as we venture downward toward the gravity crystal lens below. When we arrive at the crystal you will learn the purpose for this Epitomic structure."

Around the last inside corner the cobblestone widened abruptly to an opening at the edge of a royal crystalline frozen liquid. The crystal perimeter was surrounded by a pulsating black gravity ring coil that pulsated with two unique twenty-nine second frequencies modulations. The frequency pause was tuned to a half rotation of the Nemesis.

As Pluto passed directly overhead, the perimeter coil pulsed dark energy waves from deep within the dense soil of the inner Nemesis core and pulsed three point fourteen times. Twenty nine seconds later when Pluto was one hundred eighty degrees opposite, the edges of the crystal lake turned ultraviolet green and drastically increased pulsation to a superluminal frequency that for eight seconds sucked cold energy from space and channeled it directly back inside the Nemesis super cold core.

The Nemesis was pulsing two unique separate energy pulse waves through the immediate inner space from its corona's edge.

Firstly emitting a hot three point fourteen negative energy pulse wave that exists slightly below the subatomic frequency level in the Higgs Field, therefore producing a dark energy pulse wave frequency of three point fourteen negative beats per second in the first twenty-nine second time frame, then reversing polarity and shooting super cold charged energy through dense mass directly back into the Nemesis core in the second half Nemetar.

When the Nemesis faced the near side of Pluto the perimeter coil quickly converted energy toward the superluminal frequency level of

584,925 vibrations per second. The ultraviolet warm energy spectral field at the projection speed of approximately 584,925 miles per second reached Pluto in Nememillisecond.

In an Epitome, Johnny and Eric recognized the significance of the three point fourteen in mathematics. The significance of the pi. beats per second time from visual low frequency light speed of 186,282 miles per second to the superluminal visual spectral vibrations of more than 584925 vibrations or three point fourteen miles per seconds traveled.

That's the equivalent of pi, being that warm energy particle waves, traveling three point fourteen times faster than the low visible ultraviolet spectral wave speed of light at 186,282 miles per second.

The fact that Pluto was so very close at a mere twelve thousand two hundred miles meant, that normal radiation only took less than a one twentieth of a light second to arrive. Therefore the Higgs field wave particles arrived at Pluto at one twentieth of a second, divided by pi. Equaling almost before instantaneous arrival of dark rays that warmed and sustained Pluto.

Epitome conquered. The two followed the two Pegasus as they stepped across the coil between phases and onto the crystal blue frozen lake.

They walked on inward toward a golden upright arch light kilometers away. The crystal floor below revealed rolling green lightning bolts kilometers below the frozen liquid beneath their hooves and feet as Humans and Pegasus's progressed forward toward the center of everything.

The last half kilometer it quickly became apparent that this was way more than just a golden tuning fork arch. It was a gateway to the center of infinity itself existing harmoniously from the Alpha to the Omega simultaneously. The Sojourners came to the edge of the inner circle immediately surrounding the sky reaching golden crystal tuning fork and paused.

"Here at this boundary is where decontamination is critically finalized," Pegasus spoke. "Each of us must step through separately exactly fifty-eight seconds apart on the pi. beat frequency pulse. Only one entity per frequency pulse may enter the Epitomic realm."

"I shall step through first. Pegasus two will subsequently follow fifty-eight seconds later. Then you two humans shall follow, each fifty-eight seconds later one at a time on the negative pi. frequency pulse. Remember to step in instantly on the first of the three point fourteen beats of the low frequency pulse."

Pegasus one stepped forward and began disintegrating into a cloud of dematerializing atoms as Pegasus two stepped forward to await its exact entry moment.

Eric stepped through the mist next and saw Johnny and the Pegasus's already directly ahead of him in the distance.

"Now! How could that possibly be?" Eric pondered deeply the concept of superluminal light speed for a Nemetar. "When I followed the second Pegasus, Johnny was suppose to have stepped through the Epitomic realm fifty eight seconds after I had." Yet He'd just now materialized and Johnny with the two Pegasi were already ahead of his tag along rear point of view position. Eric scratched his head then followed on hurriedly trying to catch up. The trio ahead had suddenly vanished as they stepped upon twinkling chessboard stepping stones.

His very next step took him directly through to infinities of multiverses and they all were spiraling downward toward the center of infinity itself. Here in the center was an existence where the first big bang itself had once occurred eons upon eons ago.

Ultimately Eric and Johnny materialized in front of a flexible seemingly elastic black physical barrier. The two Pegasus emitted clicking musical tones and the four passed through into a gravity lens that revealed a splendid new solar system unlike any imagined.

Dyson spear worlds encompassed within huge ringed interplanetary translucent bead bands and surrounded by a strange star field that seemed to ooze rather than twinkle it's light from far away.

There were opposite moons that bobbed up and down along their journey as they closely circled their shielded Dyson star companion.

There were planets that performed opposite dances to their satellites journey. One Planet would suddenly change its orbital forward motion and journey backwards for a specific time then stop and reverse direction again.

There was this one amazing liquid pulsating planet system that had two opposite equal mass moons with convenient missing scoops from their round rolling muddy surface. The fast orbiting dipper moons would continuously dip downward at opposition into the fuchsia liquid surface they orbited. As one moon fell inward bounced scooped and spewed liquid inward toward a metal surrounded bright green star, the other moon rose high in it's orbit slinging the last of it's dipped cargo toward an Iris eye storm.

As the liquid traversed the distance inward and upon arrival at the metal encompassed star shield, it would instantaneously result in an outward rainbow light wave burst.

The Pegasus had disappeared from their subconscious suddenly and they immediately understood that this system is where the Pegasus's society had originated from. No sufficient words can define the beauty of this star system they named Iris.

Eric wondered just how the liquid was replenished that the dipper moons scooped up and ejected. Upon closer inspection of the Iris stars rainbow light field and at the very edge of visibility, Eric watched as the edge of the light field turned back into ice crystals and lead a direct path back to the leading face of the spinning liquid planet. Then the moons dipped their due, bounced and completed their opposite oval loops. A chime toned through their minds and they heard the fading words of Pegasus saying,

"Farewell! Oh human explorers from Earth. This is all we are allowed to reveal at this time continuum. Wisdom of the universe reveals as having been there. You have merely touched the very edge of center. Each Universe in itself is a sentient being of which is infinite. There are many infinites. If one can imagine any specific thing, Somewhere in a multiversity of infinities, it becomes truth."

Both astronauts in an instant abruptly regressed backwards in a whirlwind and the telepathic protection link with the Pegasus ended. They were instantaneously transported onto the howling Nemesis surface in front of the rover.

The explorers now back in their suits on the surface turned to each other eye to eye and knew they had just experienced something profound. No words. They both agreed. Human dialect couldn't process the ability to describe what they'd experienced.

Back aboard the rovers safety they soon unsuited speaking not a word until Johnny sat down behind the rovers idle controls.

CHAPTER NINETEEN
LANDER ONE IN DISTRESS

Looks like the Plutonians missed out on that visual Johnny stated. We should be in radio contact range of the lander by now. Try to raise the girls on the radio. Eric reached up and took the mike from its slot while still levitating and trailing the stones behind them.

"This is rover inbound on the surface," he radioed. "Are you receiving this signal?" He released the mike button and they listened to garbled static over the speakers.

Broken parts of Christy's voice crackled through their headsets as she said. "We got three hours before liftoff time and we have a major," then suddenly silence followed by a crackling static pop. The communication links dead again. "Oh well!" Eric said. "It appears she was saying that we need to get our butts back there quickly."

"Yeah this storm seems to be getting more intense by the Nemetar," Johnny replied. "Can you pick up the lander on forward radar beam?"

"Not yet," Eric replied. "I don't think any kind of dependable radio broadcast is possible on this beastly world."

"OK then! Try shooting a direct radar light power beam directly toward the landers coordinates."

"Roger that," Eric complied. "I'm charging up rovers auxiliary batteries in thirty seconds I'm gonna fire three short ten second microburst. You'll need to momentarily stop the rover while I scan for reflections off the landers metal surface."

"Roger that," Johnny complied pulling the rover to a stop in a clearing.

"Five seconds," Eric stated. Eric fired three laser beams in the direction of the landers assumed position.

They sat there quietly for a moment searching the screen for a sign that the beam had struck the lander and bounced back.

"There it is!" Eric reported. "About a quarter of a kilometer to the Southeast. Bearing point eighty six degrees."

"OK," Johnny said. "We're heading that way."

Johnny and Eric breathed a sigh of relief as Johnny steered the rover around more hot pits of matter and huge boulders. The Nemesis wind beat against the little vehicle as it struggled the last rough trail towards the lander.

"There's the ship!" Johnny exclaimed. "Over there by the rock face to the left."

"Ok," Eric said. "I was beginning to get a little worried."

"Yeah," Johnny returned. "Me too."

Johnny drove the last fifty meters up to the waiting lander and Eric levitated the heavy rocks from the cargo bay down to the ground with a thud beside the lander.

Just as soon as they'd pulled up next to the ship, Christy frantically came across the speakers. "We're in trouble here guys. We've been trying to contact you but didn't have much luck."

"We've got a bigger problem than you think," Joanna's voice came in. "Christy and I are trapped in the middle section of the lander. The Lander was impaled by an ice meteor and we were barely able to escape into the middle section before the Nemesis air rushed in. We didn't even have enough time to get our suits when it happened. We were able to escape the main deck before it filled with Nemesis air."

"I think we may have ingested a little too much of that poison air. We're a little sick but I think we'll be ok." Joanna paused.

Eric radioed back. "We're on our way in."

Eric and Johnny hurriedly suited up and prepared to exit the rover. "It's a good thing we've charged up our portable life support." Johnny said.

"Yeah, we never expected to get back and find that the lander had a hole in it," Eric returned.

"You've surely got that right. Let's hope that the girls are alright and the damage is repairable."

The two astronauts soon stood on the ground outside the lander as they walked around it to check for apparent damage.

"Look up there," Johnny said. "I see the hole in the top of the lander up near the main deck."

"Yeah I see what you mean. That's a pretty nasty looking tear in the side," Eric replied. "We'd better get inside and help the girls and then see what we can do about repairing that hole."

"Right," Johnny agreed. They climbed aboard the elevator and pushed the button to shut the door but nothing happened. "Uh Oh! I think we've got some big problems here. We don't seem to have any power on the controls at all. The elevators not working. We're gonna have to climb up the ladder and see if we can get the upper door open manually."

Johnny started up the long narrow ladder first. "It's going to be a little tricky in this wind. We'd better take it slow Eric said." Johnny was already half way up when a big gust of wind almost blew him off the ladder. Eric, just below him caught his leg in time to pull him back.

"That was close," Johnny exclaimed. He huddled closer in toward the ladder and began his slow battling climb again.

This time he made slower progress while he stopped every few seconds to look back and check on Eric's progress. The wind howled and beat against their backs as Johnny reached the platform that was at the summit of their climb.

He crawled onto the high porch and turned to lend a hand to Eric in the last portion of his climb. The two now on their knees stood up slowly and made their way over to the entry hatch. Eric dialed in the emergency entry code but the hatch did not respond.

"Looks like we're going to have to open the door" Johnny said. Eric then opened the emergency door on a small panel and took out a metal crank rod with a pronged forks on the end. The two took turns cranking the manual door opener until they were able to squeeze through the narrow entrance one at a time. Upon entry into the chamber they had to crank the outside door back shut. They had to repeat the process again when finally they managed to get the second ship door open.

The girls were sweating huddled in the middle of the ship sharing the last of an emergency air supply. The temperature inside the ship had risen to a hundred and twenty degrees and the compartment was losing its life support to the outside.

"We've got to get down below and retrieve the girls suits," Johnny ordered. "They don't have much time and this air is contaminated with Nemesis air."

"OK," Eric replied "I'm climbing down to the lower deck. I'll be back quick." He grabbed the inside ladder and hurriedly climbed downward. He reached the bottom of the ladder and momentarily had a problem with the entry hatch. He used the door crank he still had with him to open the final door. The air swished out of the chamber as Eric quickly rushed in closing the door behind him to keep the lower chamber from losing the rest of its pressure. He rushed over to the utility compartment containing the suits and quickly removed them from their charging stations. He took a quick computer check in the cargo bay of the extensive damage to the main deck and then headed back to the waiting three above.

He reached the top rung and Johnny was there to take the suits and rushed them over to the two desperate girls. Joanna and Christy were almost unconscious while they hustled to get their suits on and get them pressurized. They managed to get their helmets on and snapped them in place.

The flow of the fresh oxygen in the suit immediately brought a response from the gasping for air, girl astronauts. They breathed the air for a few moments and seemed to be recuperating and coming around to consciousness.

"OK." Johnny said. "We'd better get the girls to the main deck while we try to see what can be done about repairs." The girls still groggy managed to ascend the ladder to the main deck.

"We've got a lot of damage up here," Eric reported. "Looks like the ship took a bad hit in the main control section. We could patch that hole but I don't know what we can do about all the damage to the main computer controls. All of the ships main power is down and we're running off what's left of the reserve batteries."

The two girls rested in the main deck chairs while Johnny and Eric got busy repairing the two meter rip in the main cabin hull. "We're two hours away from liftoff time," Johnny stated. "We're not gonna make it. The repair to the hull alone will take that long."

"Yeah," Eric said. "We've got so much damage. It's impossible to repair it all in time.

"I know," Johnny said. "We've been on Nemesis for twenty two hours. Our time is running short."

"Yeah we'd better get a move on. Even if we could raise the Plutonians they can't help us."

"We need to somehow get that other lander on the surface. This one's going no where. There's just way too much damage to the computers and back up systems. What's our air supply status?" Johnny asked.

Joanna answered. "We have about six hours showing on our tanks and yours and Eric's are reading about seven hours remaining. That's if we go easy."

"Well the first thing we've got to do is attempt getting in touch with Qwerto's crew in orbit". Johnny ordered. "Eric, You and I are going to have to get back to the rover and try to get through on the radio. You two girls stay here. We'll contact the Plutonians."

Johnny and Eric again cranked the hatches to the outside open and stepped out on the deck in a ragging Nemesis storm. Eric began his descent down the ladder clinging closely to the rungs. It took three Nemetar's for the astronauts to reach the bottom rung of the ladder. In the increasing storm they jumped to the hot Nemesis surface. They leaned forward into the winds and staggered toward the rovers flashing strobe in the storm. Eventually they managed to make it to the entry door and climbed back aboard. Johnny closed the hatch behind them and pressurized the small but adequate cabin. They fell into the seats exhausted from the past long days exploration of this Nemesis stormy star.

Johnny drove the rover away from the lander a few hundred meters in hopes to get a better radio position for the emergency broadcast. He drove toward a clearing away from the lander but still in view in a now even more raging intensifying storm.

These winds are well over two hundred eighty miles per hour out there.

"This storm's getting a lot worse," Eric yelled back over the noise of the storm outside.

"Yeah," Johnny said. "Look at the lander. It's rocking in the wind like crazy. The girls are in immediate danger. That ships gonna blow over soon."

Johnny suddenly grabbed the controls and fought the storm back toward the swaying lander. "We've got to get the girls out of there," He said. "I'm going back to get the girls now. They don't possibly stand a chance if the lander blows over in this storm."

"Right indeed," Eric agreed.

Johnny drove the rover to within thirty meters of the swaying lander then quickly exited into the worst ever Nemesis storm. He disappeared into the stormy mist while Eric frantically attempted contacting the rescue party in orbit.

Johnny fought his way through extreme battering winds and fell to the ground at the foot of the rocking lander. He grabbed the ladder rungs and again fought his way up the long narrow metal rails.

The Nemesis storm grew furious and the rocking of the ship made Johnny fall to the surface several times. He hit the ground and tried to get up but extreme pain shot through his right leg. He lay there on the surface stunned and barely conscious.

The next thing Johnny remembered was Joanna and Christy dragging him across the Nemesis surface with the storm raging all around. Eric appeared from the mist of the storm and picked up Johnny. The desperate struggling crew turned into the wind to traverse the thirty meters distance to the rovers flashing strobe lights.

Meter by meter the crew fought their way through a hellish nightmare storm. Joanna and Christy led the challenge and Eric struggled with Johnny's unconscious body straddling his forward leaning center gravity shoulder.

They'd managed to fight their way back to the hatch of the rover and desperately climbed aboard and sealed the hatch behind them. They got Johnny strapped in and secured the rover away from the danger of the rocking lander.

Joanna took immediate action driving the rover away from the catastrophe. Lander one came crashing to the surface with a cataclysmic eruption of explosive fuel. Debris fell from the sky when detonation of the remaining fuel aboard the lander erupted in a tremendous explosion that left the landers skeletal remains burning violently inside a whirlwind of flame.

Joanna's nervous hands drove the desperate crew to safety a half kilometer away from the burning wreckage.

The crew sat staring hopelessly into the storm while Lander's wreckage burned in the distance. They were horrified by the burning crumpled pieces of what was left of their destroyed lander.

"What will we do? Christy asked.

Eric answered. "Let's get our emergency act together and try to contact the Plutonians."

CHAPTER TWENTY

THE RESCUE OF SACRIFICE

The crew forced themselves to settled down somewhat and the girls climbed forward into the cramped rover and charged up the lazier radio signal for the emergency s.o.s. The lander burned and the rover still rocked and shook in the raging storm as the girls desperately tried to communicate a dire straight message to the Plutonians in orbit. They'd almost given up hope when Latilia's garbled voice came over the speakers.

"We're trapped down here," Joanna radioed back. "The lander is destroyed and we've retreated to limited reserves and safety of the rover. Johnny's is seriously hurt and we only have a few hours of life support remaining. If you guys can't get that other lander on the surface soon we're surely doomed. We're gonna die."

She released the mike button and the desperate crew waited for a response to their SOS. The radio crackled with static as bits and pieces of Latilia's voice crackled a few words before the radio went dead again.

The storm raged on outside while the little rover shook and rocked in the super Nemecane. The four huddled together on the floor in space suits while their air supply dwindled down. Eric later remembered thinking. "Man! We just can't die like this. With all the knowledge we've gained and all the billions of miles we've traveled. Now to die like this on a hostile Nemesis Sun on the cold edge of the solar system."

The storm raged on and the rovers batteries were down to ten percent power remaining. The temperature inside the rover had risen to one hundred degrees and the crew of four brave souls huddled together in the tight compartment. Their air supply dwindled down to three hours remaining and the rovers batteries was down to a few hours.

Johnny looked into Joanna's eyes and felt her love and trust. He realized that he'd always loved her and the crew was depending on him being able to figure a way out of this drastic situation. Joanna stared back deep into Johnny's brown eyes and knew a respect for this man that no other woman could possibly understand. They'd traveled billions of miles together across dangerous unknown territory. They'd shared their lives with Christy and Eric in new worlds and fantastic journeys of discovery. No other four humans in this solar system had worked and lived together in their small environment and under these new life threatening conditions.

Eric and Christy held each other tight as the winds outside roared and shook the little land vehicle that sat near a pile of burning rocket rubble on this far away Nemesis. Eric was fifteen years older than Christy and realized that he must be the luckiest man in the solar system.

Christy whispered to Eric. "How can we possibly survive this?"

Eric reflected the dire straight situation for a moment then hugged her and said. "Don't worry baby. We're not about to die on this want to be grown baby star. Johnny and I have a plan. Don't We Johnny?"

"You Dang right we do." Johnny spoke up wincing the pain. "Through all the excitement we haven't had a chance to tell you about any of our discoveries. Don't worry though. Eric and I understand what has to be done."

"Yep that's right," Eric said. "I'll drive." Eric shuffled around and slid into the control seat of the rover. Johnny with his bad leg slid into the co-pilot seat.

"What are we going to do?" Joanna asked.

"Yeah!" Christy questioned. "Where are we going in this raging storm?"

"Never Fear!" Johnny ordered. "We know exactly what we are doing. We've been Enlightened. So must you be."

"How's that leg?" Eric asked.

"It hurts like Heck, but I'll manage" He responded. I've got an idea."

Eric made a silent mental connection. "If we put our minds together, we can do something about that broken leg and the pain. Do you remember what we learned in the cave? Our new knowledge."

"What new knowledge?" Joanna insisted out loud. The men were shocked that Joanna was able to hear their assumed private thoughts.

"You guys need to tell us what's going on here."

"All right," Johnny said. "First Eric and I have to do something about this leg of mine. It Hurts !" Johnny said.

He stretched his shattered leg out as much as possible in the cramped rover seat and they both concentrated their minds on his injury. Johnny felt the warm sensation instantly easing the pain considerably. The sensation continued and he felt a sharp pop in the bone when Eric mentally sat the bone back in place. Another intense sensation wave as the two mentally fussed the broken bones.

Johnny jumped up happy as a kid at a Christmas awakening and stomped his leg on the floor of the rover shouting, dang that feels super better.

Johnny back to his old self again took command and started giving orders. "We'll all right then", As if he were laughing in the face of death. "We're getting the heck out of here."

"There's about four hours battery remaining," Eric informed. "Our airs down to almost two hours, forty minutes."

"I know exactly what we must do and fast"

"Yep, me too" Eric replied and gunned the rover forward and shouted, "Hold on tight Crew." The rover made its way back through the beacon marked trail it had blazed earlier.

This time Eric knew the path they'd traveled and drove rover at full speed following the marker buoy's. The winds raged around the rover. Eric drove continuously and began explaining about the discovery of the Entity of the Nemesis cavern to the girls. Johnny began informing them of the Nemesaurus and the Pegasus's encounters. The storm began receding its intensity.

Eric drove ahead trying to make it to the cavern and their only hope of survival. He drove past one beacon then another as he watched the power of the rover dwindle down to three percent.

The storms winds had decreased to one hundred sixty kilometers per hour and had brought a new sense of hope to the brave explorers. Eric drove as fast as it would go throughout the winding path they had already traversed once. He drove on for another hour while their air supply dwindled to two percent remaining. He was getting a little worried now as he realized that it takes ten minutes of air to get to the interior of the caverns. The rover's down to one percent power and began slowing as it rounded the last beacon they'd left on the surface. It shouldn't be far now he stated. The cavern entrance should be just around that next bend.

The rover crawled as the electric drive drained the last usable electrons. Time was running short. Their air supply was down to forty five minutes and the headlights went dim as the rover crept along at a crawl before stopping two hundred meters from the cavern entrance.

"Looks like we're on our own," Johnny said. "We have to hurry. Lets get moving. We're gonna have to walk from here." They stepped onto the Nemesis soil and started walking in the direction of the dark hole in the mountain ahead. They all four stumbled forward fighting the diminished but still formidable winds. It took them fifteen minutes of hard breathing to reach the entrance to the long dark tunnel. Fifteen minutes of air left and they still had at least a twenty minute traverse to the Nemesis flowing liquid wall.

Johnny and Eric ascertained that they were going to run out of air and started communicating mentally again. Johnny began the mental conversation. "Eric I know you can hear me. We've got to come up with a way to get the girls and us to the Deity wall before our air runs out."

Eric secretly back. "Yeah I know. Why don't we try what we tried when we fixed your leg and concentrate our minds on levitating the four of us there."

"Good Idea," Johnny returned. They stopped their rushing and stood with the girls just inside the long dark tunnel. Joanna spoke up.

"Why are we stopping? We've got to hurry we only have a few minutes of air remaining."

"Yeah we know," Johnny answered. "Just hold on tight, Eric and I will get us there. That's a promise."

The two combined their mental ability and levitated the four a meter high above the floor and started moving rapidly down the long dark tunnel. In sixty seconds they'd arrived at the golden room of heavy stones and on past to where had once been the mystical flowing Deity's wall. They levitated softly down in front of the place where the two had entered before.

"Its not here!" Eric said in a panic.

"Its just an ordinary dark rock wall," Johnny said. "What happened to it? I'm positive this is the right spot."

"Yes! This is exactly where the fluid wall was." Eric said. "It's gone now and in seconds we'll be completely out of air."

The four stood at the rock wall and worried they'd gambled and lost on the Deity entrance still being in the same place. The last thirty seconds arrived and the two couples held each other in their arms as the clock ticked down to ten seconds.

"Goodbye!"

"I love you," they each spoke the words. Instantly as if they'd spoken magic love words, the wall materialized again and the flowing wall surrounded the desperate marooned astronauts.

"No air left," they gasped their last breathe and the four succumbed to the force of the Deity's protection. Christy, Eric, Johnny and Joanna stood in the presence of the Deity of the Nemesis. The protective velvet liquid enveloped the four brave astronauts that had dared explore the Nemesis.

Now they stood at its mercy in its own environment. The four became overwhelmed with emotion and jubilation at the awakening of their intelligence. Vast amounts of knowledge continued to accumulate until they were in direct communication with the Supreme Intelligence of the Nemesis Star.

The chamber was silent, allowing the explorers a moment to gather their thoughts and reflect on the past three minutes since their entrance into the wall of miraculous salvation.

Then the Deity spoke! Different words to each about their individual personal existence in the universe and their right to go on existing with a choice of either this land or the one they had known before they entered the place of the Deity. The four communicated back instantly in unison.

"We are the representation of humans from Earth. We came exploring because of a great need to know and a deep love and respect for science and natures knowledge of laws of physics and its properties and all that is yet to be assimilated by humankind. We are honored to be in your presence."

The Nemesis Deity Responded. "What proclamation has humankind from Earth learned? To what has thou concluded about your existence about the true meaning of your known universe?"

They answered. "We have concluded that this immeasurable distance of unending space filled with many worlds full of all sorts of nature and fertile grounds of the existence of all life forms are all created by higher means and are always to be revered and cherished by all that seek and touch them. Even the stars in all the heavens are full of different life forms and Deities of the most high. Life exist everywhere and all life is due to a supreme higher cause and effect."

The Deity spoke to the four humans again. "In humans I am well pleased at your response to nature and things created by supreme guidance. It is We the Deities that have reshaped solar systems of many beautiful worlds for many life forms to inhabit. Twas us that gave humanoids the inextinguishable quest for knowledge and exploration. So it is at my beckoning that humankind's thirst for knowledge has caused you to wonder of the great Nemesis that exists now and has occurred in thy ancient past. It was that act of my existence that caused two societies from different worlds and environments to band together for the survival of not one but many forms of life that exist on Earth and other worlds. So Be It. The Deity Declared. Go yeah! Oh humans of exploration and courage. Be yeah frugal and respectful in thy endeavors and bind together with appreciation for all living existence. Forever honor thy comrades and neighbors especially ones that give freely of their own lives so that others may survive and know knowledge.

Even now as I speak, Your Plutonian friends have given the ultimate sacrifice of their lives so that the four of you shall survive. I the Nemesis Entity return you humans to your second lander to honor and bury the remains of the three of your best friends. It is this kind of love of sacrifice that I most respect in living biological creatures. Go yeah and forbid to all, to stay away from this Nemesis. No more shall any come to this place that only I may dwell in with my creatures. Go then in safety back to your ship and follow my instructions. Tell others of the knowledge and the wisdom you have found. Go forth and explore but for every world of mine that thy stand upon. Give honor and respect to its present population and learn to trust and love different cultural civilizations.

Know that from now on, that all such dark suns are forbidden and are only for the Deities that live throughout the universe's. Many are the worlds that you may explore. Few are the worlds that are forbidden. These few mysterious worlds are our place of dwelling and are not hospitable to mortal life. Though I am well pleased in humanoid kind, I give thee refuge from this storm and grant your crew safe passage back to your waiting lander. Go forth and spread my message. For I am, the I Am of this dark body. I am all that is in all matter and non matter of this Nemesis. "

In an Instant the four crew members were back at the lander ship that sat near where the other lander had been before it was destroyed by the Nemesis storm. Qwerto, Zxico and Pertravio had made the ultimate sacrifice and gave their lives to land the number two lander. Their fragile low gravity bodies were only able to withstand the high gravity and radiation just long enough for them to land the ship.

They sat there dead at the controls. It was this kind of love that the deity had talked off and admired.

Johnny, Joanna, Christy and Eric stood at the head of the three graves and gave homage to three great souls that had given their lives so the four of them could survive. It was due to this kind of love that the Deity had given them reprieve from death and ordered their comrades remains buried here for eternity.

In full space suits they stood near the foot of the lander and gave thanks to their three true friends from a different culture. They climbed aboard the lander and gave one last thanks to the Deity for their survival and faithful friends.

The elevator slowly rose to the top of lander two. Christy reached forward to decompress the air lock that opened as soon as the pressure was equalized.

Nova crew took one more look down on the Nemesis surface and the three graves were illuminated with an aurora as the howling weather suddenly changed to an eerie calmness.

The Earthlings understood with deep respect about the Deities and their amazing Nemesis worlds.

CHAPTER TWENTY ONE

ESCAPE FROM THE NEMESIS

The crew readied lander for liftoff from the Nemesis. These were not the same beings that landed on this Nemesis star twenty eight hours ago. Their minds had been enlightened to a point of unlimited capacity with a new understanding of physics and nature. All this knowledge had made them more destined to explore.

Johnny sat at the controls with mixed emotions of the immediate past. He'd realized now that humans and life didn't evolve accidentally out of some gurgling mixture of DNA molecules. His very existence was the result of an ancient creation that once resulted in two humanoid cultures banding together in a time of extreme crisis. He realized that humankind had arrived in this system and discovered unique possibilities. Humans were a unique species that was an end result of an alien life not from this solar system. Humans were a generation of unique species with a devised guidance.

The ancient legends about Cydonia Mars that his great great grandfather had once told him about were somewhat true. The actual truth was that once there were Martians on Mars. The legends of the mysterious Sphinx flashed through his mind as he sat reflecting deeply on his ancient grandfathers stories.

He reminisced back to his college days at Duke University in Durham N.C. Then a lad of only nineteen he was a student of Astronomy where his grandfather lectured to students about the possibility of an extraterrestrial life that once lived on Mars.

Pictures of Mars sand covered pyramids that showed the ancient Egypt like face staring up from the Martian long ago stripped away surface. He remembered reading about the ancient pyramids to the west of the mile across the vertically pointing Sphinx. The legends about a Martian war at the fortress of the southern ninety degree wall. Johnny reflected thoughts of watching the Mars sun rise in the east using the nose of the face as a solstice to mark the summer season. He theorized of how the Sphinx lay a kilometer and a half due east of the city and at one time the face was an island buttress in the middle of an ancient Mars lake flowing south toward the Equator.

He postulated of biblical text of Ezekiel and Noah. He comprehended now how ancient Earthlings and the Martians had banned together in an extreme survival mode and built the pyramids on both worlds to protect both humanoid species from total annihilation.

Johnny assimilated how the ancient transplanted Martians were only able to survive for an era on the heavy gravity Earth. With the assistance of the Martians advanced technology and humans strong backs, they built the pyramids in the desert of Egypt and at Cydonia Mars.

Johnny then remembered the ridiculed legend of the great Nemesis that disrupted the harmony of the worlds in this solar system. He recalled it all now. It was all true.

The after Nemesis Martians that survived, by necessity soon built ships and left Earth. Mars had been devastated. Its air stripped away and no longer suitable for their existence. The few remaining Martians explored all possibilities of life in this system winding up with the discovery of the Nemesis around the once fifth planet from the sun.

All these recollections and thoughts went through Johnny's mind in seconds as he once again sat ready in the command chair of a rocket pointed skyward. This time the situation was different. Never before had humans ejected from a small fast spinning world such as this. Overhead the lavender Planet Pluto rose in the east every fifty eight seconds, then rapidly ascended to its zenith taking twenty nine seconds to rise and set in the west. Somewhere in orbit was Nova command ship where Latilia and Serdia hopefully awaited their rendezvous.

The crew of four sat buckled in as Johnny threw the breaker to ignite the mighty lander two rocket engines. A stick of fire trembled and shook as its engines roared to life taking seconds to build up enough thrust to slowly raise from the surface of Nemesis then ascending slowly at first and arching eastward over on its back chasing the direction of the Pluto heavenly body.

Thirty seconds after liftoff the ship was gaining speed rapidly. It was as if the spinning body below was slowing down as they began matching the speed of the spinning Nemesis rotation.

Nova crew were slammed back in their seats by the five gravity forces straining their individual structural integrity. Swirling massive atmosphere rushed by the forward window as the fierce lightning bolts struck near and far in all directions of their view.

"We're at ten kilometers altitude. Speed, three and two tenths kilometers per second." Eric screamed out under the stress of the high gravity. "If we're struck again by lightning it might cause our main computer to go down."

'Well lets hope the backup comes on in time." Just as Johnny finished speaking another lightning bolt struck the lander and the cabin started losing its atmospheric pressure.

"Every body had better check your suits pressure," Christy yelled. "We're losing cabin pressure fast."

Just as she spoke the main console suddenly went blank and the backup cabin lights came on and the engines went suddenly silent.

"Come on back up." Johnny punched the reset breaker furiously almost punching a hole in his index finger of his spacesuit. After thirty seconds of feverishly trying to get the back up going the ship started losing some of its forward momentum.

"We're going down," Joanna said in the darkness. Suddenly the display came back on and two seconds later the engines came back online.

The thunderous roar again filled the cabin of Nova lander two. "She's a stick of fire again," Johnny exclaimed.

"We're gaining altitude again," Eric said, "but we've obtained a small hole in our hull. We've lost all pressure in the cabin but our suits will protect us as long as nothing else goes wrong. Speed four point two k.p.s. and climbing," Eric spoke a little easier now that the G forces were subsiding. The life pod rocket rose higher as they now matched the planets spin by almost eighty percent.

"We're at seventeen kilometers altitude and climbing." Johnny eased back on the throttle and the ship relaxed from the extreme stress it was under.

Christy excitedly interjected. "We're loosing power in the main reactor. We must have taken a hit in the fuel storage section too."

Johnny glanced down at the fuel gauge. It read twenty percent and loosing a quarter of a percent per second. "We've got a big problem." He shoved the throttle forward again thrusting the four back into their chairs.

"We will run out of fuel in sixty seconds," Eric screamed over the roar.

"Yeah I know," Johnny retorted, "but we've got too get as much forward speed as possible before the remaining fuel leaks out. It's either burn it or lose it," He stated.

The rocket accelerated on forward above the spinning Nemesis.

"Five seconds until fuels depletion," Christy reported. The timer ticked to zero, as the engines fell suddenly silent.

"What's our forward speed?" Johnny questioned.

"Five point six kilometers per second," Eric replied. "Altitude thirty nine miles high. We've got just enough speed to remain in this orbit for two hours before we reenter the atmosphere. Any sign yet of the orbiter?" He asked.

"No sign of them yet. We'd better hope they spot us and come down to get us," Joanna said.

"We're already on battery back up power," Eric reported. Johnny spoke. "Christy, see if you can get us a direct line radio connection to the orbiter."

"Affirmative," she replied while reaching for the transmitter mike.

"We're in trouble if you can read us," she stated. "We have less than two hours before we fall back into the atmosphere." She released the button as quietness filled the cabin while the crew listened to a static crackling hiss. "Keep trying," Johnny ordered. "Lets hope they know we're here." Christy called a few more times and finally got a broken garbled response.

"This is Serdia," the message began and then broke up. They were only thirteen miles above the outer atmosphere and the static was intense as they sped around the dark star. The garbled message ended with, "one hour and thirty minutes" trailing off to nothingness and more static.

Christy left the radio on hoping to hear more from the two Plutonians. "If they mean they'll be here in an hour and a half, we will almost be at the point of atmospheric entry," Eric stated.

"Well," Johnny replied. "We'd better see what can be done to gain us a little more time."

"Okay," Eric said. "We've got to get rid of some of this excess weight. We can jettison the descent stage but we'll lose our cargo of heavy Nemesis stones from the surface." "Alright," Johnny ordered. "Listen up. We've got an hour before we have to jettison the descent stage. Eric lets you and I take a space walk to see if we can retrieve a few of those heavy stones before we drop the descent stage."

"Lets go then!" Eric unbuckled his belt and floated gracefully behind Johnny in a convoy heading toward the lander airlock. Johnny grabbed the entrance bar and pulled himself into the decompression chamber. Eric opened the storage compartment and took out two backpack propulsion units.

"Here put this on and help me get mine on. We're gonna need these out there."

They snapped each others clips and gave the propulsion units a little test.

"Looks good," Johnny stated. "Stay close behind me old man," he joked.

"Yeah You can laugh at a time like this but if Latilia and Serdia don't show up with that command module We're not gonna make it off of this rock and you're not going to live to be an old man."

Johnny didn't respond because he knew Eric was right. He reached down and released the latch and the door opened up to the void of space above the dreaded Nemesis. He pushed off gently and sailed out the door and activated his propulsion unit. He watched Pluto float by and turned toward the tail of the lander.

Eric followed until they reached the rear cargo storage on the bottom of the lander. Johnny took out a portable socket wrench and placed it on the latch mechanism and removed the safety bolts that held the panel in place. Holding the bolts in his hand he tossed them to the Nemesis surface below watching them disappear in the mist above the top of the atmosphere. He turned and opened the panel revealing the cargo boxes that contained the stones from the Nemesis surface. They'd managed to store five stones each in the two containers before they'd left. Eric floated past Johnny and grabbed the far railing.

"What are you going to do?" He asked.

"Watch," Johnny teased.

Johnny braced himself in the foot restraints and reached in and grabbed the closest box and slung it toward the surface. The container of five heavy stones twirled end over end and tumbled downward through the misty atmosphere of Nemesis. The two watched the spinning box until it disappeared into the atmosphere. Then Johnny reached in again taking out the other container and turned and headed back toward the open hatch. The mini-bot had repaired the small hole and slid In just ahead of Eric as he turned and looked one more time at the fascinating star below.

He struggled for words to describe the scene. The purplish green dark surface was covered by a black light violent stormy atmosphere.

There were at least ten different Nemicanes spinning away on one side of the small globe. He turned and entered the lander closing the hatch behind him and sealed it shut. Johnny stored the container away and the two astronauts floated forward toward Christy and Joanna still strapped into their chairs.

"How much time have we got before we enter the atmosphere?" Johnny questioned, as he strapped himself in again.

"About thirty-two minutes." Joanna answered.

"OK," Johnny retorted. "Lets get ready to jettison the descent stage."

"What's our air and reserve battery status?" Eric asked. Christy replied. "We've got Seventy-three percent battery power left and about two hours air supply in our tanks. Well let's hope Latilia and Serdia get here in time or they'll find us all dead."

"I'm not about to die this far from Earth," Johnny stated emphatically.

"You've got that right," they all agreed.

"Everybody, get ready for a jolt," Johnny said. "I'm going to jettison the lower descent stage. Give me a thirty second count on my mark," Johnny commanded. "Mark!"

The crew began flipping breakers disconnecting the forward section from the rear.

"Ten seconds," Joanna called out as Johnny placed his finger on the final switch that would fire the explosive bolts that joined the two sections together.

"Three, Two, One," Johnny pushed the breaker and the jolt lunged the crew forward in their seats. The rear section fell behind the lander and sank slowly in the mist of the raging atmosphere.

"What's our status now?" Johnny asked.

"Batteries down to fifty fife percent. We've gained another thirty minutes before we enter the atmosphere."

"OK," Johnny commanded. "Lock the mini-bots to the hull and bring their small maneuvering thrusters on line. We've got to gain some more altitude. Any sign yet of our friends?" Johnny questioned. "Bring up the rear radar screen. Let's see what we can see."

Christy reversed the direction of the radar, focusing it to the rear of the struggling ship. The radar showed a blip slowly gaining approximately a thousand kilometers behind and sixteen kilometers above them.

"There they are," Joanna exclaimed.

"They're coming down to get us," Christy said.

"How long at their present speed before they reach us?"
Eric asked.

"Approximately forty minutes," Christy reported.

Johnny gunned the mini thrusters trying to gain all the altitude he possibly could, before the remaining emergency fuel supply was depleted. The now half lander ship struggled with the pull of Nemesis gravity but managed to gain a few more kilometers altitude before the small reserve fuel tanks were depleted. Five seconds before fuel depletion Eric relayed. The small minibot thrusters fell silent as they burned the last drop of their nuclear injection hydrogen fuel supply.

The forward escape module drifted silently in space rolling around with low power of the remaining ten percent in its back up batteries.

"What's our altitude and status?" Johnny Questioned. "We've managed to gain five more kilometers altitude," Eric replied. "We're now thirty-four miles above the surface and traveling about seven point six kilometers per. second. We're approximately nineteen kilometers above the Nemesis's top layer of atmosphere."

"Okay," Johnny said. "Its up to Serdia and Latilia now to catch up and lock onto our module before we crash back into the Nemesis star."

Just as he'd finished speaking, Latilia came across the receiver in their helmets. "We're sixteen kilometers behind you. We should be latching onto you in thirty minutes," She radioed.

"Okay," Johnny replied. "We should be able to hold on until you get here then. We sure will be glad to see you when you do. We're almost out of batteries and remaining air supply is down to about thirty fife minutes. The ships spinning a little and you'll have to match rotation when you arrive. We're shutting down all non essential systems until you get here. We'll be out of radio contact unless we have an emergency."

"That's affirmative," Latilia said, ending the transmission with, "we'll be there in time." And the radio signal fell silent.

The escape pod rolled silently around the Nemesis Star. Christy stood staring out the window of the lifepod watching the far away ship that would spin past every forty-three seconds as the lifepod rolled in space. They seemed so far away but she knew somehow they would get here in time.

The four remained calm and as still as possible conserving the diminishing oxygen in their tanks. They all could see the approaching Nova ship getting a little larger as it rolled past the window.

Christy thought back to her childhood days when she would play with her daddy in the back yard under the shade trees. He made her all kinds of exciting gravity toys that she'd played with. She remembered the magnets he'd hung in the trees that would continuously bounce around seeking magnetic poles.

She was only three years old when her great grandpa passed away. She recollected how he had made things out of wood and the many types of balance toys he'd constructed especially for her small size and weight. Then the Idea struck her.

"I've got and idea," she exclaimed.

"What is it?" Johnny said.

"If we use a little battery power to polarize the outer hull with a magnetic field and Nova does the same thing when it arrives we'll stop rotating when the opposite poles of the two crafts seek each other out. That might save us about eight or ten minutes on docking up," she said.

"That's a great idea Christy. It'll take a little power from the batteries but it will be worth it in the long run. We won't need power once the command module docks." Eric spoke up.

"Lets do it."

Joanna programmed the power requirements to magnetize the hull into the backup computer while Christy got on the microphone to the approaching Nova orbiter to inform them of the plan.

"Nova's one kilometer away and closing." Eric reported. "They'll be here in five minutes, and our air supply is down to fifteen minutes. Looks like we're going to make it after all." Johnny said.

"We'd better hope those two Plutonian girls know how to dock a spaceship," Joanna joked.

"Well," Eric laughed. "They don't have to worry about knocking a hole in our ship. We've already had one."

The four laughed as the tension eased among the crew in relief of the approaching rescuers. Christy tracked the ship approaching closer as the much larger Nova dwarfed the remaining escape pod.

Nova hovered above the spinning pod while Johnny energized the hull and the lifepod slowed gradually coming to a rocking halt then settled down to a stop. Both Hulls became demagnetized simultaneously and the two crafts came together while the capture locks drew them inward. Johnny floated up to the hatch and turned the wheel to open the hatch to the docking bay.

The door opened almost causing him to fly through the wall but he regained his balance and motioned the two girls first into the chamber then followed by Eric and himself.

He sealed the hatch and Joanna flipped the switch to pressurize the chamber. Nova's pumps filled the chamber with breathable air. Eighty percent pressurized the crew started removing their helmets. The helmets released with a swish as they helped twist each others locks to remove them. The taste of fresh oxygen filled their lungs as they finished removing their suits before decontaminating in the two available shower chambers. Serdia and Latilia had put the ship in a slight spin so the water in the chambers would fall into the drains while showering.

The life-giving waters that now cleansed them reminded them of the green blue Earth and the Earth air that they had been so long without. They were safe for the moment. Thanks to their friends the Plutonians they'd survived the escape from the forbidden Nemesis. Thanks to the Nemesis Deity that had enlightened them on the workings of many wonders of the universe.

They knew now that all matter and matters were also sentient. They now knew that all things were like seedlings in an unlimited layered garden. That stars were the mere corpuscles of the universe and that many giant stars were the pumps or heartbeats of this humongous living, breathing, expanding, universe. That the universe itself was a living entity giving birth to many baby universes. For infinity, universes would be born and die the same way it always had in its unlimited never-ending journey of eternity through time.

CHAPTER TWENTY TWO
THE ENLIGHTENMENT OF WORLDS

The crew of four was safe aboard Nova and underwent an hour of decompression to allow their blood to be decontaminated from the hostile infections of the Nemesis. Decontamination complete, Johnny reached up to open the hatch to the Nova command ship. The door swung slowly open in the light gravity revealing the smiling alien faces of Serdia and Latilia welcoming them back.

The crew looked at the two alien women with new eyes. They realized the long ago encounter with Nemesis was due to each race uniting in a successful attempt at survival. If it had not been for the other, neither would have succeeded.

The four climbed up the short ladder back into the main command module. The light gravity was a welcome relief from the past long day they'd spent exploring the Nemesis surface. The crew of six gave thanks to their safe return and a special tribute of thanks to their three buried comrades on the Nemesis. For another race to give its lives to save a species of a different culture was one of the Deities most admired laws of nature and love. And it was through the Deities grace that they now were safe back aboard Nova.

Qwerto, Pertravio and Zxico had passed on to a new life form of unbelievable knowledge. They weren't being punished. They were soon to be rewarded for their bravery. One might also say that the Deity was testing their resolve to teach humanity humility. That life never actually ends, instead it just evolves in stages toward a more perfect life form. This was even true about the stardust that makes up all matter. For in every single speck of stardust that exists, a deity exists there also. That the Universes themselves are living breathing entities spitting out baby galaxies into the birthing void of infinite space.

That even the infinities of the black void of space itself that surrounds all forms of planet moon systems of many worlds and trillions upon quadrillion, zillion, sextillion, uncountable galaxies upon galaxies had sentience. The Deity had not forbidden humankind to explore. It was encouraged. Humankind and the Plutonians were just two of many different forms of life. This journey was just beginning. But first they had to escape from their low fast deteriorating orbit that Nova was in from the daring rescue.

CHAPTER TWENTY THREE
ESCAPE FROM THE BLACK STARS GRAVITY

Johnny made his way forward in the light gravity and sailed into the command seat of Nova. The other five crew members chattered on about the preceding events until Johnny spoke out with a direct command.

"All right crew, Lets pull it together. We're not out of this yet. We still have to get away from the Nemesis gravity well. Give me some statistics," he beckoned information. "What's our present status?"

"We've dropped to almost ten kilometers above the top of the Nemesis atmosphere. We're exactly fifty one point three kilometers above Nemesis. Forward speed five point three kilometers per second." Joanna relayed.

"Nova engines online and status is seventy three percent fuel remaining. Everybody get strapped in," Johnny ordered while grabbing Nova's thruster controls. "I'm going to bring us out of our spin." He eased the small throttles to the right to counteract the left rolling of Nova still attached to the lifepod.

The thrusters expelled hot gases and spewed into the void as they brought the rolling Nova and crew to a slow final halt with the Nemesis almost rolling to a stop.

"I'm bringing main engines back up to ready status Eric relayed.

"Ready to fire in fifteen seconds on my mark. Mark!"

The whirring of the fuel injectors filled the cabin as Johnny put his finger on the main engine igniter switch. On zero timer count he punched the precise switch and the Nova's center main engines ignited obediently. Nova shook and struggled momentarily against the resistance pull of strong gravity then started gaining momentum in its perigee of the Nemesis orbit.

"Forward speed six point five k.p.s. and climbing," Eric relayed.

"We need approximately, eleven point three k.p.s. to pull out of Nemesis orbit," Christy shouted above the increasing roar of the engines.

The deep blue flaming engines of Nova were lit up like a giant torch as the ship pulled away from Charon the Nemesis. Nova arched higher over the Nemesis until the gravity forces began releasing its grip of pressing them backwards into their cushioned seats.

"Speed nine point one k.p.s.," Eric struggled to speak. "Main engine shutdown in ten seconds." Johnny grabbed the main engine breaker against the strain of four and a half gee's. When the counter reached zero he flipped the switch that extinguished the fiery blue blaze at the rear of Nova's four main engines.

The gee forces instantly receded and Nova sailed in the void toward the Plutonians World. Joanna and Christy immediately unbuckled and floated back to check on Serdia and Latilia's status.

They'd remained silent since the ignition of the main engines. The Plutonians light body structure was more susceptible to the sudden change of gravity. The two Plutonian females had passed out in the climax of the higher gravity force during the deorbit burn. Their body structure just couldn't withstand sudden changes of velocity as well as the humans could. Christy rubbed a moist towelet gently across the pale gray forehead of Serdia while Joanna did the same to Latilia. The Plutonian females began opening their eyes in response to the attention they were receiving from the Earth females.

Serdia spoke first. "Did we make it? Have we escaped from the Nemesis gravity?" She spoke feebly.

"We're perfectly safe," Joanna consoled. "We're on our way back to Pluto," she informed.

"We're all fine now thanks to you," Christy consorted. "How about you? How do you feel?"

" I'll be all right," she said. "I'm just a little dizzy.' Then Latilia passed out again.

Serdia was also in bad shape. Barely in and out of consciousness she mumbled a few words and relapsed back into an unconscious state.

" Eric ,what's the earliest touchdown possibility of being able to land at Ultropolis?' Johnny asked.

"If every thing goes well, we should be on the surface in one hour and ten minutes. That's with an insertion orbit burn coming up in forty three minutes."

"We've got to get Latilia and Serdia medical attention fast." Joanna spoke up. "Their medical status is critical. Do you think we'll be able to land without killing them?" Joanna had a concerned frown as she spoke.

"I don't know baby," Johnny spoke with assurance. "We humans owe our lives to them. If there's any way possible we'll figure out a way to get them home safe. You and Christy do what you can medically for them. Eric and I are going to figure out a way to make the Gee forces easier on reentry. What do you think Eric? Any provisional bright ideas ?"

"Well!" Eric thought deeply a few seconds while rubbing his overgrown gray beard then spoke. "We could try the direct landing approach."

"You mean go straight in without orbiting?" Johnny asked.

"Yes! We can achieve it but it will require precise timing and quite a bit more fuel."

"Have we enough fuel to accomplish it?" Johnny inquired. "I'm absolutely sure of it." Eric replied. "Just let me inform you that you'll be required to maintain a manual strict no error tolerance landing in order to make it happen. Now how's your wet spot?" Eric jested. "Seriously though, the maneuver will require several mid course changes and we're almost at the point of the beginning challenge." "Alright then!" Johnny said. "I'm the right human to accomplish the job. Give me your program numbers as fast as you can and I'll link them into the computer for a single click execution command."

"Right on!" Eric replied. "Sequence beginning command is...." He started to configure the program to change Nova's approach and landing vector. "Ok." Eric called out. 'Here is the first set of numbers and they need to be programmed and engaged in seconds in order for the thrusters to fire on time. The symbol vectors are as follows 615* 478* 9802* 119* Regal."

"Roger that." Johnny repeated the set of numbers and symbols and waited for Eric's acknowledgment before engaging the computer execute command. Nova slowly rolled in its arrow like trajectory and turned tail first toward the fast approaching Planet Pluto.

The rockets spurted fire precisely lining the spacecraft up on a direct path to the Ultropolis landing coordinates.

"How are you coming with the rest of those numbers?" Johnny asked.

"I'll have them ready in two minutes," Eric answered. Johnny took command. "OK Joanna! I need you to get on the radio and inform Ultropolis control of our status and that Serdia and Latilia will be needing emergency medical attention as soon as we've landed."

"OK," Joanna complied floating forward to activate the radio.

Johnny and Eric finalized the programming of the number symbols into the main computer. Christy continuously monitored the status of Plutonian females condition. She read the readings out loud from the medical tricorder.

"It seems their blood is seriously infected by the exposure to the radiation they've received when they rescued us from the low orbit above Nemesis."

"We've got ten minutes before the main engines ignite," Eric reported.

"Acknowledged," Johnny returned. "I'm putting Nova on automatic pilot for a few minutes. Eric, I need you to come with me."

He unfastened his restraint and they floated over to where Latilia and Serdia were in their specially designed chairs. Johnny called Joanna to join them around the two sick alien females. They delicately placed all eight of their human hands over the Plutonian females hearts and jointly concentrated on cleansing the blood stream of Serdia and Latilia. For three minutes they infused their own blood filled with antibiotics from the resistance they'd built up.

The Plutonian girls opened their eyes. Johnny floated back to the control seat followed by Eric.

"OK," he ordered. "Eric I need those symbol digits now." Eric complied. "Everybody get prepared for the main engines firing. Three minutes twenty seconds before ignition."

Joanna and Christy finished securing Serdia and Latilia's belts and then hustled to get themselves strapped in.

"Forty five seconds," Johnny called out.

The nine chairs on Nova slowly turned opposite the direction of the tail of Nova and locked into position. A unique plan was improvised by Eric to decrease the strain from gravitational forces on their fast straight approach to Pluto's surface.

Johnny had landed on Pluto before but this was a much more difficult landing without the slowing down of orbit before landing.

Nova approached Pluto this time at twelve point three kilometers per second and they were presently less than eight hundred kilometers above Pluto when the main engines roared to life causing a sudden thrust in their belt restraints. The six astronauts then swung around facing the tail of the ship as Nova slowed from its fast bulls eye approach to Pluto. Eric's attention focused on the three empty chairs at the rear of the command module. If not for those three brave souls they wouldn't have made it this far. Nova was returning to Pluto with four humans and two very sick female Plutonians.

"Six minutes until touchdown. Eric relayed.

" Speed, six point one kilometers per second." Joanna reported.

"We're coming in too fast and a few degrees off proper coordinates," Eric reported.

Johnny released the automatic pilot from its duties and took over manual control of the reversed speeding rocket. "Yes, We're descending to fast," Johnny stated. He grabbed the throttle and gunned the four main engines to seventy five percent power. Johnny was worried about the gravitational effect on the Plutonian astronauts but he had to slow the ship down fast.

Eric reported. "Our speed is two point six k.p.s. and slowing. Altitude, one hundred fifty one kilometers. Adjusting final approach vector."

Johnny yawed the side thrusters to compensate for the inaccurate vector. Nova slid sideways to line up with the laser beacon tracker being projected from Ultropolis Control.

"Fuel down to eighteen percent," Eric yelled. "Speed one point three k.p.s., Altitude twenty three kilometers." Johnny eased forward on the throttle and Nova's tail section touched the outer mist of Pluto's atmosphere. "Speed, one half kilometer per second altitude ten kilometers," Eric continued. "Good job," Eric said. "We're slowing down nice and easy. Speed slowing to one hundred meters per second. Altitude five kilometers."

Nova sank deeper into Pluto's multi colored atmosphere. The rearview monitor showed the Plutonian city of Ultropolis growing larger as they entered their final approach. Forty five meters per second Eric reported. Altitude one kilometer. Fuel status, five percent remaining. Johnny eased back a little more on Nova's throttle trying to conserve the low fuel supply. The ship dropped to one hundred meters and he again gunned the mighty engines slowing them down to a slow approach. Bring her on down gently Eric shouted. Fuel supply is less than three percent. Johnny throttled the ships mighty engines furiously and brought Nova to a hover two meters above the surface. He eased a tiny bit more off the throttle and the returning exploration ship settled with a thump as he hit the engine kill switch that extinguished the thundering engines of Nova.

The nine seats on Nova electrically rotated one hundred and eighty degree's and locked the astronauts into upright position. Nova sat smoldering on the scorched landing pad while the engines began cooling down from their fiery reentry. Eric and Johnny immediately began shutting down systems and securing Nova's status. Christy looked out of the window and noted the barrage of Plutonians coming from the city and making a bee line straight toward them in the still smoldering rocket.

Their attention quickly turned toward Serdia and Latilia as they released restraints and loaded the unconscious females on stretchers. The crew lifted the unconscious aliens onto the rolling platform.

"Get them immediately down to the Plutonian ambulance," Johnny ordered.

Joanna and Christy rolled Serdia and Latilia into the elevator bay. "OK," Johnny stated. "There's not enough room for all of us. Joanna, you and Christy get them to the surface now. Then send the elevator back up and Eric and I will follow shortly."

Joanna punched the switch that shut the hatch and the elevator sank down the side of Nova to the growing crowd of Plutonians below. Half way down Christy began watching through the elevator window and the crowd of Plutonians chatter could be heard as they settled to the ground. The hatch opened and the two Earth females rolled Serdia and Latilia to the surface while motioning for the Plutonian medical team to come forward.

The Plutonian medical staff rushed forward taking control of Latilia and Serdia and loaded them on the awaiting ambulance. The emergency Trailapod zoomed away toward Ultropolis emitting a fading emergency tone in the distance. Joanna turned and walked back to the elevator and pushed the switch sending the elevator back toward the top of the ship. In minutes the elevator began its second descent to the surface.

Johnny and Eric stepped to the surface of Pluto once more. Now approaching was the second barrage of Plutonian dignitaries. Rominus led the pack. He stepped up to the four Earthlings and stopped. Johnny spoke first.

"We're sorry about Pertravio Zxico and Qwerto." He Paused before continuing. "We hope Latilia and Serdia will pull through alright. We did all we could to get them here quickly."

"We know you did," Rominus answered. "You must have had a rough time on the Nemesis," he said.

"Yes indeed!" Johnny answered. "It's a long fascinating story," and he turned and pointed toward the elevator and the box of five Nemesis stones on the cart. "There is a lot to be told and yes sir, it has been a hard journey.'

"Let us return to the city," Rominus said. "You Earthlings look like you could use some rest. There will be plenty of time for details after you've rested. We'll keep you apprised of the patients condition." He gestured toward the approaching larger vehicle that was arriving from Ultropolis. The four agreed and stepped toward the awaiting alien taxi.

The Plutonian Taxi was a strange vehicle that was round and about four meters in diameter. Four of the five seats were modified to accommodate the humans larger forms. The front center chair was occupied by the driver of the alien vehicle. He spoke in a cheerful demeanor.

"My designation is Penurious. I'll take you to Ultropolis and to your quarters."

The teardrop eyed gray alien turned his head forward while he extended his short left arm toward the glowing control panel. With three of his four fingers he pushed the controls that started the surface craft forward in complete silence. When in motion the ball vehicle was completely clear and transparent on the top and the bottom was semi translucent blue in color as its outer hull rolled just above and across the Plutonian roadways.

Eric was fascinated with the workings of the Plutonian Taxi. He couldn't resist tapping on the partition between the Earthlings and Penurious.

"Hey!" he knocked obtaining the drivers attention. They began their conversation with Eric asking technical questions about the workings of the mysterious craft.

"What kind of propulsion does this thing use?" He asked Penurious.

The alien driver spoke back in his musical whimsical tone. "This is called a Trailapod," He stated. "The vehicles top circumference harnesses power from the Nemesis and turns it into sort of a backward version of your electricity. The acquired power source is then focused on the bottom circumference causing the round craft to float two hundred centimeters above the also reverse energized roadway."

Eric shook his head in amazement. Penurious's answer to his complicated question had been short and to the point but certainly not satisfactory to Johnny who posed the next question.

"Are you saying that this vehicle runs on a version of black light solar power?"

"Yes and No," Penurious replied. "When the Nemesis is overhead for five of your Earth days, the craft runs on power from the Nemesis. While the craft is in use during the daylight hours it is sending all the unused energy to storage for later use in the nighttime period of Nemesis darkness."

"Are you trying to say that this thing has a battery storage capacity? Well then! Where are the batteries?" Eric asked.

Penurious looked toward the feet of the four and said. "The bottom part of the round craft is for storage and the top is for generating power from the black Nemesis rays."

"Do you mean we're sitting inside the battery?" Johnny looked concerned.

"Yes you are," Penurious said. "But it's charged powers are in a stasis dimension and are totally non harmful to either of our species."

"Well I should hope so," Joanna remarked.

The alien craft moved along the narrow road quietly and smoothly in the late afternoon on Pluto. The craft glided silently along the edge of Ultropolis to a position on the far west side of the city. The taxi glided to a stop in front of a larger than usual building that had been redesigned for human's connivance. The craft eased to the surface and the side entrance was suddenly open to their exit.

A gathered crowd of Plutonians cheered as the Earthlings stepped from the Trailapod that delivered them to the walk leading up to the half round building that they now walked toward. Hundreds of Plutonians lined the walk and immediate vicinity and cheered in a musical united voice while the four passed through the center of the crowd. They walked until they came to the front of the large green half ball building. Rominus had arrived in another Trailapod and met the four Earth astronauts at the door. Rominus held his short left hand up toward the crowd as the murmuring and cheers died down. He began to speak.

"I have news about Serdia and Latilia's condition. News from the medical facility reports that their prognosis is good. They've suffered a heavy dose of black radiation poisoning. Our physicians predict that they will be cured in approximately ten Pluto days. As soon as you've had your rest they'd like to give all of you a medical analysis to determine what effects the radiation may have caused you."

"OK," Johnny agreed. "We're glad Latilia and Serdia will be all right. And we are especially thankful for the dedication of Zxico, Qwerto, and Pertravio. They are brave loyal heroes," Johnny continued. "Our heart felt thanks goes out to them and their families. We four humans from Earth owe or very existence to them for their sacrifice rescue from the Nemesis. All the information in our ships data banks is at your disposal. While we rest I hope all of you on Pluto will accept our thanks and gratitude for all the things you did in this joint exploration of Nemesis."

The crowd cheered again and the brief welcome ended with the Earth astronauts entering the green building that had been especially redesigned for Earthlings.

"We'll continue our briefing in twenty four of your Earth hours," Rominus said to them as they entered the privacy of the building.

Joanna, Christy, Eric, and Johnny were exhausted from the past day and a half of exploration. The four opened the final door leading to the main living quarters of a fabulous suite.

The room was a huge half dome shaped fluorescent green oval chamber with four different doors spaced evenly around the half circle. Each door led to a private sleeping and shower area with its own facilities. Joanna picked the purple room, Johnny the blue, Eric the yellow and the multi colored room went to Christy.

The four went their separate quarters and in each luxurious compartment clothes began floating to the floor as they all began relaxing in the warm green heavy oxygen waters from the Plutonian multi direction showers.

Eric bathed in the relaxing shower for sixty eight Nemetar's while the warm green mist washed the Nemesis grime from his momentary soul existence that was now in a trance. He collected his thoughts on the journey to Nemesis and the narrow escape from the forbidden world.

Joanna stepped from her shower onto fuzzy blower grates that started up automatically from the weight of her beautiful body in one tenth gravity. She relished the rapid warm air that enveloped her in circles and finished drying off. The beautiful astronaut maiden stood before ultraviolet mirrors and relaxed as the mechanical devices encircled her while attending her every desire. In one round of her room existed a closet with many different garments of different colors and styles. She picked past the night garments and chose a sexy skimpy alien nightgown.

Johnny anxiously awaited as she stepped to his blue room where he lay naked on a huge human shaped bed softer than a marshmallow and warm to the touch of its soothing vibrations.

Joanna's hot body and soul touched Johnny's spirit and the long Nemehours of lovemaking began in separate quarters between two sexy, man and wife couples in Pluto's low gravity. (temporally end log) (imagination optional)

The Journey may have been physically over for the four but in their dreams they lived every Nemetar of the journey over again.

The Earth astronauts awoke from a much needed rest to a peaceful beautiful setting of the Nemesis Star. They'd slept for fourteen hours. After their morning showers the four conversed around the breakfast nook chatting ecstatically about the past mission.

"Wow," Johnny stated. "I just can't get over the Nemesaurus." Johnny laughed at Eric while shaking his head in the amazement of it all.

"Yeah," Eric answered. When we were floating that thing it was kicking and screaming while beating it's six fat blue legs in the Nemesis air." They burst out laughing at the exchange across the table.

"Try one of these Pluto sausages," Joanna teased. Johnny bit down into the tiny chicken leg looking meat.

"I sure hope that little sausage isn't a fried Plutonian penis," Johnny joked. The astronauts burst out laughing as Johnny jiggled the peculiar shaped wiener.

Eric laughed so hard he spit the meat out in the low gravity while coughing, laughing and chocking at the same time and then slinging the remainder to the floor.

"Well if it is a male Plutons penis, I certainly do feel very sorry for the alien females sex life." They all laughed.

"Hey sweetie, Try some of this Plutonian nectar and these sweet biscuits." Christy baited Eric's eating prong while pouring his juice into a flask.

Eric bit the cake turned up the flask of nectar spilling a little on his beard and nightshirt.

"Ahhh shucks!" He let out a burp. "Food ain't half bad way out here on Pluto. Is it?"

"It's pretty good stuff," Joanna spoke up while grabbing for one of the sweet biscuits before Eric could eat the last three.

"Try one of these Pluto chicken legs," Johnny waved the small meaty concoction in Joanna's face. "It might look gross but it sure taste good." Johnny was finishing his third while Eric was on his second meaty alien chicken concoction.

"No thanks," Joanna retorted. I'll stick to pastry stuff. "You guys can eat all that dead Pluto chicken you want. I'm not eating that stuff."

"Awe shoot," Johnny replied. "You girls don't know what you're missing here."

"Yeah! I may even carry some of those Pluto chickens back to Earth, Eric said. 'Maybe I'll start myself a Pluto chicken ranch outside Dallas Texas when we get home. Possibly I may even settle down and raise me a couple two dozen youngans. I must inform you sweetie that this stuff makes me extremely horny." Eric spoke with a cowboy John Wayne voice while looking over and winking at Christy who was blushing at his jest.

The four laughed again together out loud before the conversation turned to a more serious tone. Johnny spoke up his concerns.

"Listen up you guys. We've got a meeting with Rominus in a few hours. We'll be going through an intense debriefing about the mission. We'll also find out about the dedication ceremony for Pertravio, Qwerto, and Zxico. So I guess we'd better get our act together and get dressed ready to roll." They all agreed and went to their rooms to prepare for the debriefing ordeal.

CHAPTER TWENTY FOUR
CEREMONY OF FRIENDSHIP

Rominus and his barrage of eleven rang the bell precisely on time. The four explorers filed out the door toward the awaiting Trailapod. It was early night time on Pluto and the non glare red lighting illuminated the City of Ultropolis. Penurious the same driver that had transported them here sat behind the controls. They greeted him with a cheerful hello and loaded aboard his hovering taxi. Johnny spoke.

"Do you think possibly that I may be allowed to drive your Trailapod?" He asked.

Penurious chuckled in his musical voice. "I think maybe that can be arranged at this moment."

Penurious was amused that an Earthling would want to do such a thing and for the first time he now asked a question back as he motioned Johnny forward to the copilot seat and explained the controls.

"What was it like on the Nemesis surface?" His question caught the four by surprise.

"Oh man!" Johnny began speaking about the adventure of the Pegasus's, Nemesaurus, and by the time he's reached the middle of his driving sojourn he'd reached the part of the adventure when the lander was destroyed and the brave Plutonians rescued the Earthlings giving the ultimate sacrifice. He'd merely half finished the condensed version of the flowing wall when he drove into the courtyard of the headquarters of Plutonian Science's Facility. "I'll have to tell you the rest later,"

Johnny patted Penurious on his alien shoulder and thanked him. The humans headed up the walk to the welcoming crowd of Plutonian dignitaries.

Rominus was the first to extend his alien hand in congratulations of the successful mission. By now they were use to the cooler touch of the aliens palm. Rominus spoke with dignity and distinction as his voice rang harmonically throughout the foreign auditorium.

"We the inhabitants of Ultropolis and the four from Earth have gathered here on this momentous occasion to honor our fallen brethren Qwerto, Zxico and Pertravio. Let us hope and pray that their remains shall be returned to Pluto soon and placed in suitable high place of honor to be admired martyrs for generations by all beings who pass their way."

The speech continued. "We begin now a new voyage to understand and study the data and matter from The Nemesis. In the coming days it is our intention to contact the officials of Earth to ratify the agreement between worlds. We hope to persuade officials of Earth to still one more landing on the Nemesis surface for religious purpose of retrieving the remains of Zxico, Pertravio and Qwerto." The coliseum grew quiet as Johnny stepped up to the mike followed by the other three humans.

Then he spoke. "I hear your wise words your majesty." He looked at the King Rominus and paused. "I'm sure I speak for the four of us from Earth. We're not afraid to go back to Nemesis but what of this command that the Deity gave that the Nemesis from now on is forbidden?. It was that Deity that told us to bury their remains on Nemesis. I think I speak for the four of us when I say we would be honored to retrieve our fallen brothers remains and return them to Pluto once an agreement has been re-ratified."

The auditorium filled with musical voices as they rose to their feet and applauded the content of the conversation. The crowd calmed and Rominus ended his statements.

"In the future days, We as a team will endeavor to rebuild the Nova and also a new vessel to return to Nemesis if this is all agreeable with Earth officials. Together in six Earth months or approximately eighteen Pluto days, the new ship we build will return again to the Nemesis. Therefore in this immediate Nemehours, I proclaim to let the celebrations began. Tomorrow, when the Nemesis rises, we will began our work on the new ship and begin deciphering the data about Nemesis matter. So be it declared by I King Rominus, that the rest of this Pluto night is for celebration and relaxation intended for the entire population to participate. Let the festivities begin." The crowd of grey teardrop eyed aliens erupted in merriment and exuberating laughter.

Shortly there began a carnival of amusements, shows and many a feast of exotic alien foods. The Plutonian night had just begun. The four stayed together moving through the alien outdoor carnival delighting at some of the amusing sights they were seeing along their way.

"Look over there!" Christy darted off in the direction of a peculiar group of alien musicians playing strange instruments but creating a danceable tune that was hard to resist. She grabbed Eric by the neck and pulled him closer to the round projection speakers.

The bass pumped and beautiful music resonated through the sweet atmosphere as the four danced several tunes inside a circle of amused giggling aliens. A few Plutonian couples joined in and began attempting the hot bump dance Johnny and Joanna were dancing. Johnny danced Joanna toward the bandstand and grabbed one of the aliens spare guitar instruments and began playing a rift in the music key of A of the ancient song Johnny be Good and the entire group of aliens began boogieing all over the carnival to his singing of the words and playing hot guitar. He returned the smoking guitar to its stand and thanked the applauding crowd and the musicians and the four departed into the crowd of Plutons.

Joanna took the lead dragging Johnny by the hand to a colorful game of chance on a Plutonian color blob wheel. They watched as the Plutons placed their wager on the three dimension color blob as it began to spin in two directions at once.

The object of the game was for one individual to throw a small colored paint balloon at the spinning section of the giant three meter diameter ball that was the same color that filled your paint balloons.

They laughed at the aliens and their short arms trying to throw at the dodging jello ball blob. The ball upon a missed toss would turn and bounce into the center ring and tease and ridicule the attacking player calling them names and trying to make them lose their temper.

Johnny stepped forward as a hush came over the crowd at his approach to the alien three meters tall colorful jelly blob.

The hideous blob burst out laughing at the strange looking creature that stood before it. He sneered his wrinkle puss nose at Johnny, daring him to try his luck at the crowd pleasing game.

"You aliens sure are ugly," the blob teased. "I'll bet you can't even hit near me much less my individual colors. Your Mama probably kicked you in the weenie when you were little because your puppy dog already had four broken legs. Then she smacked you in the face and tied a pork chop around your neck so the puppy would play with you. You're one ugly Earth alien," the blob teased at Johnny.

Johnny stepped forward and spit toward the blob saying, "you'd best leave my mama out of this," while dropping down a few alien coins that the officials had furnished them earlier.

Johnny reached forward and picked up three purple paint balloons and stepped toward the clearing to begin his test of skill and fun.

"Look at this!" the blob jeered. "This Earth creature thinks that he can hit me with those three purple blobs. I bet that homely creature won't even get near me with one."

Johnny leaned forward placing two of the balloons on the ground and stood up facing the hideous creature tucking the one balloon behind his back like a baseball player and starred the thing right in the eyes.

The blob started its ritual of spinning and bouncing flashing a sequence of colors toward Johnny in his frozen pitcher stance. Johnny watched, motionless for a few moments while the blob jeered and called him more names.

Johnny waited until the proper sequence of colors had passed and he let go with a fierce forceful throw that whisked centimeters by the blob's head just as it turned purple.

The blob laughed out loudly and ducked the mighty blow that splattered the white wall behind it.

"What! Possibly your ugly mama raise a blind boy?" The blob teased. "You're not going to hit me with those other two either."

It started its musical teasing dance again as Johnny reached to the ground picking up the second volley.

"Ugly, nasty little Earthling," the blob sang blinking its color scheme at the perched motionless attacker. Johnny threw the second balloon so hard that the speed caused the balloon to disintegrate in mid air missing the blob by a half meter.

"Ha! Ha! It jeered. I told you that you were ugly and blind, now you're stupid too. You haven't got but one more shot remaining you ugly Earth human. You'd just as well go on home to mama now, before you make a bigger fool of yourself." Johnny reached down to retrieve the last salvo and watched silently for two Nemetar's while the blob jeered more humiliation his way.

This time Johnny reached all the way back mustering all the force he could, then let go with a mighty, rolling pitch that smacked the blob dead between the eyes while it was purple knocking it to the ground and the blob let out a cry much like the sound of a squalling baby.

"Awe now! What's the matter big fat ugly Pluto blob? Looks like it struck you just as you turned purple. You must not have seen that one coming blind blob. I guess you forgot I'm from a planet with ten times this gravity."

Johnny reached down this time and grabbed Eric's yellow salvos who was awaiting his turn. He jumped six meters high in the Pluto gravity and swamped the crying baby alien blob with three more paint balloons.

The crowd of Plutons cheered as Johnny walked away and left the blob crying in the distance.

"I guess we showed that thing," Johnny said as the others followed him away through the alien night carnival.

"Well! You could have let me have my turn," Eric reputed. "You owe me for those three balloons. They cost me a lot of plutatoes."

"Yeah, How much is that in earth money?" Johnny laughed. "About eighty-two cents," Eric laughed back.

Joanna yelled out "Over here you guys." She pulled Johnny toward another Plutonian exhibit.

"It's some sort of scary ride," Eric said stepping up to purchase tickets for the four.

"It appears to be some sort of alien haunted house that you ride through." Christy clutched closer to Eric's arm. The four got into a line behind a dozen Plutons waiting their turn to enter the Fright house coaster.

Each car held six Plutons or four Earthlings and the four finally got their turn to strap into the small vehicle that started its ride on rails.

Johnny and Joanna pilled into the front and Christy and Eric sat directly behind them in the alien roller car. The Plutonian attendant helped them fasten their safety harnesses.

"Hold on tight," he implied, while blinking one black teardrop eye at the Earthlings.

The ride began with a jerk and accelerated quickly to a fast speed then climbed up high disappearing behind a curtain in the top of the giant tent dome. The whir of its motors increased in pitch as the contraption climbed higher and higher into total darkness. Suddenly the ride accelerated again like a rocket had been ignited behind it. They burst through the clouds into the night air of Pluto's purple darkness just as the tracked roller sled approached its peak again and almost stopped before it crested the hill.

It seemed as if time stood still and they were in slow motion as their bodies floated in zero gravity for an instant before slowly starting to fall faster down the tracks in Pluto's one tenth gravity.

At first the fall was slow but then gradually began gaining momentum. The four were whirled through a series of loops and turns then remained upside down through a long inside loop spiral. The sound of screeching brakes could be heard, rubbing drums as they suddenly slowed down to a speed that brought them into another dark tunnel and then exited cautiously into a giant cavern barely lit with dull luminous blob lamps.

Out of the darkness jumped an alien hairy three headed spidery creature with fangs oozing smelly puss drops as big as the front of the car. The disgusting phlem was secreted out of a slit just below one eye in each head. Christy and Joanna screamed and clutched their partners by the arm while ducking down low in the buggy. The roller car passed through a curtain into another room full of huge serpent creatures that spit imitation fire toward the approaching vehicle. Joanna shrieked and ducked while Johnny shot a spit ball at the hideous thing that disappeared behind the car as it bumped and turned through the maze of tracks slowly making its way toward another doorway of pinkish glowing colors.

As the cart passed through this curtain, it suddenly shot upward again at great speed twirling clockwise through thick clouds of multi colored steamy mist. They shot high over Ultropolis propelled now in a crystal like ball, that flew under its own power. The altimeter showed they were two kilometers high and sailing above the city slowly making its way around a ten-kilometer diameter circle. "What a great ride!" they all exclaimed.

They sailed past the College of Plutonian Science's and onward toward the beautiful green waters of the rivers that ran through Ultropolis. The lighted waterfalls that slowly tumbled in the light gravity gurgled off green bubbles as the water tumbled in slow motion eastward toward the awaited three and a half day wait of the rising Nemesis. The crystal ball took them across the city to the homes of the Plutonian residents that were aligned perfectly in geometric formations.

Abruptly the craft took off in a different direction zipping back toward the carnival atmosphere below. In ten Nemeseconds they were back in the trolley and burst through the last curtain and slowly rolled to a stop at the carnival ride exit ramp. The attendant helped unstrap their restraints and the four thrilled Earthlings departed the ultimate ride.

Eric now led the pack heading toward a precarious little booth across the midway.

"Hold up!" Christy yelled above the noise. "One of my shoes came off."

Eric waited patiently for her to replace it. Catching up she marveled at the fuzzy looking artificial stuffed creatures that hung above the games of skill waiting to be played.

"Awe baby, would you look at that? Please try to win me one of those." She pointed up at a slimy fuzz monster hanging over the attendant's head.

"I'll try," Eric said stepping closer to view the game and watching the Plutonians play.

This was a jelly pyramid structure game. The rules were that you placed two arms into a jelly like substance in any two of the separated three sides. The object being, to construct the meter long jiggle sticks, inside the jellies ice crystal structure in a three-point connection at top. Then once balanced in the center, to win your prize you must then remove both arms very cautiously without disturbing the crystalline structure of the jelly crystals surrounding the balanced meter jiggle sticks. Any abrupt moves and the crystals would tumble down into a pile causing you to lose the game and your wager.

The booth was full of unsuccessful aliens trying their luck at the almost impossible puzzle task. Eric slapped a double bet of his plutatoes down on the counter and stepped forward to try his luck at solving the equation. His larger human hands plunged into the crystals of transparent particles as he started his balance of the three jiggle poles in the center. The time limit was five Nemetar's with a flashing digital counter at the top of each invisible sided triangle container.

The crystals slowly dissipated from the triangle shape container as Eric struggled to stack them gently. Suddenly the pyramid of crystal pieces tumbled to the bottom ending his first attempt at the game.

Eric quickly reached into his pocket pulling out more plutatoes and placed his second bet attempt at the allusive game. Again he plunged straight into the sides of the triangle jelly flask and immediately started methodically fitting the wobbling puzzle sticks together. The last jiggle stick in hand, he gently placed it against the quivering but still stable stacked sticks and methodically removed his hands three Nemeseconds before the timer ran out.

Bells and chimes alarmed above as the quivering puzzle did a little dance and turned into a kaleidoscope of colors. "Congratulating to the solver of the tricklix equation puzzle," a robotic like voice exclaimed.

Christy jumped up and down in delight pointing at the little green fuzzy monster as her prize. The alien attendant came over to congratulate Eric and pulled the prize from the pile and handed it to the little lady Earthling.

Johnny laughed at Eric and was ready to try his hand at the puzzle when the game attendant hung a sign saying No Earthlings Allowed. Puzzle solved. Gone Home for the night and then the lights went out around the puzzle game.

"Oh let it go," Eric said. "Besides, you owe me eighty-two cents anyway. Where's my money?" Eric snatched the paper bills from Johnny's hand and took off through the crowd saying, "Come on Guys. I'm hungry."

The three followed Eric, finally catching him at the entrance of a place called, City on the edge of Forever Gardens Restaurant.

"Wow! It's beautiful," Joanna said as they caught up to Eric and Christy. "Lets go in." Eric led the way down the ramp to the beautiful restaurant establishment.

The head waiter greeted them with a smile and said, "Welcome to the Forever Gardens Restaurant. My designation is Orataso." He blinked his black teardrop eyes saying, "follow please," then turned and led the four to a larger table that was meant to seat eight Plutonians.

They pilled into the booth table and Orataso passed out four menus, politely bowed and turned and darted away saying, "I'll return in a Nemetar."

What a beautiful place indeed Christy remarked. Look at the lavish plants and running water falls. Plutonians filled most of the tables and the place was alive with cheerful musical laughter. Orataso returned shortly bringing sweet rolls and warm nectar drinks on a tray while laying out the plates and alien table settings then quickly darting off around a grassy bush and disappeared into the crowd again. "Well!" Eric said. "I'm certainly hungry. I'm glad I found this place," he said, as he began attempting to read the menu out loud. "Take your pick people. We've got Plutonian plate specials one through eight."

The description words were in Plutonian.

"Oh shucks. Who cares?" Joanna laughed. "Order a one through four and we'll see what they bring."

Orataso returned with drink refills bearing a peculiar looking pen and pad.

Johnny ordered the one through four specials and the waiter scribbled away writing with his four-fingered hand, then curtseyed and darted back toward the kitchen.

While they chatted about the carnival adventures, four Plutonian waiters came from the kitchen carrying platters of steaming hot exotic foods and a cold platter full of Plutonian fruits, nuts, berries and vegetables. The platters were placed in the center of the tables and the waiters were gone as fast as they had arrived leaving the four Earthlings staring at a feast of Plutonian exotic food and drink.

Johnny and Eric grabbed for the meaty steak patties and some peculiar vegetables that resembled flat potato fries. Christy and Joanna sampled the delicious fruits and sweet rolls and sipped warm nectar milk. They laughed and joked again about the jumping fat blob and the hairy green monster doll that sat between Christy and Eric. They all ate until they could hold no more.

A pulsating search beam appeared from the balcony and focused on a tiny stage that began the entertainment show. A female narrator's voice introduced the Humorist named La'fi'fu'can and out onto stage walks a female alien clown character dressed in skirts that bounced as she walked while she shook her peculiar, branched, tickle stick at the audience. Delightfully she touched a little Pluton child with the stick and the alien child giggled uncontrollably and bounced in her chair. She winked at the Earth table and began her dialog.

"Yeah You Earth women think you have it bad, but on Pluto females giggle while having sex. Well it tickles!" The crowd laughed. "But what Earthlings don't understand is that once a female is impregnated by a male, His thingy curls up and becomes useless except for use at the tasty treat sausage factory for those brave enough to eat meat. You see we Pluton females can only have one child."

She reached over and touched the twelve inch giggly child again and it bounced and laughed as the comedian bowed and thanked the applauding audience and exited behind a curtain. Dispelling a huge burp while stretching his legs, Johnny yawned and grabbed Joanna then winked.

"Hey baby, I'm for getting back to our pad and taking a shower together. Maybe do a little something something, he said, as he kissed Joanna in the nuzzle spot teasing her and laughing softly.

"Yeah," Eric spoke up. "I'm a little tired myself but certainly never too tired for that," he growled, as he snuggled and winked at Christy.

She grinned and said. "Let's go then!"

The four then sprang from the booth while Johnny and Eric threw a wad of Plutonian bills on the table and they departed toward the exit out into the cool moist dark night air.

They stood a moment on the curb looking up at the tiny Thimbus moon reflecting its feeble purple light. Just past the corner block Penurious in his Trailapod appeared zooming up to greet the four. He exited the driver seat and ushered the four aboard.

"I hope you had an enjoyable evening," he smiled, as he sealed the door behind them.

"Home Penurious, take us to our quarters please." Johnny slumped down in his seat as soon as he had fastened his belt and grinned back at Penurious.

The Trailapod accelerated silently into the city streets of Ultropolis. Johnny awoke from his doze when the Trailapod bumped a little settling down in front of their Plutonian temporary home. The four exited the cab, thanked Penurious and walked slowly through the night toward the door of their private little palace on Pluto.

They were exhausted from the nights activities. Within an hour of their return both couples had showered and snuggled up in the warm beds. Within another hour the lovemaking was over and they all slept for nine continuous hours before their alarm sounded waking them to another Earth time night period on Pluto.

They all met over breakfast discussing the night's adventure on Pluto. All four agreed to go their separate ways and explore Ultropolis.

Johnny experienced the thrill of piloting a Plutonian fighter craft in aerial tag games with the Pluto fighter teams. Eric experienced driving his own Trailapod around exploring the barren void side with a Plutonian explorer friend named Melianas. Christy and Joanna drove their own vehicles to the many different unique shops in Ultropolis. The five Earth-nights of darkness on Pluto was a time of celebration and relaxation for the whole population.

The four from Earth were well rested when they found themselves standing on the Eastern edge of Ultropolis with a whole Nation of Plutonians greeting the slow rising of the spinning Nemesis. The Plutonian military stood in full dress and armament facing eastward toward the bright purple light of the slowly rising Nemesis.

The early twilight of sky was bathed in fluffy colored clouds moving south across the horizon. They stood on a podium among many high ranking Plutonian officials on this early new day on Planet Pluto.

Their chief military commander gave the signal for the trumpet to sound its first note and the soldiers raised three tall straight thin mast of metal and pointed it toward Nemesis. On his second long trumpet note three continuous laser beams of light shot skyward in a salute to the fallen Plutonians Zxico, Qwerto and Pertravio. The chatter from the crowd died down as the reflected light bathed the morning audience in ambient lighting. Rominus began his speech during the twenty-nine Nemesecond reflection of light from the Nemesis.

"It is because of their bravery, that both worlds owe these heroes our future's survival. This new dawn on Pluto is hereby proclaimed to be in honor of our fallen comrades and to the honor they chose as martyrs of Plutonia. With the agreement ratified between worlds, we now begin a new journey together. These brave heroes from Earth along with five courageous Plutonian scientists will return to the Nemesis in a new ship to retrieve the fallen hero's remains. Be it decreed that once their mission is successful, soon they will be buried to rest in peace on the highest eastern mountains of Pluto. This day is hereby decreed, A Thorius day."

A loud cheer erupted as he paused a moment. He began again as the applause died down.

"For the fallen heroes, their humanoid form has progressed. Their souls have been cast forward into a new realm of physics. A science that mere mortal humanoids are incapable of achieving at the moment. May their new journey be officiated with a Nemetar of silence in their honor." (58s Pause)(One Nemesis rotation).

Rominus continued. "Today, is a new beginning for the beings of Earth and Plutonia. This day we begin building a new ship. A ship of scientific technology beyond any yet built by either race. We will employ all our forces and technicians to work around the clock until the day of the completion of this new vessel of space exploration and with the Earthlings help once again return to the Nemesis only for the purpose of the retrieval of the remains of our three Heroes, Pertravio, Zxico and Qwerto."

A loud roar again erupted in the Plutonian air as they cheered for their fallen heroes.

"And now!" King Rominus concluded. "Let us once again join together in agreement and let the hard work begin on the construction of the new ship that will be the best ship possible. We will also endeavor to replenish the Nova for its return trip home after the Earthlings return from the Nemesis. Let it be written. So shall it be done! He proclaimed. Let the preparations begin."

His Honor Rominus of Pluto finished his speech and the Plutonians scattered toward the city on that early morning rising of the Nemesis sun.

CHAPTER TWENTY FIVE

THE NEW SHIP THORIUS

By now on Pluto the Earthlings had learned most of the societal cultural traits of the occupants of Pluto. They'd learned their way around Ultropolis and drove their own specially designed Trailapods here and there monitoring the progress of the newly designed ship. Early in its planning stage it was named Thorius One, In honor of the Omnipotent Dweller of the inner Nemesis. After the first five Plutonic days the Thorius skeletal framework stood assembled on its future launch pad.

A beautiful ship indeed! Saucer shaped and made from a special lightweight metal alloy created from the Nemesis minerals. Luminescent green its hull was translucent in color and when inside the ship you could see through the hull to the outside. The ship's diameter was sixty meters and the height of the upper crystal dome body was ten meters high above the lower body of the saucer. Thorius's main deck sat directly on top of the body and was thirty meters across. The main deck was a clear dome resembling a thickened crystal on a watch and was made out of all new elements of the Nemesis matter that was brought back from the first expeditions daring escape from the Nemesis surface.

The technicians were presently installing the new engines in Thorius and soon would install the Nemesis reactor core that would get its power directly from the Nemesis. A total new group of technologies from discoveries assimilated from the exotic Nemesis matter, allowed huge steps forward in their combined physics knowledge.

The mysterious new elements discovered would allow advances that would not have been possible had the first mission failed. All was going well on the construction when on the sixteenth Pluto day, the new Nemesis Starship rose up slowly on a pedestal base. This would be the first day of testing Thorius's newly installed systems.

Johnny, Joanna, Christy and Eric arrived at the base together and it had been one hundred sixty-five Earth days since they'd returned from the Nemesis and now they boarded Thorius One along with a crew of ten Plutonians to start the power acquisition test.

Johnny sat in the center command chair awaiting the go ahead from Plutonian command base two kilometers away. Before the beginning of systems checks five of the Plutonian technicians departed Thorius and the four Earth Astronauts and five Plutonian scientists remained strapped in their

launch cubicles

A green light illuminated on the panel in front of Christy and the intercom system came to life with static at first. The signal soon became clear and perfect communication was established with the Plutons base.

"You've got a go light, on power up engage," came the voice over the speaker.

"Roger that." Johnny radioed back, placing the new operations cap on his head.

Each cubicle had its own operations hat that folded down over their foreheads and directly tied all of their brain wave activities into the ship's main computers. All nine aboard sat ready with their visors down, as Johnny gave the mental command to bring the engines on line at idle frequency.

Thorius whirred like a top and rose above the surface one meter while it's three landing gears retracted and folded gracefully into its bottom. Eric's visor projected a schematic of the immediate surrounding area on the view screen.

"All systems and stations checking in and reporting nominally,' Eric reported.

The beautiful Thorius ship hovered just above the ground absorbing the morning dawn dark rays from the Nemesis and converting them into energy. The Plutonian named Quota reported engines at three percent idle in hover mode.

"Roger that."

Johnny acknowledged all the reports coming in. Serdia reported all ultraviolet solar fuel cells working properly and Latilia reported inside pressure status of the ship Nominal. The other two Plutonians were named Shata and Phalo and they were busy executing the commands that Johnny was issuing.

"Let's take her up," Johnny relayed to the rest of the crew. "It's time to find out just what this ship can accomplish."

Johnny visualized the command to accelerate skyward at forty-five degrees. For the first twenty-nine seconds the ship went from zero speed to sub sound Pluto speed to equalize the effects of g forces. Thorius then shot skyward at incredible speed while leveling off at ninety kilometers altitude and equalizing proper orbit around Pluto.

It was a glorious ride inside the crystal dome on top of Thorius. The green luminescent ship sailed around Pluto silently and gracefully. It was as if they could reach out and touch the stars through the crystal canopy. The ship performed almost flawlessly for it's first three hours of testing in Pluto orbit. Then the decision was made to bring Thorius crew back to home base until a few minor technical issues could be resolved.

Johnny settled Thorius softly to the ground just outside the base and the crew departed the ship, happy that all had gone so well.

Ten more Earth days passed while preparations were maliciously made and all was assumed ready for the beginning of the new mission to return again to the beckoning Nemesis. It was a brand-new dawn on Pluto.

The base was alive with activity as the Plutonians hustled to and fro in the final preparation of Thorius and its crew of nine. The four Earthlings boarded the large Trailapod that awaited them outside the door of Pluto mission control. In three Nemetar's Penurious sat the Trailapod down in front of the Earthlings apartment complex. They thanked him and departed inside for a few hours rest before the mission.

"Man," Joanna sighed. "That Thorius sure is a fantastic ship. Don't you think?"

"Yeah," Johnny looked thoughtful. "It's a good ship all right. Don't get me wrong. But I'll take Nova any day to get us back to Earth over Thorius."

"Yeah," Eric spoke up. "I've got to admit that Thorius is well suited to the task of landing on Nemesis. The ship is constructed from the new elements discovered from the heavy matter. It draws its power directly from the Nemesis Star."

"By the way," Christy broke in. "Latilia's report reads that their scientists have now discovered a total of nine new elements in the Nemesis matter. Every thing in Thorius is made from five of those new elements. A total of five small stones were retrieved from the surface and all the material that makes up Thorius is made out of one and a half of those stones. The matter is packed so tightly together that one two-inch stone on Earth would weigh more than four thousand pounds."

"That's amazing," Eric said. "So I guess that tells us that the total unoccupied weight of Thorius is six hundred Pluto kilograms. Lets see, That would be equivalent to approximately three thousand Earth kilograms or 6613 earth pounds."

"I really do like the way they've fixed up Nova for our return trip to Earth though." Christy smiled.

"Yes, you're right." Eric responded. "Thorius one is a very good ship indeed as long as it's in the immediate one hundred million kilometer vicinity of the Nemesis. But I'm like Johnny. I'll depend on Nova to get us back home to Earth."

"You've sure got that right," Johnny agreed. "But Thorius is a mighty fine vessel. We don't even know what its potential is. In a few hours we'll check it out thoroughly."

"I concur," Eric replied. "I really do like the way the Thorius's main controls are hooked directly into the visors. It's as if our brain waves were tied directly into the Thorius main computer."

"Yeah," Joanna spoke up. "When we had those visors on, the whole crew pulled together and everybody functioned as a perfect efficient team."

The conversation continued through the feast of food they devoured.

"Johnny, How do you like the two landing pods Thorius has for the descent to the surface?" Eric asked through a mouth full of food

"Oh, I think they'll be OK. They work on the exact same principal as Thorius just on a smaller scale. We'll test the landing pods tomorrow before we take Thorius to the Nemesis."

"Yeah," Eric said. "We'll see tomorrow. I'm ready to explore some more."

"Me too," Johnny replied. "There's only one thing that bothers me."

"Hey man! What could be bothering you? What's on your mind?"

"Well," Johnny hesitated. "Well, remember how the Omnipotent being of the Nemesis warned us that from now on all Nemesis's were forbidden territory and not to be trespassed on ever again?"

"Yeah I know what you mean," Eric sighed. "But I don't think the Deity would punish us if we're only there for the soul purpose of the retrieval of Qwerto, Pertravio and Zxico's remains. Besides! I do think the entity was challenging us to test our resolve and see if we humans would risk our lives the way the three Plutons did for us."

"I do agree it seems logical and I certainly hope we're right about all of this," Johnny said. "We will know in a few hours that's for sure."

"Yep! So true."

Eric got up from the table and winked at Christy.

"I'm a little tired. I think I'll hit the shower and get some shut eye after snuggling up with Christy. I'll see you guys in about eight Earth hours."

"Yeah," Johnny said. "Don't eat too many biscuits. I'll see you in a few over a breakfast." They laughed and the two couples retired to their personal territory and did some things of marital discern.

CHAPTER TWENTY SIX
THE TESTIMONY OF NIMBUS

The four astronauts awoke on the eloquent planet of Pluto while The Nemesis sun was about forty-eight degrees above the horizon. The Earth astronauts finished their breakfast and hustled to board the waiting Trailapod to transport them to the launch base. Penurious greeted them with his usual pleasant tone and the four departed on a three Nemetar ride to the beginning of more exploration.

The nine astronauts gathered at the final briefings room and prepared to board Thorius and strap into and connect the visors that totally linked the nine of their thoughts directly to the ships main computer. Johnny followed by three humans and five Plutonians walked the crystal gangplank to board Thorius the wonder ship. Finally all the technicians began to depart and the last one sealed the hatch to the outside as she left.

The four from Earth sat in the forward cubicles that would become one of the descent vessels when Johnny gave the mental command. The nine buckled harnesses and lowered visors that brought them in total communication with each other. Plutonia control came across the speakers with a status green light for lift off.

Johnny sat for a moment while focusing his attention on the Nemesis on the forward view screen.

"All systems reporting in go status, for engine idle up."

Eric's words brought Johnny back from his momentary distraction.

"OK," Johnny ordered. "So be it. Everybody, hold on. I'm engaging Thorius One idle."

He sent the mental command and Thorius immediately hummed to life and sprang from the surface a meter and retracted it's three spider legs that disappeared into the bottom of the saucer craft. Johnny pointed the ship's nose upward and the pink clouds of Pluto sailed by the crystal dome that the nine astronauts occupied on top of the great ship Thorius One.

In less than a Nemetar they'd accelerated into the blackness and void of outer space. Johnny eased the super efficient Thorius into orbit and they circled the globe fifty kilometers above Pluto and thirty kilometers above the pink cloud tops. The crystal dome above their heads was as clear as a glass panel allowing them a vision of billions of stars shining through the crystal canopy.

Johnny gave the mental command that soared Thorius ahead of Pluto and past its Thimbus moon in orbit.

"I think we should to run a few tests on Thorius before we attempt to go to the Nemesis," Johnny announced.

"What do you have in mind?" Eric questioned, upon hearing his mental thoughts.

"Let's take Thorius out a ways in space. We'll give it a speed test run around Pluto's orbit of the Nemesis."

"Ok then," Eric immediately replied with the proper numbers required for the computed course. "Pluto is approximately seventeen thousand kilometers above the Nemesis. That makes its total circumference in its orbit of the Nemesis to be approximately 106760 kilometers."

"All right," Johnny commanded, "hold on. I'm going to take us out ahead of Pluto in its orbit around the star. We're going to give Thorius a little speed test to see what it will do."

Johnny sent the mental command that sent Thorius zooming away from Pluto at half speed. He watched the monitor as Thorius passed one-quarter light speed. In a very brief second Thorius had sailed all the way around the Nemesis and was now approaching Planet Pluto again after a full Pluto orbit. Johnny commanded Thorius to slow down to orbit speed around Pluto.

The crew of nine sailed silently toward Pluto's tiny sixteen kilometer diameter moon and gently began approaching its surface. Johnny sailed to within fifteen meters of the surface and hovered momentarily over the small round little moon.

"What do you think crew? Should We land?"

"Hey!" Eric replied with a grin. "We're this close. I don't see why not."

The seven others agreed.

"OK! So be it," Johnny said. "Let's set her down easy. Maybe we'll do a little unauthorized early exploring."

Johnny eased Thorius to within a meter and the three legs deployed from the bottom and Thorius settled ever so gently to the tiny moons slight gravity surface.

"What's the gravity on this little moon?" Johnny asked. "Hardly any at all," Christy reported. "Gravity is so little. We'd each weigh about one tenth kilogram on the surface."

"Yeah," Eric chimed in. "If you're not careful, you can accidentally jump completely off of this moon into space." "That's right," Johnny said. "But I think the new space suits that were developed from the Nemesis matter will work well out on the surface. We'll all have to wear gravity spike boots to dig into the surface and hold us down."

The Plutonians aboard Quota, Phalo, and Shata, and the two females Latilia and Serdia were all excited now as they donned their protective shield spacesuit and were the first in line to exit upon the lowering of the ramp to the surface.

The smaller Plutonians eased cautiously onto the surface followed by the four larger Earthlings. The new spacesuits protected each astronaut with an invisible pressurized umbrella shield. The gravity boots worked well and dug into the fine powdery soil. Never before had the Earthlings ever been on such a world so small and beautiful. The extreme curvature of the horizon was breathtaking. Pluto's dark side loomed huge in the overhead sky and the Nemesis purple light lit the entire system with an eerie glow.

Moving around on the surface became a little easier as the crew got better accustomed to the way the boots dug into the Thimbus soil. It wasn't long before Joanna eyed a mysterious glowing rock a hundred meters away and started toward it. Eric and the others fell in behind her as she was the first to approach the three and a half inch rock. The area was filled with smaller splash craters and this rock lay directly in the center of the largest crater that was about twenty meters across.

A blood-red ruby stone lay at the feet of the nine explorers. They circled around the pulsating red ruby stone.

"It's beautiful," Joanna exclaimed. The five Plutonians chattered excitedly in their native musical language.

"Hold on," Johnny said. "There's no telling what that thing is. We've got to be careful."

Eric spoke up. "I'd better go back to Thorius and get a containment box. I'll be right back."

Eric shuffled off back toward Thorius kicking up the moon dust and creating a cloud of slow settling soil in his wake. The remaining eight stood there in awe as the wonderful moon ruby pulsated hypnotically.

In a short while Eric shuffled back toward the circle of explorers pulling an alien version of a floating container. Johnny opened the box in the center and removed the surface tongs to pick up the jewel. He eased toward the pulsating rock holding the tongs out in front. He flicked the switch to open the claws of the tongs and settled the tool gently in place closing the claws around the mysterious Thimbus stone. He cautiously picked up the rock and placed it inside the containment box.

"Nice job," indeed Eric said. "Whatever that thing is, it certainly didn't originate on this moon. It's probably been perched in the center of this large crater for a very long time."

The team of astronauts moved on picking up other small interesting stones along the way toward a huge boldface cliff. Johnny led the line of eight followers while Eric guided the flotation cart in the rear.

Johnny, Joanna and Christy at the front of the line approached the valley below the tall rock face. Quota, Phalo, Shata went around the right corner followed by Latilia and Serdia. Johnny and the three Earthlings followed the face of the cliff until they came to a sharp right turn that trailed off into total darkness. Johnny from his hat projected a green photon beam of penetrating light into the dark ravine and it landed on a dark structure three point fourteen meters high. Johnny followed by the others now with their helmet lights on proceeded cautiously down the steep slope toward the bottom. Ten meters away in total darkness stood a perfect pyramid pitch black in color.

Suddenly more lights flashed on the walls off the far side of the ravine. It was the Plutonians approaching from another direction. They chattered excitedly as they stared at the pyramid from the opposite side of the clearing.

Johnny eased cautiously closer and knelt down to the base and brushed away the moon dust that covered the inscription that read.

(FA INKARNYA DE Milo) (^^^) (^^) ((^)}

Shata stood beside Johnny and began translating the Plutonian dialect into English. (translation) "We worked, endured and survived." He continued. "Three sides to a pyramid (3.14) = pi."

Johnny was now intrigued at his explanation and asked Shata to continue.

"It was placed here many thousands of your years ago by our ancient ancestors when they first landed on this moon that you have named Thimbus. This platinum pyramid was left as a monument to the struggle and survival of ours and your ancestors that endured for many years," Shata began, reading the ancestors names inscribed on the black pyramid.

The four Earthlings made their way around the pyramid to where the Plutonians were standing and began discussing the history of their race.

Johnny asked a question to Quota. "Why many years ago on Earth were the pyramids built?

"When the ancient ruler King Ra, ruler of Cydonia Mars learned from his astronomers that in three Earth years the Nemesis would pass very close to the five inner worlds, He immediately mobilized his colony to build escape ships sending almost a hundred Cydonians to a Earth colony to mobilize the then primitive desert humans to help build the three large pyramids in Egypt. The Cydonian colony of refuges arrived on Earth thirteen months before The Nemesis arrival near Earth."

"They immediately bonded and allied with the then primitive Earthlings and lived temporarily in the five ships they'd arrived on. In nine more months time with the help of their advanced technology and machines they accomplished building the most stable large structures possible in the short time that they had to prepare."

"In the first three months a large concrete stone cutting factory was put into operation and with the strong backs of the Earthlings the blocks were manufactured from the then surface materials available and smelted in large stone molds."

"In another month's time production of the bolder blocks was already up to more than a hundred, one and a half meter square blocks per day. By the time the larger base stones were made and placed the production was changed to one meter by one and a half meter stones. Three of our ancestors ships were re-engineered to work as both a flying transport and upon landing near the pyramid construction site transmuting it's function into a hovering crane. The flying block transport ships started out small but it was sufficient to carry one stone at a time. Every Earth night while the Earthlings rested our mechanics would continuously modify the flying cranes so when they landed and as the pyramid got larger the hovering cranes hovered higher."

Quota continued his lengthy answer after a short pause.

"It is hard for me to explain all the details but you must realize, before the Nemesis this whole solar system was different then. It was the Planet Jupiter's strong gravitational pull that hurled the Nemesis inward. It passed within one million miles of Jupiter achieving extreme speed then continuing on inward dragging the then fifth Planet Pluto behind it when it passed. The cataclysmic collision with the then fifth planets moon caused a huge chunk of the moon to vector outward toward Jupiter producing the giant red spot storm that rages on even today."

"The pair of falling worlds and debris then passed within twenty-five thousand miles of Mars almost completely destroying the civilization colonies on Mars. Cydonia Quoerea and Thaldesia were the three bases our ancestors once had established on the then in its springtime Mars. They were all destroyed."

"The two inward falling worlds while dragging all kinds of space debris rocks and frozen and molten matter, rained down on Mars almost completely blowing away the atmosphere and taking one Earth days to pass. The Nemesis then three months away from Earth fell inward on another close encounter with the then much different Earth. One month ahead of the Earth encounter the three pyramids were finished and stocked and by then only one hundred and fifty of our race remained alive on Earth. Our ancestors quickly supplied the survival pyramids with food and water and saved as many Earthlings and animals as possible from the approaching devastating Nemesis."

"Then Earth was a hotter dryer planet with surface water covering only forty-five percent. Its atmosphere was only half as thick with condensed oxygen content. Earth's rotation rate was much slower taking four twenty-four hour periods to rotate once. By the time the Nemesis thundered pass Earth, the colony was tucked away inside below the ark pyramids in fear of the terrible fire rock and ice ball raining storms. The whole Earth shook from within and hell's fury fell from the sky while the Nemesis took twenty-three present Earth hours to pass within a hundred thousand kilometers in front of Earth as it orbited the sun. The quick and close encounter with the high gravity Nemesis and Pluto caused the Earth moon to almost stop rotating and the rotation rate of Earth to increase four times to it's present twenty-four hour period."

Giant ice and fire balls struck the Earth and exploded vaporizing instantly into steam lava causing it to rain hot acid rain. It took a while before the steaming new oceans eventually cooled and turned to water clouds. With the sudden increase in the rotation the surface stayed completely covered with water for a hundred and sixty new Earth days and nights. Finally the water began to recede and catch up with the faster planet rotation and in approximately forty more new Earth days it began settling to form the Earth's present oceans and thicker atmosphere. The pyramids withstood the rolling waves of water for a total of two hundred new Earth days and it was these three-sided pyramid arks that allowed what was left of the two races to survive."

Quota paused again before continuing to read from the sacred altar. The nine astronauts listened intently as Quota read the Nemesis Chronicles about the destructive of the Nemesis journey through this solar system. Quota read on aloud.

"The fast passing in front of Earth caused the planet to speed up in its orbit of the sun and distance from the sun was increased by approximately four and a half million kilometers causing its year length to increase from the before, two hundred fifty eight new Earth days to approximately three hundred sixty five present Earth days." "Since the passing both Mars and Earth rotate at approximately the same rate and their wobble is approximately the same in their yearly procession around the sun."

'The devastating Nemesis then fell even faster toward the sun passing even closer toward the backside of Venus causing that world to flip its poles and reverse it's rotation to it's now slow backward two hundred fifty new Earth day rotation in a clockwise direction. A huge percentage of the remaining matter that trailed the Nemesis duo struck Venus and caused its atmosphere to increase drastically from its original amount."

"The Nemesis pair passed behind Venus's orbit barely missing the world by a mere sixty thousand kilometers. Venus's orbit distance changed from seventy-three million miles to sixty-seven million miles causing the run away greenhouse effect to build up excess heat and pressure on the now backward rotating Hellish Planet."

"The Nemesis was gaining greater forward rotation speed from all of its close encounters with each planet as it continued inward toward the opposite side of Mercury's orbit and fell to within thirty-six million kilometers behind the sun."

"Nemesis duo passed so swiftly curving behind the then younger hot star. It was this extreme fast close passing to sun that super charged the Nemesis in infrared radiation. The Nemesis and Pluto were slung furiously slightly out of the ecliptic plane toward the eventual encounters above Uranus and Neptune."

"The fast spinning Nemesis and trailing Pluto were eventually attracted by Uranus's gravity and slung again very closely above Neptune. The pair of spinning worlds were almost captured by Neptune's system causing the cold liquid world to wobble almost one hundred eighty degrees in its yearly axle tilt."

"The two worlds Pluto and the Nemesis were then ejected into their present day out of plane oval orbit by Neptune." Quota paused one more time before he read the final two paragraphs on the altar book. He continued.

" The destructive passing of the Nemesis on Earth was survived by one hundred ninety-seven Earthlings and more than twenty-two thousand Earth animal species and thousands of seedlings."

"Only ninety-seven of our ancestors survived in ships from Mars and in the immediate years after the passing they fled to Earth to join up with the one hundred fifty-three of our race that survived in the three life saving pyramids. Earth was battered and scared from the one day passing of the Nemesis and when the Earth's rotation was increased suddenly by the close passing all the waters of the planet was pulled to one side by the heavy gravity of the Nemesis. So be it ! The final few paragraphs were written in the hand of Ra. The Architect and surviving ruler after the era of the passing of the terrible Nemesis."

"So be it as it is. Ye who read this truthful history of the journey of the system changing Nemesis. Let they also be aware of the new life Nemesis created in it's frightful but glorious passing. For out of the three arks came this colony to this tiny moon with only sixty-six original survivors of the Martian species. Fifty-three new Earth years had passed when seventy-three departed in three ships from Earth. Earth's gravity and new heavier atmosphere had slowly killed all but these of our race. We arrived at this small moon twenty three years from Earth and one hundred seventy-six new Earth years after the encounter of the dreadful solar system changing Nemesis."

"We worked, endured and survived. In the ten years we first recuperated here. We procreated and had our first new born young on this moon. Together our kind departed to what once was the fifth planet from the sun that was now in its new close orbit around the Nemesis."

"Our survivors studied and learned the science of the Nemesis sun and harnessed this great new powers to teraforming the captured Pluto in orbit around the dark star. Be it truthful that out of the ark pyramid's came two species of sentient beings. Humans of Earth had survived to the number of nine hundred fifty of different cultures at our departure from Egypt. Of us. Originally from Ultropolis and then Mars whom had to leave Earth to ultimately further survive. It was on this Moon that we first landed our crippled three ships and regained our strength and recuperated to settle to the better suited Ultropolis ten years later."

"This memorial has been here for ten thousand three hundred fourteen of your Earth years," Quota stated as he finished reading the memorial history book then resealed it in its protective clear cover.

The nine astronauts stood in a moment of grand respect in memory of all that had sacrificed and worked so hard for these two races to be standing on this moon together.

Johnny broke the silence with a command that brought everyone back to reality and pointing toward the Nemesis past Pluto.

"OK team, We all need to head back to Thorius. We've still got the biggest mission ahead."

They all acknowledged and quickly made their way out of the dark ravine of the memorial on Thimbus.

In a short trek back toward Thorius, Eric brought up the rear guiding the flotation cart that carried the beautiful red stone and others of different sizes and shapes. They turned the corner and in five Nemetars they'd arrived back at the loading ramp of their grand new ship Thorius. Eric and Johnny stowed the stones and cart away and were the last two to board Thorius raising the ramp and sealing the cabin from the zero pressure outside.

The door sealed and Thorius hummed to life pumping air through the cabin and idling its engines. The ship automatically retracted the three spiked legs that held it to Thimbus. Johnny and Eric installed their visors and ran a status check of Thorius's systems.

"Everything looks good," Eric relayed.

" Everybody, buckle up," Johnny ordered. "Now comes the big test of Thorius and its crew. Stay alert." Johnny quipped.

Thorius hovered three meters above the surface for a moment then suddenly fast accelerated away from Thimbus gaining forward speed by the second. Inside Thorius the nine sat strapped into their individual cubicles under the crystal dome.

CHAPTER TWENTY SEVEN
BACK TO NEMESIS

The moon sank far behind them looking similar to a basketball hanging just above Pluto's dark side equator. Thorius fell behind Pluto curved and then exited toward the Nemesis from the far side. At impulse speed in ten minutes the crew approached the fast spinning dark star.

They fell inward toward the direction of the suns rotation. Johnny directed the ship to zoom to within fifty-five kilometers altitude and started chasing the Nemesis in it's once every fifty-eight second spin. He buzzed in closer skimming the cloud tops as the ship began matching the rotating star's speed. Eric sent the command for the proper coordinates and the Thorius was in a close orbit with the landing site directly below the ship.

"OK," Johnny said. 'We're almost here. It's time to board the lander."

"You know we'll come and get you if we have to." The Plutonian Phalo told the Earth crew.

"We know!" Johnny returned. "Let's hope that won't be necessary this time. We will just land and retrieve the remains of the three bodies and hope we don't offend the Ark angel of the Nemesis. OK," Johnny said. "Girls, I want you to stay in orbit with the Plutonians, That way if any thing bad does happen You'll still have lander two to rescue us." They all agreed that was a good idea and Johnny and Eric stepped aboard the new Thorius lander one.

One third the size of the mother ship this was a miniature version of Thorius.

"Thorius lander here."

Eric checked the communication as the two strapped themselves in and put their control visor's on.

"Loud and clear," Christy replied over the radio. "Ship to ship communication is good."

"OK," Johnny radioed back. "Here's the mission schedule. In five minutes on my mark. Eric and I will drop away from Thorius and descent to the surface in lander one. Presently we're only ten kilometers above the top of the Nemesis atmosphere. You won't be able to maintain this close gyrosyncronous orbit much longer so as soon as lander one falls away put Thorius into a more stable orbit at approximately five hundred kilometers altitude. That will also reduce the immediate radiation that is so lethal to Plutonians. We may loose contact due to the extreme weather down there but under no circumstances attempt a rescue unless you've haven't had any response from Eric or I in twenty-four hours. Agreed?'

"Yes," came the reply from the crew.

"OK," Johnny captained. "Three, two, one, MARK!"

The timers on the display started counting down from five minutes. Johnny and Eric breathed a long deep breath taking a moment to reflect on their surrounding environment inside and outside. He brought the landers idle engines on line as the clock ticked past three minutes they watched above as Pluto sailed across their view in about thirty seconds then disappeared behind the Nemesis then again in twenty-eight seconds popped up on the other side as they traveled at a great speed matching the dark star's spin.

The beautiful deep blue purple Pluto with it's hazy pink clouded atmosphere sailed by again as the clock ticked past fifty-eight seconds and brought their attention into focus. Eric radioed a farewell to the seven aboard Thorius and Pluto sailed by again as a ten-second countdown began.

The lander catapulted away from Thorius and engines purred to life sinking gradually away from the mother ship toward the swirling clouds below. In a few seconds they'd skimmed the outer atmosphere and increased their descent into the whirling storm's of rushing atmosphere.

"I've got the landing coordinates programmed into the computer," Eric reported. "Altitude twenty nine kilometers high."

Lander one's presence in the atmosphere caused a calming effect on the outside environment as the Thorius lander sank deeper into the violent storms. Johnny's mind link with the lander was precise and almost under complete control. He'd blinked his eyes for a moment and lander shook a little until he regained control of the swirling descent. Up until now they'd been spinning clockwise with the rotating clouds until Johnny reversed the rotation of lander causing the immediate inside of the funnel storm to slowly stop and then reverse rotation.

"We couldn't have done that with Nova," Eric joked at Johnny.

"That's right," He retorted. "Don't forget though, as good as this ship is, It can't get us back home to Earth. But you're right. She sure is a mighty fine ship indeed."

Thorius Lander dropped quickly through the funnel clouds hovering fifty meters above the burial sight while Eric mentally programmed the computer with the proper number sequence for the final landing approach. The video projected an infrared view of the landing site and the lander battled winds while easing forward toward the burial site. Three cork screw spider legs on lander unfurled and the connectors spun and dug into the soil for stability. Lander sat spinning its outside circumference ring anti clockwise resting thirty meters away from the heroes graves. Johnny issued the mental command for Lander to go into surface mode operation and the ship came to life with data from the surrounding environment.

New data appeared all over the view screen. Look at that Eric suggested. The outside ring is producing anti rotation in the immediate vicinity and the weather outside is fairly calm and the temperature outside is relativity cool compared to before. Fascinating Johnny replied. Johnny issued a command for the protective shield overhead to retract and the iris mechanism opened as if it were a large eyeball on top of the lander. The shield retracted and they stood in a crystal bubble on top of the lander and looked out across the grave sight to where the remains of Nova's lander one lay almost obliterated on the surface.

In another Earth year the abrasive air on Nemesis will have completely destroyed the rest of that old ship Eric stated. Yep Johnny replied. Let's get out the new surface suits and get this job done before something malfunctions. They both suddenly realized the return of the heavy gravity when they unbuckled their restraints and walked the few steps toward the back of lander where the suits and gear were stowed.

They stowed their visor's in the cabinet base then placed peculiar shaped excursion beanies directly in the center crown of their heads. They activated the suits and a glowing black light shield formed around them that was opaque and completely sealed to the surface when they moved.

"You'd better adjust that head band," Johnny suggested. "While we're on the surface, we can't allow our excursion suits to become dislodged from our heads for any reason what so ever. In a quick tenth Nemetar you'd be totally dead on the surface without its protection."

Eric pushed the breaker that opened a hatch on lander and the ramp extended straight out then lowered slowly to the surface. The two astronauts walked down the slanting ramp and stepped cautiously back on the Nemesis surface.

"These new suits are providing a perfect protective pressurized bubble around us as we move about on the surface." Eric reported.

"My suit is working fine also," Johnny radioed back. "Let's hope they keep working properly. Let's get to work and get this job over with. We're here under more stable circumstances this time."

"It sure is spooky here though."

"The anti rotating force field on TL-1 seems to have a calming effect on approximately one hundred meter diameter circle extending almost to the edge of the old Nova landers remains."

"Let's go check it out."

Eric's curiosity had succumbed to temptation as he walked toward the booster's tail fin sticking through from the swirling storm outside the force field.

Johnny used a tricorder from his tool belt and placed it near the metal frame that had been savagely eaten away by the Nemesis sand particles.

"The atoms inside this metal are oscillating excessively." Johnny noted. "The electrons are literally being stripped away as they collide together."

Eric pinged the metal with his rock hammer and it broke in half and crashed to the ground with a thump and then further disintegrated into orange metal flakes of matter. "Man oh man!" Eric exclaimed. "It certainly would have been nice to have this force field when we landed with Nova."

" Yep! We'd better get busy and get this job done," Johnny said as he looked up to the traveling Pluto above. "Do you think we still have the power of enlightenment and can float those stones off the bodies?"

"I don't know," Eric replied. "There's only one sure way to find out."

They walked the short distance to the three burial plots and stood while they joined thoughts and mentally focused on the bottom heavy Nemesis stones. In a few Nemeseconds the stones rose from the body bags that contained Pertravio, Qwerto, and Zxico's remains.

They floated the rocks down just to the left of the graves and the ground rumbled and lightning struck the stones when they touched the Nemesis surface. The rocks settled and shot lightning bolts and they both were immediately overcome with a deep emotion that compelled them to pick the stones up again and move them to the right side of the graves. As the rocks touched Nemesis again the ground began to rumble and shake violently.

Standing in the exact spot the stones had occupied was the Omnipotent Ark Angel of the Nemesis expanding skyward until it reached a height of thirty-three meters.

The dust and debris soon settled from the Angels rumbling arrival. The two held onto their excursion beanies as the last of the falling pebbles bounced of their shields and fell in the dust all around them. The Nemesis shook again harder and the two astronauts fell to their knees during the quake. The surface vibrations subsided and the air cleared.

"Rise Yea whom have returned here to the Nemesis despite my warning," came the overpowering voice from the Angel. "Why have you humans disobeyed my command?"

Johnny struggled up to his feet and helped Eric regain his stance then cringed his neck upward toward the Angel anomaly.

The Angle then decreased its size and shrank down to the height of the two humans. "I repeat," The voice more tolerable now but still stern. "Why have Earth beings returned to my Nemesis?"

The astronauts regained their composure and Johnny spoke first to the Angle.

"Eric and I apologize for disobeying your command. We have returned out of love and respect for the remains of the three buried here. If not for their love we would not be alive today. It is their race's wish and ours that the remains are allowed to return to Pluto for burial on its highest peak. These heroes gave their lives for us and we are willing to do the same for their remains so that their race will know that our friendship is equal."

Eric nervously spoke next while the Angel remained silent.

"Please Omnipotent One, If You allow us to retrieve the remains we will leave here never to return again. We're a long ways from Earth and neither of us wishes to die way out here on the edge of the solar system. We want to return home to planet Earth. We meant no harm. I hope you can forgive us."

The silence was long as the two from Earth awaited the judgment of the Angel.

"Your reason for being here is valid," the angle spoke in a softer tone. "It was I who told you to leave them here. It was a test to see if your love and courage was as strong as the three that lay in these graves. I the Angel of this Nemesis commend you for your courage and love of your fellow race. I shall allow this retrieval in hopes that your memorial on Pluto will be the beginning of a true friendship between cultures. And I decree that at no time ever will you allow your technologies to bare arms against one other. If this is agreeable between cultures, then you may take the remains and leave this Nemesis without taking any more stones from this place." With the finish of those stern words the Angle disappeared into the mist and left them alone on the Nemesis surface.

Mighty winds howled outside their force fields as the two concentrated on levitating and loading the remains into the cargo storage bay. The compartment closed as Johnny turned to Eric and said.

"Let's get out of here. I'm ready to get back to Pluto and ready Nova for the trip back to Mars base."

"Yeah Me Too," Eric replied. "I'm right behind you."

The two climbed the ramp of the Thorius Lander. Eric stepped inside last and pushed the breaker to raise the ramp and closed the hatch behind him as he kicked the Nemesis dust from his boots.

Thorius lander buzzed to life as the two astronauts removed their outside beanies and activated the decontamination procedure.

Two of the ship's three floating mini-bots rolled around them saturating the pair in ultraviolet light to kill any Nemesis microorganisms. The round robots started at their heads and revolved around each seven times before sinking to feet level retracted their probes then buzzed away toward the front of Thorius lander.

Eric finished securing the utility cabinet's and joined Johnny in the command section of Lander.

"We've got what we came for," Johnny said. "Let's get this ship out of here before the Nemesis Angel changes its mind."

Johnny and Eric took their command seats and strapped themselves into the ships control chairs. The three saucer shaped mini-bots buzzed the circumference of Thorius on the inside then two of them departed to the outside airlock and in twenty Nemeseconds they'd locked to the outside hull of Thorius lander. The third robot stationed itself into a locked position between Johnny and Eric's headgear.

They'd only been on the surface for sixty-eight Nemetar's and so far no attempt had been made to contact the mother ship. Eric radioed a laser message upward toward the small satellite that the mother ship had left in low synchronous orbit.

Joanna came right back crystal clear over the speakers of the new communication system.

"We were getting a little worried," came her reply.

" We're all right," Johnny returned. "Everything's fine. We'll be lifting off shortly. We're going to attempt a slow ascent so don't worry if it takes us a while. We'll be in touch, Thorius lander out."

"Every thing is go for launch," Eric reported.

"Roger that!"

Johnny sent a quick mental command to close the canopy above their heads. The view screen came online showing the video of the outside of the ship with the two mini-bots locked tightly against the hull.

"Thorius works so well in this hostile environment. I think we'll do a little experimenting on the way up. We're going to try something different this time," Johnny said "Thorius's shield has a calming effect for about a hundred meters radius. As long as the shields are working fine we should be able to do a little flying and exploring before we leave."

"Sounds good to me," Eric stated. "After all, like I said before, we may never get to come this way again."

The two laughed at the phrase Eric had stated on the first mission as Johnny engaged the hover mode and landers legs unscrewed then jumped from the surface ten meters high while the three legs disappeared into its bottom.

Eric activated Thorius's advanced radar screen while Johnny adjusted the light filters and the contrast of the cliffs ahead came into sharp focus.

Thorius moved slowly hovering twenty five meters high while maneuvering left and right around high jagged rock walls on both sides. The view of the below canyon opened up as they flew further into the valley of the Nemesis where they had first encountered the Nemesis

Angel on mission one. They flew past the entrance to the caverns and around a bend in the cliff face.

Suddenly, without warning the ground below began to vibrate and rumble violently. Their search beams fell on the two fire belching Nemasaurus's in furious battle. Johnny brought Thorius to a quick halt and hovered silently while they momentarily watched the thunderous battle of reptile giants. One Nemesaurus grabbed the other by the neck and slung it one hundred eighty degrees in the air and slammed it to the ground causing a cataclysmic air disturbance that shook Thorius as the shock waves rolled around the field. Johnny regained control and shot up to one kilometer well out of sight of the dueling beast. Every fifty eight seconds the blurry image of Pluto passed overhead through the thick atmosphere of the Nemesis star.

Johnny again dropped Thorius down to five hundred meters above the battling monsters then moved slowly ahead and above the top of the canyon walls to where it opened up into a huge crater one hundred kilometers diameter.

"Look at that," Eric said, his eyes grew wide open as Johnny brought Thorius to a hovering stop.

"There must be at least three hundred Nemasaurus's down there," Johnny said.

"Wow! Check out the other huge tear drop crater to the right of the herd. It covers almost twenty percent of the entire Nemesis surface. That crater must be exactly where the Nemesis made contact with Pluto's moon when it was the fifth planet from the sun."

"Yeah, I surmise you may be right," Johnny said. "A fast rotating glancing collision with a small moon would certainly make a teardrop crater like that."

"That's absolutely amazing." Eric stated. "Now it's full of Dinosaur creatures living in huge herds."

Johnny moved Thorius in closer to the main attraction near the middle where fifty or so smaller creatures sipped the bubbling hot liquid that spilled from a geyser that spewed blue jelly blobs.

"They eat that stuff," Johnny said.

"Yeah." Eric replied in amazement. "That one large geyser feeds all the creatures big and small that live on this world. And most of them live in this gigantic crater made by the collision eons ago."

They hovered a hundred meters above the larger reptiles head and watched for a moment the amusing scene that was taking place below.

Another family of ten meter tall alien creatures were grazing near the side of the bubbling food pond when as Johnny drooped down to fifty meters a smaller three meter creature looked up and spotted Thorius. It Immediately let out a high pitch scream that registered on the landers shield.

Johnny became aware that the vibration of their shields was hurting the small aliens ears so he hovered Thorius back up to two hundred meters just out of range of the vibrations and magnified the view screen to zoom in on the creatures. The alien creatures were elephant like in appearance with long thick trunks to suck the thick liquid from the pond. A baby elephant creature pointed its trunk skyward at Thorius now higher overhead and blew a trumpet scream that brought the larger Nemasaurus's running toward the food pond.

The ground below quaked as the giant charging Nemasaurus's thundered closer. Johnny immediately gained more altitude and again magnified the viewscreen of the creatures below. The larger creatures began firing volleys of fireballs that bounced off landers shields but still shook the craft.

The artillery increased as more of the larger creatures gathered around and joined in on the attack. Hundreds of fire balls now were striking the ships shields by the second and the vibration increased as even more joined in upon the assault of Thorius. Johnny commanded Thorius to gain more altitude just out of range of the arc of the hot fireballs.

He again magnified the view screen that showed the fireballs arching and falling back toward the surface. The hazy view of the creatures was obscured somewhat by the misty atmosphere but they could see that the furious attack had ceased and the creatures were settling back down to their normal routine of feeding from the pond.

Johnny zoomed the lens in on the little elephant creature that had alarmed their presence and the animal rolled playfully down the ponds outside embankment. Other creatures his size joined in on the playful activities of Gabriel a name that Johnny now called it.

"Look at that little rascal," Johnny commented. "I sure would like to take one of those back to Earth with us."

"Me too," Eric replied. "But I don't think the Nemesis Angel would like that at all. Besides we're the aliens on their world. You do remember what he said. Don't You?"

"Yeah," Johnny said. "You're right. These creatures belong here. The Nemesis Deity provided them this place to live and prosper. Dinosaurs of Earth are a thing of the long ago past. They couldn't breathe the air we breathe any more than we could breathe theirs."

"Yep, you're right." Eric stated. "I wont ever forget the lens way passage that enters into the Pegasus galaxy."

"That was a fascinating place indeed. You're so right." Johnny replied. "I guess we'd better leave this world and get back upstairs."

Eric switched the video recorders off and focused the radar antenna skyward toward the passing blurry Pluto as it passed in it's ever rolling traverse.

"OK," Johnny said. "We're going up and out sideways in the direction of this rolling star so we can stay matched up with the fast rotation for a gyrosyncronous orbit."

Thorius lander shot off at a forty-five degrees angle through a funnel storm that reached up high into the top of the Nemesis atmosphere.

The ships operation on the Nemesis had been impeccable until now when suddenly a sharp jolt violently shook the small vessel knocking both astronauts momentarily unconscious and spinning Thorius dangerously out of control ten kilometers above the top of the Nemesis atmosphere.

Eric sat unconscious as Johnny strained against the force of the spinning ships centrifugal gravity. He tried desperately to grab his visor sliding back and fourth with the ships out of control wobble. Eric began awakening while grabbing his head and trying to orient himself in this sudden serious situation.

CHAPTER TWENTY EIGHT
THE ICE METEOR STORM

The shields had been struck by super fast moving ice missile that came out of nowhere. A meter size ice intrusion stuck out of the top of the spinning Thorius just above Johnny's head.

The inside air supply hissed out slowly around a fracture in the damaged crystal hull. The computers were all off line from the jolt of the collision and they continuously tried in vain to reboot themselves as the ship spun madly out of control. Johnny's right arm was also broken but through excruciating pain he somehow finally managed to crawl up and grab his visor with his left hand.

Eric unbuckled, then managed to make his way to the storage cabinet and retrieve the two e.v.a. beanies that would soon save their lives.

Johnny managed to get the visor back on but realized he needed to get back to his console in order to bring the backup computers on line. He finally managed to crawl his way forward to his cubicle and climb exhausted into it. Pressure had leaked down to sixty-three percent and the air was getting thinner by the second. Eric came crawling from the back and climbed into his seat passing Johnny his outside excursion beanie to create a forcefield around himself. They activated the beanies and immediately had a fresh supply of oxygen.

Everything was down on the damaged ship. Thorius's main computer screen was blank as Johnny repeatedly tried again to reboot the back up computers. It was hard for them to concentrate with the lander spinning violently out of control a few kilometers above the Nemesis's atmosphere.

Finally, Johnny got the panel open and reached in to reset the ship's main breaker. The panel flickered briefly and lit up screaming with alarms displaying the malfunctioning ship's status. Johnny quickly sent a mental command through his visor to try to regain some control of the ship. The little side thrusters suddenly spat short burst of propulsion trying to stabilize the spinning wobble. Slowly the back up thrusters managed to stabilize the lander.

"Ship's main engines are dead," Eric said. "We've reached the apogee of our orbit."

"I know," Johnny replied. "If we don't get those main engines going quick we'll start to reenter the atmosphere."

The two mini-bots attached to the outside hull constantly fired their thrusters and finally managed to bring Thorius Lander to a stable condition but the main engines still wouldn't restart.

"The Main computer is fried," Eric reported. "I'd better try the radio to raise our comrades out there."

Eric sent the S.O.S. through his visor and they listened to the static in their headphones.

Johnny was able to bring up emergency power and the low frequency lights now lit the cabin for the first time since the collision. He then ordered the two outside mini-bots to detach and examine the damage to the outside of the ship.

The two mini-bots immediately broke away from the hull and whirred into action showing a visual image of a jagged chunk of frozen meteor ice three feet in diameter sticking out from the canopy of the ship.

Johnny ordered the robots to lock back onto the side of ship again and engaged their ship's small thrusters pointing them downward to gain a little more altitude. Their small efficient Ion engines pushed at full power for three minutes giving the lander an increase of altitude of six more kilometers.

"Good job!" Eric said. "That gives us a couple of hours before we reenter the atmosphere."

"Yep that's right." Johnny replied. "Lets see what we can do about getting that chunk of ice out of the ship's dome." He then ordered the two mini-bots back into action and they instantly went to work with tiny torches cutting the spear of dirty ice away from the canopy. The water particles melted and refroze instantly as they drifted away from the ship's hull.

The two industrious mini-bot torches took ten minutes to finish cutting away the remainder of the ice rock then studiously started welding the jagged crack closed that the ice ball had left in the canopy above Johnny's head. Eric made his way back toward the storage cabinets and retrieved a medical kit then floated back to his station beside Johnny.

"Let Me take a look at that arm and leg," he told Johnny giving him an injection to ease the pain.

Johnny immediately felt relief as the medicine entered his bloodstream and offered his injured arm up for Eric to examine. He continued to monitor the progress of the mini-bots while Eric set the bones and made a temporary braces and slings.

The mini-bots were half way through welding the plate when the radio crackled to life with Christy's distant voice. "We've located you on our radar," the message said. "Our estimated time of arrival is forty three minutes."

"That's a dang good deal," Johnny radioed back. "Our main computers are off line and all we have are our mini thrusters. We should be all right though until you get down here."

"We're on our way," Christy returned. "Glad you're OK. Don't worry. We'll be there. Christy out."

The radio fell silent and the flicker from the torches lit up the area outside the ship. The robots were finished with the weld and slowly circled the lander looking for further damage before locking back to the hull of the ship.

The ships inside pressure rose to normal as the emergency compressor pumped air back into the cabin allowing the two astronauts to remove their EVA beanies. Eric locked the radar onto the mother ship showing the distance between the ships decreasing by the Nemetar.

"It looks like we're going to be OK," Johnny stated. No sooner than he'd finished speaking his monitor lit up with a warning of incoming meteors.

"Oh my goodness," Johnny screamed. "Would you just look at this?"

"Estimated time of arrival three minutes," Eric reported back.

"How many ice balls are coming at us and how's your wet spot?" Johnny's tension rose.

"Looks like a shower of about ten thousand ice rocks ranging in marble size to two meter boulders and yeah I gotta pee bad."

"What the heck are we going to do?"

Johnny looked at Eric as if it was the end of all known. Johnny activated the mini thrusters and the ship struggled against Nemesis gravity to attempt getting out of the way of the fast approaching meteors. Our shields are down to eight percent Eric injected. Johnny struggled with the mental controls to get the crippled lander out of the way. Eric tried furiously to switch backup batteries to the starboard side shields in the direction of the incoming missiles of ice.

"Thirty seconds," Johnny shouted.

Suddenly in the forward view was Thorius command module running ahead of them activating a huge torch of fire toward the ice missiles approaching the crippled lander.

Thorius extended its fully functional shields around Thorius lander and desperately began melting the ice missiles that managed to penetrate the shields and threaten the ships.

The starboard side of the lander was splattered with a wall of hot misty water that resulted from the melting of several ice missiles that would have collided with Thorius lander. The fast moving wall of water struck the lander rocking it as if it were being run through a steaming spaceship wash. When the wall of water had passed the ships field it instantly refroze leaving a black hole imprint of the Lander. The frozen ice ship outline mass fell toward the swirling storms on the Nemesis. Several more walls of water struck the lander and repeated the same refreezing process as before.

"We're only three kilometers above the top of the atmosphere," now Eric reported.

"All that missile pee has caused us to loose more altitude." Johnny retorted. "Look out the window."

The lander had a coat of ice that had frozen to the surface of the ship. Eric complied and saw the fascinating sight that Johnny was referring to. Thorius lander was out of commission temporally but the small lander glistened with colors of the rainbow surrounded by the black light spectrum of the Nemesis. Out ahead was an even more beautiful sight. The Thorius command ship glistened with rainbow ice colors also. In the dark light of the Nemesis all the colors of the rainbow and many more toward the dark end of the spectrum trailed off into the most beautiful colors that one could imagine. From the purple indigo black end of the spectrum came darker more brilliant colors than human's eyes had ever seen before. Johnny had to shut his eyes a moment and shake his head to withdraw from the hypnotic trance the colors had his mind focused on.

Johnny focused his attention back toward Mother Thorius that was still battling with the barrage of ice meteors. Thorius command ship had activated a tractor beam that enveloped the smaller ship a kilometer above the top of the atmosphere. The mother ship flew five kilometers ahead of them gradually decreased the distance as it continued to melt the frozen in coming meteors.

With the activation of the beam the lander instantly started recharging its reserve batteries and the communications system crackled back to life.

Joanna spoke. "Hang in there you guys. The rest of the crew is busy destroying incoming meteors. The two ships will dock in four Nemetar's and twenty seconds."

"Ok," Johnny returned. "We're OK now but it sure will be good to get back aboard Thorius."

"We're glad you guys are OK, and as soon as we get docked I'll set those broken bones and fix you up."

"Eric's already set the bone but I sure could use some of that fixing up and tender loving care you've got."

Joanna laughed and ended the conversation with "I've got to get to the docking controls and bring you in. I Love You too. Joanna out."

The pair of astronauts looked out of their patch welded crystal dome as the mother ship glistened beautifully firing multicolored lasers at the meteor storm that was finally decreasing in intensity. Thorius was about seven hundred meters away growing larger in their view as the bottom of the mother ship was slowly opening up to accommodate the wounded lander.

The lander locked into the bay with a magnetic click and the outer door on Thorius's bottom slid shut thrice faster than it had opened. Pumps began filling the lander bay and the pressure soon equalized when the lander hatch opened. Joanna rushed into the lander happy to see her two favorite astronauts. Hugging Johnny carefully and examining his arm. "I'm all right," Johnny said as he looked deep in her eyes then kissed her long and hard.

"Hey you guys! Save that stuff for later. I'll see you upstairs." Eric's mind was on Christy and the main deck crew.

Eric climbed the ladder poking his head through to the main deck where Christy and the five Plutonians still manned their post firing at the last of the ice missiles that threatened Thorius.

Christy looked up with a smile as she noticed his head poking through the hatch. Eric finished climbing the ladder and they fell into each others arms and kissed. The Plutonians chattered musically in their native voice at the embraced couple. The meteor crisis almost over the Plutonians turned the defense over to the computers and rushed over to great the astronauts as Joanna and Johnny climbed the ladder and entered the main deck.

Thorius was full of jubilation and cheer but the moment was short before Johnny brought the crew together with a command.

"We'll celebrate later. Right now everybody must get to their cubicles while we do still have a ship left above this dreaded Nemesis."

The crew hustled to their stations and fastened their restraints as Johnny and Eric installed their visors. Present Status Johnny Questioned. The ship's vitals filled the screen as the crew reported their station's data.

"Ok," Johnny ordered! "I'm taking us up and getting us the heck and out of here. Hold on crew."

Thorius's engines powered up with a quick oscillation hum of the main power feed. The ship's computers continued to sporadically fire at the now trailing shower of meteors. Thorius one eased away from the Nemesis and gained altitude in a reverse direction spin until it had reached a five hundred kilometer higher stable orbit.

The ship still glistened with a coat of ice on its hull but was in excellent shape considering the battle it won with the star and the ice meteor storm.

Easing into a safer parking orbit, Johnny sang a few words of an ancient Earth ditty sonata.

We swim out in space,
like fish in sea.
To sail to the stars,
is our destiny.
Our home is so far,
across a black sea.
We're safe for the moment,
My good crew and me!)

"We're a bit safer now and can relax a little," Johnny grinned.

The crew burst into chatter as they all joined in singing the ditty and converged into the dining compartment on Thorius and celebrated their mission accomplishments of the Nemesis. They were all jubilant. Their mission had been a tremendous success this time with only minimal damage to the lander and the most important thing this time was there was no loss of life.

The remains of their fallen comrades were safely tucked away in the freezer bay of the damaged lander and they all ate and laughed while discussing about the events of the past few Nemehours.

Shata had established contact with the officials of their world and notified them of their successful mission and the fact that the crew had decided unanimously to take an additional twenty-four hour delay in their return to Pluto.

Johnny ordered a twenty-four hour break for the crew to relax a little and review some of the data of the stones they'd earlier retrieved from the Thimbus moon. A short ceremony entailed in the bay of Thorius Lander for the remains of their fellow astronauts Zxico, Qwerto and Pertravio. Their sarcophagus hung attached to the inside of the lander freezer as the nine bowed their heads in a moment of silence and show of respect.

{sixty Nemetars later)

Johnny shut his eyes and let the warm waters run over his body and thought about the day's exploration of Thimbus and Nemesis. He thought about the red crystal stone they'd found on Thimbus and pondered the possibilities of finding even more new elements.

"After We get a little rest he thought, We'll study that red crystal to see what we can learn. Right now," he thought. "I've got something more important on my mind. Johnny's mind drifted to the beautiful woman that waited for him to finish his shower. He was so lucky he thought. To have a great girl like Joanna to follow him all the way out here to Pluto.

"She must really love me a lot," Johnny thought. "I sure do love her."

Joanna waited as he dried off from his shower and the sight of her beautiful body always stimulated Johnny as if he were seeing it for the very first time. Joanna was so gentle being very careful not to hurt his healing bones. They made passionate love before they fell exhausted asleep with the flicker of the pulsating black star flashing through the porthole window. Eric and Christy slept soundly after repeating their own love making adventure. Eric now exhausted fell into a strange but wonderful deep sleep.

CHAPTER TWENTY NINE
ERIC'S TIME TRAVEL DREAM

He was a small boy again. He could push with his tip toes, draw his elbows in tight to his side and he soared high above the town of his childhood. The gravity bonds of Earth held him no more as he sailed high above the oceans of Earth and landed on a foreign shore to do his exploring.

Suddenly his dream converted to a flow of light speed acceleration through a black ocean and then away from a big blue beautiful marble planet that was falling away behind his destination. Eric traveled at light speed.

"Just imagine," he pondered. 186,282 miles in one earth second of time has elapsed. He orbited the Earth more than seven times in a second. Then shot toward Earth's cratered gray Moon and in only one and a half second he was there. He slowed down to five kilometers per second for a slow orbit of the mysterious hot cold deeply craters almost airless gray Moon.

Slowly he descended to the surface in an ancient place called Tranquility Base. The time was July, 1969 and two brave astronauts Neil Armstrong and Buzz Aldrin walked upon the moon for the first time while their comrade Michel Collins orbited above. A historic occasion indeed. Eric now nineteen years old watched as the two well trained bulky astronauts traversed and bounced with joy in the immediate vicinity of their spider legged lander cocked slightly sideways near the rim of a twenty meter crater.

His light dream took him on to the last visit of the Apollo 17 landing site in a mountainous valley called Tauruus-Littrow in December 1972. By the time Eric had arrived he was a twenty three year old young man watching the last two brave explorers Eugene Cernan and Harrison Schmitt blast away from the moon on December 14th 1972 in their tiny craft.

In the beginning twelve brave men had walked the Earths Moon while their command module pilots remained faithfully in orbit. Then there was the Apollo thirteen mission that thanks to the ingenuity of a well trained NASA crew they barely managed to limp home and survive to tell a brave cold survival adventure. The dedication of the Challenger and Discovery shuttle crews that lost their lives so future generations could explore. All were there with them in spirit. All of a moments time past suddenly relapsing into a different direction.

Eric's dream to the past launched away from the Moon and in four light minutes he'd approached a red rusty planet Mars and again slowed down to a orbit eighty kilometers above the low pressure desert barren land that dwelled the largest mountain in this solar system called Olympus Mons. (Nix Olympica)

His spirit descended down toward the mountains and to the valleys below where the remains of ancient earth robotic machines stood rusted in place on the cold barren rocky surface. He traveled past these earth relics to an even older ancient civilization called Cydonia Mars where the ancient Martians ancestors had long ago departed this once springtime world in frantic terror.

Ejecting from mars at light speed in light minutes he'd already crossed over the asteroid belt that was once the remains of a small five hundred kilometer diameter moon that once orbited Pluto the then fifth planet from the sun. Above the floating herds of fragmented rocks he sailed toward a Humongous gas world called Jupiter. Many moons of all sizes and shapes chased the fast rotating mammoth planet. Yellow gold, orange brilliance filled his view as he stood bathed in Jupiter radiation on a small asteroid two miles across and watched the giant red spot that was eighteen degrees above the equator.

The Jupiter storm was huge compared to Earth and had raged on for well over fifty centuries since the passing of the Nemesis. The cold Jupitercane raged below swirling counter clockwise from the spin of the largest remaining piece of the once fifth planets moon. The two hundred kilometer moon chunk was spiraled into Jupiter spinning furiously and causing a storm that would rage its furry for eons to come.

Eric at light speed accelerated from his perch on the big stone and traveled toward the huge ringed beautiful yellow brown white world of Saturn. In several light minutes he'd arrived and circled the giant many mooned system of glorious Saturn. He perched himself on another small asteroid and viewed the musical dance of the many crystal ice rings and fast orbiting frozen bodies.

The asteroid he stood on orbited the ringed world three times in Saturn's ten and a quarter hour days time as he watched the bobbing dance of the snow rings and many moons that orbited the large fast spinning Saturn.

Thirty five years old now Eric journeyed from Saturn passing the pair of mini voyager crafts that sailed their own historic directions slowly toward another giant blue hydrogen world called Uranus ahead. He sailed around the big cold green world several times and then sailed on toward another large blue gas giant planet further away.

As the kilometers distance ticked away he became older and in a few minutes he'd sailed over Neptune and past to the largest moon. Through all of his journeys he'd watched all of the planets wobble slightly in their axle procession and now this planet Neptune lay almost on its side from the result of the ancient catching of the Nemesis and Pluto as it sailed by very close.

Eric orbited Neptune and looked out toward the edges of the solar system at the far away tiny pair of orbiting purple dark worlds that seemed just out of his reach for the moment. He grew rapidly older as he peered past Quaoar and Sedna and at least fifty more Kuiper belt worlds on the very outside edge of the solar system.

His spirit yearned to travel past Pluto and Charon toward the Kuiper belt objects Quaoar and Sedna. To explore these mysterious worlds he somehow suddenly realized that is was simply not his time and his soul began falling back toward his Earthly body and he fell swiftly silently inward toward the bright yellow class m star that centered all these worlds seen and unseen.

At light speed he regressed inward again past the Jovial worlds and past Mars then on past a pristine beautiful marble Earth. Then he arrived at a hot greenhouse high pressure world called Venus.

Venus the only world in this system that had an almost perfect circular orbit was rotating slowly retrograde from the result of the extreme close passing behind of the Nemesis that reversed the planets poles as it fell close behind Venus.

He then sailed further inward toward the suns closest planet Mercury that luckily was on the far side of its 88 day orbit when the Nemesis rapidly passed.

Eric watched the Nemesis duo plunge near the sun and was slung at great speed toward its eventual encounter with Uranus and then it's capture in this solar system by Neptune the planet that wobbles almost ninety degrees in both directions as it traverses around the yellow sun while presenting opposite poles on opposite sides of its yearly orbit.

Eric's dream took him to within thirty seven-million miles of the sun toward a battered hot gray metallic world called Mercury. He slowed down and looped around Mercury looking down at the hot pools of boiling metal gurgling in the pits of several sun scorched craters.

In a light flash he flew back past Venus and toward the big beautiful marble Earth and slowed down to a gyrosyncronous orbit between the glorious planet of life and the dead gray airless moon. Suddenly Eric realized He was not a young man anymore and he was now seventy years old. He capped his hand to his ear and listened in on the communications taking place on Earth below. The year was late February two thousand and one. Thirty two years since Aldrin Armstrong and Collins had made that historical first giant leap for Mankind. Earth had struggled for thirty-six years trying to heal the wars of mans past. President, George W. Bush Jr. had taken office and was making an announcement of great importance to the world. This

Nation must make a firm commitment toward revitalizing our manned space program. In the years ahead I intend to lead this Nation and it's future generations in a commitment to return to the moon and then on to colonize Planet Mars by the year two thousand twenty nine.

In this worthy quest we have reached a unanimous agreement with fellow participating nations of Earth to modify the International space station. With appropriate modifications, space station Alpha will become a stepping stone in space to study physics and launch brave humans to the outer planets. We must make this commitment now to enable the future generations the proper tools to meet these grand challenges. The young adults that occupy our classrooms today will be the ones who colonize Mars. It is to these children and their children's children that will someday visit many worlds and discover many valuable new elements that will revolutionize humankind's destiny.

I George W. Bush make this commitment to the revitalization of space research and dedicate its name Project Challenge in honor of the Challenger and Columbia crew and all others that so bravely gave their lives so that humankind could evolve and prosper while exploring. His historic speech ended with, As a great President Named John F. Kennedy once said. We do this not because it is easy, But we do this because it is hard.

With all the empty political words spoken, It was President Donald Trump that finally got humankind back to the Moon in 2024.

Eric descended backward from the void of space into his conscience awakening state next to the beautiful Christy whom was the distant descendant of Neil Armstrong the first human to walk on the moon. He kissed her gently on the forehead taking care not to awake her from her Cinderella sleep.

CHAPTER THIRTY

THE FASCINATING DISCOVERIES INSIDE THE NIMBUS STONE

Eric met Johnny coming out of his quarters and they grinned at each other and quietly headed toward the galley where Johnny already had bacon and eggs on his mind. They greeted the five Plutonians chatted briefly about the ships status and excused themselves toward the galley. Eric sipped his coffee and in a few minutes the smell of bacon and eggs filled the galley of the ship. Johnny popped a pan of fresh biscuits out of the microwave and the two men sat down to their hearty breakfast and gave thanks Twelve hours had passed since they were rescued above the Nemesis. They began eating as Johnny started the conversation.

"We've come a long way and it's still a long way back home."

"Yeah," Eric said. "You and I sure do go back a long ways together before this mission began."

"Hey Eric, Remember our old college days?"

"You were seventeen years old when I first met you and I was thirty years old and had already been thrown out by two wives while I was trying to get a little education and experience." Eric snorted.

" Remember that time we went fishing and got lost at Kerr Lake?"

"Oh shucks man. We weren't lost. I was just testing you to see if you could survive in the wild outdoors."

"Well If that's true, Why did we have to be rescued from Buggs Island?"

The two laughed and reminisced about their younger days before Eric turned the conversation toward a more immediate tone.

"I'm about ready to get down to the lander bay and check out that red crystal stone that Joanna discovered on Thimbus."

"Me too!" Johnny replied as they hurriedly finished eating and headed toward the laboratory bay where the containment box was stored.

"We'd better engage a force field around us and set it on a small dispersion field of high energy particle protection," Johnny said.

"OK, "Eric made the adjustments and they both put on their excursion beanies. "There!" Eric replied. "That should protect us from a nuclear explosion."

He laughed as Johnny placed the box on the table. Gravity on board was set at ten percent Earth gravity. The Plutonians fragileness couldn't withstand much more than that for long.

"On Earth that box would weigh over two hundred pounds," Johnny said. "Sure is nice to be able to regulate gravity without spinning the ship."

"What do you mean?" Eric comically asked. "The bottom of the ship is always spinning." The two laughed again as Eric grabbed the tongs and Johnny opened the Thimbus moon sample box.

A red ruby glow filled the laboratory as the lid bounced slowly in the low gravity and then came to a stop. They stood back engaging eye shields and stared into the mysterious glow of the red Nimbus stone. Eric eased forward with the tongs and plucked the glowing rock from the box of other Thimbus stones. He eased toward the table and placed the stone on a pedestal perch. Johnny activated the inside mini-bot and the robot they'd named Zulu zoomed into action buzzing around the pedestal clicking and chattering steadily as it began assimilated data facts.

Zulu extended its probe sensors touching the Thimbus jewel and clicked rapidly as it began consuming large amounts of information.

"Zulu sure is working hard," Johnny noted. "It should have finished analyzing that rock by now."

The saucerbot continued to make contact with the red stone clicking even faster now as massive amounts of data flowed through the probe that touched the stone.

Johnny became concerned for the mini-bot as it clicked faster and faster.

"Its filling up its data banks."

Johnny adjusted its computer bandwidth to allow more room for the fast flowing data stream. Finally after twenty-five minutes of fast data recording the little mini-bot almost exhausted withdrew its probe and settled for a minute on the floor as it recuperated from a very strenuous task. After a Nemetar of recharging its power source the robot flew to its place beside the main computer and plugged into it's receiving port for further uploading of the data. Zulu frantically clicked its data into the main onboard computer. Thanks to Thorius's advanced technology it only took two minutes to upload. The mini-bot dumped the information and zoomed back for another twenty-five minute analysis of the ruby stone from Thimbus.

Johnny and Eric began analyzing the first batch of data while Zulu continued another analysis of this mystifying seven sided double triangular stone.

"Tryoxis, is what we'll call it," Johnny said, as they started reading the data that was the first of twenty-seven more uploads from the mini-bot yet to come.

"Man this is absolutely incredible," Johnny emphatically stated.

The two stared hypnotized into the spectral analysis of a single atom of Tryoxis. Johnny looked over at Eric and shook his head in disbelief at what the first data was indicating. "Eric, this is absolutely revolutionary. A discovery of such a significant magnitude that it's hard to describe."

Eric was speechless also. He knew Johnny was right and just shook his head right back saying nothing as the data kept assimilating. The new data filled Thorius's computer screen.

"There are a several million pages of data after that on this single disk," Eric shook his head. "Then twenty-seven more uploads from Zulu yet to come."

"Yeah that's going to make about twenty million pages of data."

"This is going to revolutionize science as we now know it. Look at these amazing statistics on the new data."

Eric started reading some of the facts of the properties of the Thimbus stone.

"To begin with it's exactly three point fourteen inches in diameter and its habit has seven sides while every point on its surface is exactly three point fourteen inches from every other point. It contains more than seven thousand new elements and combinations of matter that makes existing science seem like cavemen's perspective in comparison. He continued. There are several kinds of new atoms that are unexplainable in that, there nucleus revolves around the positive charged electron with a negative charged proton that orbit's the nucleus also. There are many more particles in orbit around the electrons and protons that are too tiny and numerous to state."

"Man I just can't believe this. It seems impossible," Johnny scratched his head as he looked at Eric with disbelief. "There's another whole universe in that incredible Tryoxis Gem."

Johnny was reading the second upload batch as he began to realize the significance of this fantastic find. The computer screen projected galaxies upon galaxies concentrating their revolution around a deep red inferred center of brilliance.

"How could anything such as this exist? How can it contain a whole universe of large galaxies?"

Eric looked at Johnny with complete astonishment before asking his third and fourth questions.

"Have we discovered a Holy Grail of Science? Are there sentient life forms that exist in that miniature universe?" "Yes to all of those things and more. It would seem that we have indeed discovered great knowledge that will take decades to decipher and unlock all of the mysteries."

Johnny increased the magnification around a single yellow star near the edge of one galaxy and focused in on a miniature Earthlike planet.

The blue planet revolved around its sun every thirty seconds and wobbled slightly as it progressed around the star. He increased the magnification more and a blue green white brown world filled the view screen. Eric was astonished as he watched the miniature movie of the planets thirty second yearly circle around its star.

"Unbelievable," Eric said.

The blue world revolved so fast that you can't quite make out the surface features. Eric programmed the numbers to slow the recorder down to five hundred times slower than normal.

The planet stopped its fast revolve and spin and now rolled slowly around its star.

"Look!" Eric exclaimed. "Now I can see four more planets between the blue planet and the star."

"Yeah," Johnny said. "There are six Jovian planets outside also. That makes a total of eleven worlds circling that star."

"There are billions upon billions of other stars with numerous planets in orbit around them are all inside this fantastic Thimbus Stone. And We thought the Nemesis stones were a big find."

"They were, Johnny replied, "but compared to this discovery one is a lit match and the Thimbus Stone is nuclear fusion. This certainly is the most significant find of the twenty-third century. Wait until both our civilizations hear about this Tryoxis Jewel. It will take centuries to decipher all the data from the Tryoxis."

Johnny excitedly opened the mike to the seven on the main deck and they could tell by the two's excitement that something fantastic had happened.

"You guys are going to have to slow down a little," Joanna interrupted.

Both Eric and Johnny were exuberant with talk as they both tried to explain the discovery to the crew.

"Joanna, send out another message of ((Eureka}} to Pluto and Mars base. This fantastic discover we call the Tryoxis Stone will keep both of our cultures scientists delighted for centuries."

"You've got to be exaggerating," Quota shook his small gray head. "How can a rock contain a universe? Is that possible?"

Eric was the first to answer.

"We don't know how. We just know that it does."

Johnny projected the view of the blue planet to the main deck and for the first time the other seven viewed the fantastic solar system that orbited a yellow star inside a tiny space inside the Tryoxis Stone.

The Plutonians alien musical chatter filled the main deck as they began analyzing the fantastic amount of data that Johnny and Eric had been reviewing.

Instantly the data was transferred to Pluto and from there onto a more powerful transmitter in orbit pointed at Mars and in a few hours the Message of Eureka and the Rosette Tryoxis Stone would be relayed to their own beautiful blue white world Planet Earth.

Johnny and Eric entered the main deck of Thorius and found the crew hard at work and deeply entranced in the data that was still being radioed to Pluto Command.

"OK," Johnny questioned. "What's our current status?"

"We'll have the remainder of Tryoxis data transmitted in fifteen minutes," Joanna reported

Phalo reported, "The tremendous data we've read so far is only one trillionth of the actual data in the Tryoxis Stone. The rest will have to be done back at Ultropolis." Quota resumed the report. "We're presently in a slow orbit one thousand, three hundred kilometers above the Nemesis." Serdia chimed in "Ships overall status is excellent. There is an unusual amount of strange radiation coming from the remains stored in the cargo bay freezer."

Latilia ordered "Shata, You and I will have to go down to the cargo bay and see if we can determine the cause of the radiation."

"If it's all right, I'll come with you," Christy said

Shata and Latilia agreed.

"Alright," Johnny spoke up, "but keep your radio links open so that we can monitor your progress."

CHAPTER THIRTY ONE
THE DEITIES REWARD

The three astronauts headed toward the ladder that took them to the lower deck of Thorius. Christy followed the Plutonians down the tunnel corridor to the freezer storage compartment. Shata scanned the freezer compartment with his tricorder device. There are unusual high beta gamma rays coming from within the three storage sarcophagus containers.

The three engaged containment fields as the radiation level began increasing by the second. It would seem that the three bodies are drawing some sort of mysterious power from the vicinity of the Nemesis. Latilia, Christy and Shata stood before the freezers now in a trance from the increasing vibration of the scanner device.`

The chamber suddenly glowed in an eerie green light that seemed to alarm the three yet instantly calmed them at the same time. Christy stood between Latilia and Shata trying to activate her communication link but she was unable to make her body obey the commands of her mind. Shata and Latilia stood paralyzed also as the eerie light seemed to further relieve their anxiety and they settled into calmness when the presence of the entity appeared.

Christy could hear Johnny's voice frantically calling to her and the two Plutonians as it echoed off into nothingness. The expanse of time seemed to drift away as Christy realized that Johnny's voice no longer was calling her. She realized also that the whole crew of twelve including Qwerto, Pertravio, and Zxico now stood in a circle in the chamber of the freezers.

Majestically in the center of the mesmerized group appeared the deity from the Nemesis. The walls of Thorius fell away from them as their surrounding changed from the storage bay to a beautiful pristine world teeming with colored mist and lavish running water. The mesmerized two culture dozen stood on top of a gorgeous flat plateau that rested high on top of giant cone shaped mountain with the tip flattened out. Babbling brooks and a sweet songs of exotic birds filled the air and a beautiful world of sunshine flowers and lavish fruit trees surrounded the circle of twelve with the deity still occupying the center.

The beautiful glowing Deity now motioned toward the sky and in an instant the whole vastness of time fell silent as they stood in the beautiful Gardens of the Deity on a heavenly Planet embellished with the sunshine of a golden huge from the two smaller golden suns.

The twelve were not able to distinguish form in the Deity but the visual experience was one that words or thoughts were incapable of describing. Now the silence of the frozen moments ended as the Deity spoke to the representatives of both cultures.

"You twelve of two different humanoid cultures, in whom I am well pleased, have been brought to this Planet billions of light years away from where you were. I have returned to you the lives of the three who bravely rescued you in appreciation for the love that you have shown toward each other."

" Oh yea of humanoid form , Let these things be known to you in which you are about to be apprised of a few wonders of the Vast Multiverses."

The Omnipotent voice fell silent again as the sweetness of the fresh air filled their nostrils. His mesmerizing facial eyes focused on the group of twelve now bidding his parabolic words.

"You my daughters and sons have the red blood of my essence in your veins. So are such corpuscles that are so vital to your human blood also are the vital elements in stars and galaxies that fill the many Multiverses."

"There is always life upon life to the grandest scale down to the sub atomic level of atoms. Many Universe's exist and many dark matter worlds such as the one your ship now orbits are the main energy corpuscles that enrich the fabric of space itself. This is why you are forbidden from exploring these Nemesis bodies scattered through the vast universe. These dark energy corpuscle worlds are susceptible to infection by contact with you and any other species throughout the Universe. All that both cultures have become is due to a long process of cooperation and endurance by evolving to this point of shared existence."

As quickly as the Deity appeared, It now disappeared from the center of the stunned dozen. They now stood on top of a great mountain and the waters and time began to flow again as the gentle sounds of the Planet returned to their ears. One last echoing message from Deity resonated through the air as the Eden planet returned to normal.

"For eight hours the twelve of you will be allowed visitation to this docile peaceful place that is the most beautiful and fascinating of all my known worlds."

The peaceful voice of the Deity trailed off into nothingness as the enlightened group found themselves in a most magical mystical world. A place like no other imaginable beckoned their exploration of the mysteries of this world many light years from Earth on a planet the Deity referred to as East of Eden.

CHAPTER THIRTY TWO

EAST OF EDEN

The dozen double culture group stood atop the flat plateau forest among the lavish wildlife and cool running waters. The soil beneath their feet was of the consistency of astro turf neatly trimmed and stretching as far as the eye could see slopping gently down to the beautiful valleys below. The two golden suns circled each other over head as they orbited each other every two minutes constantly changing the hew as the early morning on this fantastic planet Eden had just begun.

They traversed the slope to the valleys below pausing here and there to admire some exotic trees and plant life growing wild on the long slope of Eden Mountain. The four Earthlings and the eight Plutonians chattered happily and separated into two groups as the two teams approached the valley floor. They agreed to meet back together here at the foot of Mt. Eden in seven hours. Then wished each other luck and each culture followed a separate path away from the East side of Mt. Eden.

The four Earthlings paused for a moment before entering the alien forest ahead.

"Wow," Eric exclaimed. "This is the most beautiful place ever imaginable. No words in any language could ever do justice to describing the beauty of this world."

The running waters falling down the gentle slopes of the mountain that split apart into two separate streams leading into the fruit laden forests ahead. The Plutonians had taken the path to the right and The

Earthlings strolled into the forest alongside of the branch that lead to the left.

Sparkling waters the color of crimson yellow gold gurgled around the colored stones in the stream. Flying birdlike animals inhabited the air and vegetation as the four Earthlings walked along beside the golden river. Johnny led the group as they made their way through the thickening alien forest.

A peculiar sound was heard from the distance and Johnny lead the group forward through the misty forest of alien plants and lavish exotic trees. The two small revolving suns through the trees beamed their rotating amber colored brilliance through small spaces in the thick alien canopy above. Eric brought up the rear of the single file astronauts and ahead of him were Christy and then Joanna. Eric checked his watch as he struggled a little keeping up with his younger peers. It seemed like they had been walking through this forest for at least an hour but he was shocked to realize factually that only two minutes had passed since they had departed from The Plutonian group and only twenty-two minutes had passed since they'd departed the mountain top. This was amazing. He thought suddenly realizing that time on this planet was an extended version of earth seconds to earth minutes. Meaning that one minute of their actual time took only one second on Eden. Meaning also that in total they would have 20 Earth days to explore this fantastic Planet Eden.

It seemed so absolutely obvious to him at this very moment that suddenly the same facts occurred to all the visitors to Eden at the same precise moment. This mental link about time difference was known to all as they became aware of what the Earthlings and the Plutonians each were experiencing. The Plutonians across the river were seeing what the Earthlings were seeing and visa versa.

Eric and the others realized that they had been traveling over 22 hours in real time and had covered a vast distance in what seemed like twenty-two Eden minutes.

Johnny paused the group in a gorgeous clearing beside the babbling stream and they began discussing how they would camp realizing that the planet had rotated until the twin stars were starting to approach Eden's dusk.

"I think we should make camp right here for tonight." Their attentions focused toward the east where an even more mystical destination lay just out of sight toward the growing darkness.

The four began assembling their provided gear and in a few Eden moments they'd set up their tents and camping equipment. They began gathering what looked like alien scrap wood in a pile in the center of their campsite. The twelve campers on Eden had an Eden minute or Earth hour before nightfall and the two separate groups started to prepare their campsites lighting a fire for warmth and campfire cooking.

Johnny and Eric went hunting in the forest to find cooking game while the girls tended the campfire. The chattering faded away as the two instinctively made their way toward a clearing along a path that led to another small clearing in the now dusk light of Eden.

Johnny and Eric stood quietly at the edge of a clearing and peered through the shrubbery watching creatures the size of a rabbit grazing in the open. Instinctively they knew these little varmints would taste excellent cooked on an open fire.

The pair brandished their palm weapons and each aimed toward a different spot in the clearing occupied by a dozen of the alien critters. They simultaneously fired a beam toward their target and each shot three critters while the remainder scurried away into the forest brush. They retrieved their bounty and laughed about the weird shape of the alien creatures they deliberately named Grubs. The round Grubs had small fury tails and were plump with meat. Grubs had a tiny one-eyed head and their pelts were soft brown fur. They made their way back toward camp as the suns now started the finale process of dusk on Planet Eden.

The two stepped through to the campsite clearing to find the two girls already cooking exotic vegetables they'd harvested from the surrounding territory. The sweetness permeated the air and the aroma filled their nostrils. "Mmmmm! Aunt Bea!" Johnny said as he smelled the tantalizing brew. "That stuff sure smells tasty. Eric and I will have our Grubs skinned and mounted in a few minutes. Then you'll smell something tasty indeed."

The two picked a spot near the fire and started skinning the six alien critters. They washed the meat in golden waters and mounted the plump alien Eden grubs to the grill rotating above a bristling campfire.

They sat around the campfire as the two suns fell below the horizon in the west and in a few Eden seconds the grubs were well done.

The animals and foul of the forest had settled down to a murmur as night fell on the two groups of astronauts.

Johnny not being able to resist any longer removed one of the grub from one of the rotisserie prongs and slid it off onto his plate along with some exotic vegetables of the forest. Cutting off a piece with his laser pocket knife he sniffed the meat that revealed a delicious odor of steak meat on Earth. He slowly blew on the hot meat and placed a good size chunk of the grub into his mouth chewing slowly savoring the delicious taste.

"Wow!" Johnny exclaimed. "This is the best stuff I've ever tasted."

He bit hungrily into the grub meat and the others followed suit seeing how much he was enjoying the grub.

"Oh yeah!" Eric said, devouring some of the grub and sampling the wonderful vegetables that the girls had prepared. "This is the best dang food I've ever tasted too."

The girls joined in on the feast and marveled at how delicious the alien food was. After a few minutes of enjoying the feast everyone started realizing the stimulating effect that had come over their being. Suddenly, they were taken to another magical mystical enlightening environment. Before Christy realized the stimulation she found herself nibbling Eric's neck and blowing sensuously in his ear. Eric held Christy ever so gently and kissed her passionately until the two broke their long kiss and made their way toward the privacy of their campsite tent.

Joanna and Johnny were also embraced in passionate lustfulness and they didn't even notice that the other two were missing. The Plutonians at the second campsite were also experiencing similar exotic passions and ultra high enlightenment.

Christy and Eric floated in each others arms inside the privacy of their portable space tent. Shivers and chills ran up her spine as she experienced satisfaction to the extent that she now embraced in a passionate romance dance with Eric doing things to her she'd never imagined possible. She suddenly started returning his attentions and caused Eric to moan loudly as she enticed him with exotic teasing and lustful passionate kisses.

The teasing and ultimate climax intensifies by the moment but they realized the time difference and continued their passionate romance for another three Eden minutes. It all ceased with exhaustion after the passionate moment of conception of the miracle baby to be later christened Eric Armstrong Alley. They fell exhausted into a peaceful restful existence in each others arms.

Their first early dawn on Eden began with a golden glimmer of frosted light toward the eastern almost straight lined horizon. Johnny and Eric were the first to awaken and exit their tents on this Planet called Eden. Johnny relit the campfire that had dwindled down to hot ashes smoldering in the early morning hours. Eric gathered up more scrap fire wood and brush and soon they had a brisk campfire burning again.

The girls were up and about now as the four gathered around the morning fire sipping the juice that came from the exotic looking coconuts on this world. They all laughed and reminisced about there past voyages and discussed their soon to be homeward journey back to Mars base.

Many hours passed on the wonderful planet Eden and after many days of exploring and camping on the finale morning they packed up gear and walked back toward the rendezvous point to meet with their Plutonian Comrades.

Experiences they shared on Eden brought a new sense of optimism to the Earth crew. They'd all needed this time of rest and relaxation to bring into focus all the fantastic events and discoveries they had made. Every moment since their departure from Mars base was full of excitement and adventure. They returned that last morning to the meeting place while their friends the Plutonians were just approaching the edge of the wonderful colored forest on Eden.

The group of twelve astronauts greeted each other again and the moment they stood arranged in a full circle they were instantaneously transported back aboard Thorius One.

The sleek quick ship Thorius sailed inward looping a final lap around behind the dark sun before heading in the direction of Pluto. The Nemesis grew larger as Thorius pushed them swiftly around the black star then looped outward toward Pluto.

In a time span of thirty Nemetar's, they were entering the hazy atmosphere and settling down at Ultropolis airfield. Thorius sat steaming and exhausting vapors into the purple Pluto twilight of daybreak. A Large delegation of Plutonians made their way toward the black green ship. Their journey had been extremely successful. The three that had died in sacrifice were now alive and home again. They had seen many new things and had been many places that no humanoid souls had ever been before. The fantastic discoveries would keep both worlds busy for decades to come.

A new connection of super fast laser light wave was connected between worlds and information now flowed at a superluminal fast rate of speed. The immediate days after the journey were full of excitement and great expectations.

The newly reengineered Nova sat ready on the launch pad awaiting the upcoming departure of the four Earthlings that had been Earths delegation to the new found allegiance of friends. The enlightenment of mysteries of the past Nemesis that had settled into this orbit eons ago was now solved.

Many eons had passed and the two alien cultures had met on this once fifth Planet we call Pluto around Charon the infamous Nemesis. The long ago threatening Nemesis that almost destroyed both civilizations was a super compressed high gravity black light cold fusion star of fantastic new elements and rare minerals.

A Super compressed cold core mini star with a density of forty-two at its surface. So compressed the rare minerals and new elements created there had turned this small planetoid into a black light sun that Pluto now orbits on the edge of our solar system in it's highly eccentric orbital plane.

CHAPTER THIRTY THREE
THE JOURNEY HOME

The longest Plutonian night ensued as the four Earthlings spent their last night on Planet Pluto. All the good-byes had been said in the preceding times and the four awoke to an early morning purple twilight on this alien marble jewel that was now the home of the descendants of the former Cydonians of ancient times.

Johnny and Eric sat at the table feasting on morning delicacies while Joanna and Christy packed their bags for their departure approximately six hours away. After a fantastic morning breakfast the four sat around the table and reminisced their past days since they'd arrived here. Then Christy feebly spoke up and the mood of the room changed to a more somber environment.

"Eric I have a surprise for You," Christy looked across at him with a sly gleam in her beautiful brown eyes.

"What?" Eric Looked at her in a curious, concerned way. "Well," Christy replied. "I think I'm pregnant."

Eric's jaw fell open as the look of surprise over took his concerned look.

The two embraced in each others arms as Eric kissed then hugged her tightly.

"Awe Honey, that's fantastic."

He danced a little jig as Christy giggled about his excitement. Then Eric stopped and thought a moment about the nine-month trip back to Mars base.

He scratched his head slightly and asked, "How long have you known and how far are you along?"

"About a month," Christy replied. "It happened that night on Eden."

"Wow!" Eric exclaimed. "That means our baby will be born a month out from Mars base."

"This will be the first human child ever conceived this far out in space," Joanna spoke up.

"Yep That's right," Johnny said. "Dang ole Man, I really didn't think you had it in you. I guess you proved me wrong."

Johnny laughed and poked Eric in the arm.

"Yeah, right," Eric answered. "There's a whole lot this ole man has that still might surprise you." Laughter broke out among the four.

They celebrated the remaining hours away until the chime sounded announcing the arrival of the Plutonian escort party that would take them to the launch pad. The crew took one last look around at the Plutonian apartment then climbed aboard the Trailapod that waited just outside in the early dawn of a slow purple Plutonian Nemesis Sunrise.

Thousands of cheering Plutonians lined the roped boundaries to the walkway that led toward the newly renovated Nova Ship. The beautiful early twilight glistened around the Earth Ship Nova as the crew approached the end of the red carpet that was blocked by the Plutonian King Rominus and his staff.

The crowds cheers subsided as the alien king rose his four fingered hand in a gesture toward the crowd. A short calmness ensued as he paused a moment in reflection before finally speaking. The crowd grew quiet. In a divine moment of silence Rominus began his speech.

"Let it be written of this moment in time for our two different cultures, that we shared the great knowledge of both the ancient Cydonians and all that had and will be learned in the future of the Nemesis Chronicles. He paused another moment in reflection then continued. These brave four that depart from Ultropolis and all humans of Earth, from this day forth are forever our new found friends."

"If not for their great courage and the ability of humans to survive heavier gravity and radiation, the great discoveries of the Nemesis Chronicles would never have been known. Therefore we of Pluto honor them greatly as they leave us now to return home."

"I King Rominus hereby proclaim this to be a great day that will live through infamy as we bid our five Earth friends farewell. May their journey home be completely safe and prosperous he proclaimed. And may our two civilizations become even greater friends in future times."

The clatter of alien applause grew steadily louder as The King ended his farewell proclamation and cut the silver thin thallium ribbon that opened the gateway toward the beautiful Nova Ship in the middle of a fenced in airfield. Christy, Joanna, Eric, then Johnny stepped into the elevator hatch and for the last time the four turned and waved to the thousands of Plutonians still cheering and slapping their short armed hands.

Johnny took one last look and breath of the sweet Plutonian air and closed the newly designed hatch to the elevator that started a slow ascent up the sides of the newly painted red white and blue Nova Ship. Higher they rose over the crowd of alien spectators that were there to witness the impending launch of the Earthlings.

At the top entry hatch to Nova, Johnny couldn't help but notice a concerned peculiar look on Eric's face. The hatch door to Nova opened as the two girls headed inside the ship Johnny closed the door behind them and asked. "What is it Eric? Is something bothering you? Tell me what's on your mind."

"I don't know Eric replied. Something just doesn't seem right here."

They gazed out the clear window of the elevator at thousands of Plutonians in silence a moment before Johnny spoke.

"Yeah, I think I know what you mean. A few things seem peculiar to me also. Did you notice that back at the ribbon ceremony Rominus and his immediate staff were there but We didn't see any of the other Plutonians we shared our mission with? I wonder Why."

"I don't know Eric answered. You'd think they would certainly want to be here."

"Yes, That does seem peculiar," Johnny replied.

"Something just doesn't seem right about all this. I mean, Well I don't know exactly what I mean," Eric struggled with his words.

"Yeah, You're probably right," Johnny interrupted. "Anyway, Let's you and I just keep our suspicions to ourselves and we'll give Nova a thorough systems check before liftoff."

"There's no need to upset the girls unless we find evidence," Eric replied. "That is of course unless something obvious turns up."

"Agreed then."

Johnny patted Eric on his shoulder and again opened the hatch and boarded Nova.

Eric took one long last look at the breathtaking view of the Pluto environment then stared down at the crowd of scattering little gray aliens. He'd been here before. Possibly in a dream he thought to himself.

I know that seems impossible but somehow I sense that the essence of my atoms have experienced this moment in the fabric of the time-space continuum before.

Eric was the last to board Nova as the automatic locks began engaging and the pressure started equalizing. A gut feeling told him that this was a unique moment to always be treasured. They were going home.

Johnny had Joanna and Christy performing checks on all of Nova's computer systems while Eric worked below checking out Nova's newly designed parts that the Plutonians had helped to install. He'd checked every fitting on all the fuel connectors and every single one was at torque specification. He'd removed all the lower panels checking computer mother board connections then meticulously checked the status of Nova's nuclear hydrogen fuel and oxygen supply. After several exhausting hours Eric had found nothing out of the ordinary and proceeded up the ladder to the main deck.

"Everything seems to check out perfect," Eric reported as he mounted his station. "I've thoroughly been through all the systems below and inspected everything I could possibly think of."

"Excellent my friend!" Johnny replied.

"I've performed a thorough virus scan on all three main computers and Nova has a green light and is Go for lift off, "Joanna reported

"Ok Then!" Johnny retorted. "Let's post lift off time for one hour while we final systems check to make sure everything is up to standards and communicating properly."

For the next forty five minutes the crew worked diligently calling out calibrations and systems checks to each other.

"Ten minutes until launch!" Johnny ordered everyone to their to their stations and the countdown began.

Nova was a newly designed vessel now. The Plutonians had incorporated the new Thorius drive system into Nova and that system would be Nova's main propulsion within a million kilometers of the Nemesis.

"Alright," Johnny called out above the chatter. "Lets pull this team together! We need to get precisely organized and ready. Three minutes until liftoff," he warned.

Silence filled the cockpit for the next Nemetar's while the crew sat strapped in. Johnny used a moment to reflect on the past adventures and took one last look around at the alien launch complex. They'd traveled a long way he thought. They'd been through some fantastic experiences. It had been almost an Earth year since they'd arrived.

They crew sat perched atop Nova within a few seconds of lifting off from Pluto. Earth was well over fifty astronomical units inward toward a bright yellow hydrogen helium star. The solar star was visible through the forward port in the early Pluto twilight. From this vantage point the sun was yellow and ten times brighter than Venus appears from Earth.

"Thirty seconds," Christy reported, snapping Johnny back from reminiscing and instantly into reality.

The red digital display clicked past seven as Nova's Thorius drive began whirring to life. At two seconds the latches released and Nova achieved buoyancy then began a slow ascent over Ultropolis in the black light of a twilight dawn. Gradually gaining altitude and velocity Nova climbed away from Pluto falling eastward toward the Nemesis sunrise.

G forces are increasing to one point seven Earth gravity Eric reported over the pulsed whir of Nova's thorium drive. Joanna leaned forward to check on Christy who seemed to be bearing the stress of the gravity well.

"Are you ok girl?"

"Yeah Christy laughed a little. Me and little Eric are doing just fine."

She laughed again rubbing her belly a little and winking at Eric as he grinned back at her.

"Alright." Johnny yelled. "Stay sharp. We still have about two minutes before we reach orbit."

"Roger that." They agreed and set to their task of monitoring Nova's ascending progress.

Suddenly without warning there was an explosion and Nova's nuclear hydrogen engines engaged as the four were fiercely thrust back into their seats with sudden extreme G forces.

"What the heck's going on here?" Johnny bellowed above the roar as Nova shook and vibrated.

Smoke began pouring from a control panel and sparks shot past Johnny's face as he struggled and tried to disengage Nova's powerful chemical hydrogen nuclear engines.

"Speed, one hundred fifty-three kilometers per second and climbing," Joanna screamed out above the engine roar.

Eric unbuckled his belt, fell out of his seat and slid heavily toward the rear Of Nova's cockpit and hit the floor with a thud as Nova's four main rocket engines expressed violently.

"Speed, one hundred eighty-one k.p.s and still climbing," Joanna yelled above the infernal engine roar.

"We've gotta get those hydrogen engines shut down," Johnny yelled down to Eric, who by now had the panel off the main wiring harness and had taken out his pocket knife and began cutting a main command connection to Nova's fire hot engines.

A shock knocked his arm away when he cut through the main command wire and Nova's blazing hydrogen engines feel silent.

Johnny quickly shut down all main breakers. The cockpit was full of smoke settling to an eerie silence. Eric glided back toward the forward cabin.

"Backup power's coming on line and the baby and I are fine," Christy reported.

"Is everybody else alright? Report your status," Johnny ordered in the smoke filled cabin. "What's our speed and course?"

"Speed, two hundred thirteen kilometers per second. Course. We're headed straight for a collision course with the Nemesis. Arrival time, one minute, six seconds," Joanna reported.

"We've gotta get some serious controllable engines online quick," Johnny ordered. "At the speed we're traveling, the Thorium drive won't be enough to cause us to miss the Nemesis."

Eric hastily crimped Novas main command wire back together as Johnny vectored Nova's hydrogen engines toward the fast approaching black Charon.

"Twenty-eight seconds until impact." Joanna's nervous face looked back at Christy to check her status.

"I'm doing fine," Christy said, looking back at Eric struggling with a welding arc and trying to get Nova's hydrogen engines back online.

Suddenly with a powerful flash the engines roared to life again and the abrupt force threw Eric against the wire grill.

"Alright," Johnny yelled. "We've got controllable hydrogen engines as a huge bead of sweat exited his brow and fell backwards."

The engines fell silent after pushing the falling Nova and crew barely past the leading edge of the Dark Nemesis whose strong gravity grabbed the ship and slung it hard into the darkness of outer space and Pluto and the Nemesis fell away silently.

"Ok,' Johnny said in a moment of stress relief. "We've been ejected out into deep space. We need to get Nova back under precise control. I need damage and status reports ASAP. Let's find out what happened."

The two worlds were now only fading specks in the distance. The purple strobe disappeared suddenly into nothingness as Nova drifted spinning out of control but safe for the moment in the black void of unknown cold space.

The crew was trying desperately to regain control of an obliviously sabotaged desperate ship. Eric and Johnny struggled with the hydrogen mini thrusters trying to bring the, out of control ship into a stable unknown destination drift.

"There! That's about got it," Johnny said looking over at Eric who had a trickle of blood running out of the corner of his mouth. "Is everybody alright? What the heck were those aliens trying to do to us? Somebody down there had a hidden Trojan virus in our computer and tried to kill us. We were rocketed within sixty-three kilometers of the Nemesis and then were slung into who knows where by the sling shot effect."

Christy floated forward and began wiping the small amount of blood off of Eric's face.

"How are you doing, baby?" Eric asked rubbing her belly as she leaned across to get another tissue.

She laughed a little and said. "We're fine now that the ship is under control. Something told me those Plutonians were not on the level," she said while shaking her head.

"Yeah," Joanna spoke up. "We've been thrown on some crazy outward course that takes us way past the outer edge of the solar system and we're still headed away from the solar system two hundred thirteen kilometers for every second that goes by."

"Ship's status?" Johnny questioned bringing the focus back on Nova and it's momentary desperate condition. "How are the engines and the remaining fuel status?" he asked looking over at Joanna and her console.

"Hydrogen fuel's down to fifty-eight percent and we're now well over a half astronomical unit past Pluto's orbit and on a highly elliptical path that will reach its apogee in five Earth years." Christy reported in.

"Main computers are offline due to all the overloaded breakers. We should be able to repair them in a few hours with a little luck."

"Ok," Eric spoke up. "We're venting hydrogen fuel into space at a rate of a half liter per second."

"We'd better get suited up and get outside to make repairs before all our fuel is gone." Johnny ordered.

The two floated toward the back of the cabin and in a few minutes were in the airlock and soon along side the ruptured fuel line that spewed frozen hydrogen crystals into the void of outer space. Johnny skillfully cold welded a sleeve around the ruptured line and in twenty minutes they were heading back aboard Nova.

Inside the airlock they privately discussed their status situation while Joanna and Christy attempted to bring the main computers back on line. The Crew worked diligently for the next four hours repairing the ship. Nova drifted extremely far from their home world. With no Communications and navigation abilities these four brave souls were at the mercy of their wits and the ships remaining sustenance of life. They had enough oxygen, water and food remaining to survive for a year before perishing. After six hours of ship repairs the timeline brings them to the point of firing Nova's main engines and putting them back on a proper course inward.

There had been no time for sleep and the exhausted crew now readied the ship for the three hour continuous firing of the engines that was required to correct their run away orbit.

Johnny gave the order to bring the computers back online. Nova's display screen lit up with digital lights on the control console.

"The main engines will require a three hour and six minute burn," Eric said. "Just past half way through the firing we should reach our apogee and begin to head back inward towards our sun."

Eric flipped the breaker bringing Nova's engines to ready status and Johnny placed his right hand on the ignition breaker.

"Thirty seconds," Eric relayed.

The cabin grew quiet as the numbers drifted toward zero. The rumble was immediate as Nova began to tremble and roar a half second after Johnny engaged the engines. All four mains firing nominal Christy reported. Gravity forces pushed them back into their seats as the ship strained against the force of the outward sling they had received from the escape vector of the Nemesis Star.

Suddenly a warning alarm occurred that was barely audible over the rumble of the engines.

"There's an anomaly on the forward radar," Eric said, leaning forward against the two gravity strain.

"What is it now?" Johnny inquired anxiously.

"Looks like a volley of ice chunks in the Kuiper belt," Eric replied. "But we're above it in our trajectory. Were gonna glide over the top of them."

"Bring the aft camera online," Johnny ordered.

Joanna activated the video. Novas view screen lit up with a beautiful sparkling ice crystal belt of particles showing on the monitor.

"Wow!" they all exclaimed together.

"Would You look at that." Christy was the first to comment.

"It's beautiful," Joanna exclaimed. Eric and Johnny just sat and marveled at the beauty of the many colored ice crystal belt that Nova sailed thousands of kilometers above while burning it's engines in the attempt to save their lives and get them headed toward home.

"That's one beautiful ice belt," Eric stated. "There are ice crystals down there as big as mountains and all different shapes and sizes too. Bringing the rear radar online," Eric reported.

An alarm sounded and immediately projected the video of the dreaded anomaly. The visual divulged a huge black hole in the center of the screen. Nova ship strained against the, growing by the moment, stress of the heavy gravity pulling them from behind.

Johnny yelled above the roar. "I'm gonna have to bring the engines up to full throttle or we're gonna be sucked into that thing."

He reached forward against the strain of four gravities and grasped the handle and slid the throttle control all the way toward himself. Nova's mighty engines came to life with twice the fiery glory. The walls of the ship began to creak and pop under the stress of the tremendous forces that tugged at the fighting for survival lost ship.

"We're reaching apogee in one minute if the engines can just hold out," Eric bellowed above the thundering roar. Seven Gee forces and the crew blacked out as Nova kept up its fiery struggle with the black hole way past the edge of the solar system.

Eric opened his eyes to a silent cabin as he regained consciousness first and saw the screen display reading course correction complete. Remaining Hydrogen fuel thirteen percent. Systems Nominal. Mars base distance is fifty one A U's.

Johnny shortly regained consciousness and began reading the data status. Eric floated free checking on the girls now also coming back from the blackout.

"Are you alright honey?" He asked Christy as she opened her eyes.

He kissed her on the forehead and hugged her gently.

"I'm alright," she stated. "Just a little woozy that's all."

Joanna now taking in the present scene spoke up. "We've made it. We've escaped from the black hole she cried with joy."

"Yep," Johnny said, "and in two hundred ninety-six days we'll be at Mars base. Ole Nova sure came through for us. We should have just enough fuel to retro fire when we reach Jupiter in a little more than six and a half months from now."

"The recorder reads that Nova fought against the black hole for three hours after we all lost consciousness. We've been unconscious for almost twelve hours. Man!" Johnny exclaimed. "That was a close call. If we had waited another minute before engaging full throttle we couldn't have escaped from that black hole before Nova would have ran out of fuel."

The next few days the crew were busy repairing damage to Nova and getting ready for a six-month cryogenic sleep. They still had not regained communication with Mars base but they had improvised by sending out ahead a radio beacon projectile satellite that should arrive near Mars base in four months announcing their situation and arrival time of nine and a half months from their present stardate.

Christy's sleep chamber was specially calibrated for the required nurturing of the growing fetus and the crew now adjourned to their final goodnights before they all enter the suspended animation chamber.

Eric was the cryogenics officer of this mission and he sealed Johnny in his chamber and engaged it as Johnny grinned at him through the glass Tektronix shield. In seconds Johnny closed his eyes and went into a peaceful restful sleep.

Eric floated gracefully through the silent cabin and final checked the ships status one more time before programming and sending ahead another messenger satellite as backup just in case the first one failed to arrive at Mars base.

He watched the projectile fire ahead of the ship out of sight falling faster inward toward the bright solar star. Half way between his position and the sun Jupiter was but an orange globe that was easily visible to the left of the sun. As he squinted at the orange world and visualized the red spot he thought out load.

"That's our destination. We should pass five million miles behind Jupiter and use its gravity to boost us toward Mars base with one major course correction after we wake up from the cryogenic sleep."

Eric took a few moments to reflect as he watched the final message buoy disappeared out of sight ahead.

"Imagine," he thought to himself. "All the adventures we've been on. All we've learned. The Plutonians whom had betrayed them over the Tryoxis stone and tried to destroy them after they claimed they were their friends. Well anyway," Eric thought. "For now they were all safe."

They'd survived through great perils of danger. Home was where they were headed.

"And the baby," he smiled as he thought. "Imagine that. At my age of fifty-six. I'm gonna be a daddy again."

He grinned ear to ear as the chamber closed around him and sleeping gas filled his compartment.

"Thank You! God." He whispered in the silence of the sleeping crew then closed his eyes.

Dreams unfolded and the four drifted peacefully in sleep while Nova's mini-bot monitored their survival and counted the days until their awakening. Six uneventful months later Nova's sleeping crew had traversed the blackness and a glorious Jupiter system loomed in the forward monitor.

Fifteen minutes away from awakening, Eric's chamber deactivated first and in a few seconds the canopy retracts and he floated free into zero gravity. He sleepily floated forward ascertaining that everything appeared to be in order and they were as planned presently five days away from passing behind Jupiter.

"Wow," He exclaimed to himself. "The Jupiter system is like a miniature solar system of its own."

He engaged the opening valves to the ships fuel scoops and even at this distance of twenty million miles from Jupiter, hydrogen molecules were present and the ships extended scoops began sucking in the particles to replenish Nova's fuel supply.

Eric deactivated. Johnny's capsule first then quickly floated to free the girls from their deep sleep. "Everything's perfect," Eric reported as Johnny first floated free.

The girls yawned as their canopy opened and Eric floated over to Christy and held her. The four gathered their senses and Johnny, after hugging and kissing, Joanna immediately floated forward to his command chair.

"Yeee haaaaa!" Johnny yelled out sleepily, from the forward cabin. "That sure is one humongous system rotating out there."

He pondered on a bit as the others floated forward to view the immaculate giant Jupiter system spinning in the blackness of space. Sixty-three moons showed up on the opaque radar gracefully sailing around the solar giant in different vectors. The orangewood western edge revealed twelve, twenty to fifty kilometer asteroid bodies on the same orbital plane as the Giant Red Spot.

Johnny thought to himself. These were the facts that twenty second century knowledge hadn't revealed to Astronomy. That these twelve asteroid bodies were the remains of the once fifth planet Pluto's moon. According to the mass structure remaining in the Red spot orbital plane trajectory, the once Pluto moon was approximately five hundred kilometers in diameter and only one third of that mass remained in the orbital twelve bodies. That meant that two thirds of that mass impacted Jupiter at a high spin velocity causing the Red hurricane storm that rages on until this very day.

Now the present brings the crew around the galley nook just behind the four command chairs in the cockpit.

"There's fifty hours before our trajectory firing," Johnny said chewing on his morning protein pop tart and sipping on some warm coffee.

"Yep," Eric returned. "As long as the critical burn goes alright we'll be on the final vector of our journey home." "Yeah," Joanna chirped up. "So we must be sure to make that quick right turn after we pass Jupiter not before."

They burst into laughter.

Eric put his hand on Christy's tummy and the fetus kicked his hand as if to say, "hey daddy! I'm playing in here."

He grinned at Christy, kissed her lips then gently hugged her again.

"Hey baby," he whispered. "Unless things have changed since we've left Mars. Our child will be the first baby conceived and born on a journey in space."

Christy kissed him teasingly and said. "That's right ole man. I guess You must have gotten it right huh?"

She winked then floated forward toward her station looking back to see his reaction. Eric felt a little guilty about having sexual thoughts but, "oh my," He thought. "She is even more beautiful pregnant."

He quickly finished his morning snack and joined the others on the main command deck.

"What's up?" Johnny said as Eric floated into his copilot seat and started the task of checking configurations. "What's our status?"

Eric returned quickly. "We're exactly forty-seven hours and three minutes, thirty three seconds from our retro burn. The scoops already have been able to replenish our hydrogen fuel supply back up to twenty-one percent and will be at twenty-nine percent status just before we fire the engines for the final loop vector home."

"Cool," Johnny replied. "I hope mars base has received at least one of our probes and know that we're coming home."

"Wow," Christy exclaimed. "Would You just look at Jupiter's moons circling that enormous orange yellow brown and white Planet."

"Yep," Joanna spoke up. "It sure is something to see Callisto, Ganymede, Europa, and Io from this distance. They certainly are beautiful moons indeed."

"Yep, they sure are," Eric replied. "We're now approximately seven million miles distance. That's over twenty-eight times as far as our moon is from Earth. That's certainly a giant system indeed."

Johnny laughed. "Yeah! Check this out! You could easily fit two of our Earths into the center of the giant red hurricane."

"Man, You're right. That sure is a vision that is hard to explain with words," Christy spoke up with excitement. "Look at that," she exclaimed.

Suddenly Callisto the cracked frozen white moon entered around Jupiter's edge followed seconds later by Europa with it's frozen ice caps. Then Icy Ganymede followed as the smaller but more violent hot Io puffed its mushroom red billows of volcanic ash into its own hazy atmosphere.

The four Galilean satellites were discovered in the year sixteen ten by Galileo Galilei.(1564 1642).

Dozens of other smaller worlds immediately chased the four larger worlds as Jupiter turned swiftly completing half of a revolution in only four point nine hours.

The days pass and the time line brings the crew to the point of firing the final transmars burn that would assure them of getting home.

"Fuel supply, twenty-nine percent as projected," Eric reported. "Liquid oxygen supply at a little over thirty-three percent. That's as good as it gets," Eric quipped.

"I hear You," Johnny replied. "Alright girls, give me some trajectory readings as I proceed and get ready. Main engine firing in 50 seconds."

Christy reported in. "Our speed is in excess of nine hundred ninety-eight thousand kilometers per hour. That's about twenty-eight kilometers every second. We're gaining momentum fast."

"I hear you," Johnny replied. "I intend on slowing us down around a curve. Hang on to your wet spots," he shouted. "We're gonna experience about six Gee's again in our slowing down loop."

Joanna counted down. "Three, Two, One."

"Engines purged." Eric said, as Johnny threw the breaker to explode a thunderous sound of Nova's four main engines.

The four chairs spun around and locked into position as the gravity began to thrust them back into their padded console chairs.

"We have four good engines burning,' Eric reported. Johnny grabbed the controls and sailed Nova backwards along the projected radar tract that was displayed for all to see. "Atta Boy, Johnny!" Eric said. "Follow that curve man," as he strained to talk in the intense gravity. "Speed down to six hundred ninety thousand kilometers per hour, nineteen point one k.p.s and dropping. We're in the curve of the heaviest Gee forces."

Johnny fired the side thrusters to push Nova around the arc as the main four engines thundered passing over the largest hurricane in the solar system.

"We're seven point two million kilometers above Jupiter's atmosphere," Eric said, as they sailed on and the engines thundered as Nova fought against the great forces of their momentum and Jupiter's massive gravity sling.

"Speed's down to seventeen k.p.s," Christy quoted.

Johnny clutched the steering rocket control and with his other hand on the main throttle he increased power to speed Nova up along the slingshot curve.

"Gee forces still at maximum," Eric spoke above the strain and the roar. "Five point nine Gee's right now."

He struggled to turn and check the girls status but was quickly overcome by the gravity forces.

"We're ok," Christy's voice came through the headphone speakers.

"Fuel down to eight percent," Joanna reported. "Present speed now increasing along the curve to nineteen K.P.S and gaining at the rate of one quarter kilometer per second." "Main engine shutdown in fifty seconds," Johnny relayed. "Looks good so far,' Eric replied. "Right down the trajectory."

The rumbling decreased the last thirty seconds as Nova now in Jupiter's gravity slingshot began to relax against the receding gravity forces.

Johnny threw the breaker and Nova's battle with Jupiter was over. The silence was immediate as the fire disappeared from Nova's main engines.

They sailed away from the Jupiter system moving swiftly now at twenty-nine kilometers per second.

"Not Bad Eh?" Johnny and Eric slapped hands in celebration.

"Yep," Eric quipped back. "And that's just enough speed to let us escape Jupiter's massive gravity well. We still have about seven billion, four hundred million miles to go to Mars base though. It seems our sabotage and close encounter with the black hole has delayed our arrival time by almost a month more."

A detection alarm began filling the cabin. Long range detectors are picking up two extremely distant blips on the radar screen.

"They must have gotten our probe message," Johnny spoke up. "What's their distance?" he asked.

"One moment while I calculate,' Eric replied. "They're way out there. Seems those two ships are about a month out of Mars base and are heading toward us."

"Try the radio." Johnny ordered. "Focus the forward antenna ahead of us and try full power on the transmitter. Lets see if we can contact them."

Eric modulated the controls and brought the antenna on line as Johnny grabbed for the mike and waited for his ok. "Almost ready," Eric said. "But remember this. Once You key the microphone, It's going to take about thirty-three minutes for our signal to reach them. Then thirty-three more minutes before we receive a reply. So we're looking at about an hour before it's possible to know if they hear you. Ok Your microphone's hot," Eric nodded as he brought the wattage on the antenna up to its maximum.

Johnny's excited messages began.

"This is Johnny Wilkins and Crew of the U.S.S. Nova exploration Vessel. We've broken free of Jupiter's gravity and have five aboard safe. Our Hydrogen fuel supply is down to six percent and all five of us are alive and well. Remaining oxygen is sufficient to sustain us unless an unforeseen situation should arise to changes that. We are temporarily ok. Anxiously Awaiting Your reply. U.S.S. Nova Out."

The two girls slapped hands in celebration as Johnny unkeyed the microphone and for the first time since the ordeal of the black hole they finally realized that they had a good chance of making it back home to Mars base and then on to Earth.

The four hugged in celebration. They knew that they were still months out from Mars base but if those were ships headed their way, they'd be seeing humans again. The crew was anxious to find out what their rescuers knew about Plutonians and what would be the politician's reaction to the suspected sabotage of Nova and their betrayal that they had earlier radioed ahead about in the forward satellite beacons. But first they had to be sure contact was established.

Thirty minutes after the message was sent the crew broke open a bottle of Mars red champagne that they'd stored away just for this moment. Johnny had put Nova in a spin and for the first time in quite a while they had gravity on board Nova.

"Here's to our return from the Nemesis," Johnny raised his glass in a toast, turning the tubular flask up in one gulp devouring the rum red misty ale.

The others followed suit and toasted the occasion. Yep Our message should be arriving right about now Eric spoke up after drinking his toast of success.

"We're not out of the woods yet though," Christy jested with her ale. "But Me and this baby sure are glad that we're a lot closer and help is possibly on the way."

Joanna giggled from the tickly bubbles she'd received from the ale mist and said.

"Girl You're going to be the envy of every woman on Earth and Mars. You're going to be the first to conceive and give birth on a space mission. And you got knocked up on Eden too." She laughed again saying "Dang girl. That little boy child right there will go down in the history of humankind."

"A toast to the baby then," Eric filled their flask again. "So what shall we name him honey?" Eric asked looking over at Christy and grinning.

"I don't know yet," Christy toasted back. "But I think I'll let you decide that, baby." She kissed him softly and waited for his response.

"Well," Eric replied after a long moment of thought. "I have given this some thought. I think that we should name the child Eric Armstrong Alley. After Your great, great, great grandfather Neil Armstrong and Me."

"So be it then baby." She kissed his lips and smiled.

The crew laughed away the minutes after becoming somewhat inebriated while anticipating an answer to their message. A faint crackle of static began to grow louder and in the distance a voice was heard almost lost in the static sound. The same instant they all became quiet listening deeper to the garbled faint reply.

" Ahoy U.S.S. Nova Crew . This is Admiral Jack Kepler Of The U. S. S. Research Vessel Challenger Seven, along with Admiral Richard Dunn Captain of the U. S. S. Tranquility cargo supply vessel. Welcome back from the edge of the solar system." You could hear a faint crowd of happy celebrating voices in the background as Admiral Kepler paused in his reply.

"We have you on our long range radar and have set our course to intercept with yours in fifty days. We have a total crew of twenty-three. We have launched ahead a relay buoy that should allow our communication to get better by the hour. Welcome home Nova crew! Admiral Kepler out."

The messaged crackled and broke off suddenly disappearing into the silent darkness ahead. Silently they sat waiting to see if the static voice of Admiral Kepler would continue.

"Oh well," Johnny said. "That relay buoy must be a long ways out there. But at least we know now that they'll be here. That's a month before Christy gives birth to Little Eric too."

The empty darkness ahead showed Mars a tiny red speck with planet Earth a further blue green dot in the distant background.

Behind them giant Jupiter had released its gravity hold as Nova sailed far away from Jupiter's icy white moon Callisto. The cracked frozen moon in the ship's rear view screen fell toward Jupiter in its orbit. Gradually it receding away as they watched Jupiter's whole lunar system dance their orbits around the Giant of all Planets.

"We've made it," Came the celebrated laughter inside Nova.

"Yeee Haw!," Eric did his cowboy imitation.

For the first time in a long while they knew that help was on the way and in weeks they would meet with them. Then only another month and a half back to Mars base. As long as everything went as planned, Christy's baby would be born a month out of Mars base. Supplies were low but as long as nothing unexpected occurred they'd all be just fine.

Nova twenty fours hours later had settled into a more leisurely environment. The ship was in a slow spin to induce light gravity while coasting into the darkness. The crew settled down to the task of conserving Nova's remaining life sustaining elements. They'd slept for six months. Morale was high and the mellow sounds of Eric playing a classical guitar filled Nova's cabin.

The Crew of Nova had truly been where no humans had been before. Their bravery was the catalyst of many great discoveries. If not for their exploration the Plutonians and the Nemesis would still remain a secret.

Since their departure from Pluto not even a whisper of communication was heard from the mysterious aliens. Little did the far away explorers know but Mars base and all of Earth were in an uproar over the recent events of the attempted sabotage. Not one single message had been communicated between the Plutonians and humans since their departure.

Earths and Mars defenses were at full capacity considering all that had recently happened. The next few days aboard Nova passed mostly uneventful until twenty-three days before rendezvous. Nova and the rescue team grew closer by the hour and return communication on world events and their status were exchanged in five minute messages every six hours. Christy's pregnancy was going well and the low gravity on board Nova made it easy for the crew to get around.

It was presently twenty-three days before rendezvous with rescue ships. Morning aboard Nova had begun routinely as the smell of coffee and pastries filled the air. The four gathered around the table sleepily eating breakfast and barely speaking.

Suddenly a loud defense buzzer alarmed that sent the four sailing toward Nova's cockpit in a hurry. Johnny sailed into his control chair and the others followed close behind. "What is it now?" Johnny questioned, as the buzzer grew steadily louder.

"We've got numerous incoming targets straight ahead," Eric reported while bringing long range radar online. "We've got thousands of incoming objects. Looks a lot like a huge meteor storm to me," Eric yelled above the buzzer. "They're headed straight toward us at eighty-three kilometers per second. They're two minutes out and approaching fast," Eric reported.

Johnny reached over and brought Nova's main engines online and Nova roared to life.

"We're going to attempt going over that storm," Johnny said taking immediate action. "Hold On!" He yelled.

He quickly keyed the course and angled Nova outward toward the edge of the fast approaching rock storm. Nova's four main engines thundered pushing Nova outward as the storm approached swiftly on the port side.

"Contact with the edge of the storm in twenty-three seconds," Joanna reported.

Pings of small rocks could be heard hitting the hull. "Fuel supply's down to four percent," Christy reported. "We'd better save what little fuel we have left."

Johnny Shut Nova's Engines down and the pings grew louder as larger rocks began bashing the ship. Rock chunks were battering Nova as it passed close to the outer edge of the violent storm. Nova rocked and jerked as the ship engaged the full force of the outer gaseous edge of the storm.

"We'd all better get suited up," Eric shouted above the noise of the colliding ice chunks.

The four hurried to the cargo locker and as the ship shook and rocked from the storm they all hurriedly got into their suits. The ship rocked harder now from the blows of larger meteors.

The crew had just finished pressurizing their suits when suddenly an explosion occurred in Nova's lower cargo bay. The blow was so intense the crew was thrown to the floor and knocked unconscious from the concussion blow to Nova and loss of atmosphere occurred instantly.

Their suited bodies floated freely in the un pressurized Nova. The ship appeared lifeless as it rolled slowly end over end off course and lost in unknown space.

Eric awoke and felt the trickle of warm blood over his right eye. His head and leg was throbbing with pain as he opened his eyes to the blurred vision of the other three unconscious astronauts floating freely around the dark interior of Nova's upper cargo room. The escaping air from his suit was the only sound he could hear. He became aware of the coldness around his right leg. The pain was so intense. Blindly he labored to accomplished a task of extreme heroism.

Then the pain ceased and the coldness enveloped his soul as he closed his eyes and drifted off into a forever unconsciousness. Eric drifted in a deep sleep among white misty clouds. His eyes opened momentarily to a misty welcome environment. Far away voices in the distance seemed to be calling his name. No more pain, just totally peaceful calmness and white tunnel mist toward the bright light. Voices grew louder as he floated toward the direction of Christy's voice.

His momentary vision of her beautiful face slowly came into focus as he regained consciousness. She kissed him gently on the lips and asked as he opened his eyes.

"Are You alright baby?"

The words echoed inside Eric's mind as Christy asked again. "Can You hear me baby? Are You alright?"

Still unable to speak, Eric managed to smile a little at the recognition of her face. He mumbled softly.

"Yeah Baby. I'll be alright."

He now became aware of the presence of Joanna and Johnny floating into the room.

Eric looked into Christy's eyes and said. "Are you alright? How's the baby?" He looked down at her now almost due condition.

"The baby's fine." She kissed him again on his forehead. "I'm fine too."

Eric starting to recall the events of the storm now looked over at Johnny and asked.

'What happened man? Where are We? We're aboard Number one Lander." Johnny began. "Nova's Main ship and Lander two were destroyed by impacts with large ice asteroids. The ships video tape shows you pulling us into Lander one with air escaping from your suit around your right leg. Eric," Johnny looked him square in the eyes. "We had to amputate your right leg to save you man."

A tear rolled down from Johnny's eyes as he hesitated saying the words. "I'm so sorry man. We were going to lose you. We had to do it."

Eric for the first time looked down in disbelief now realizing the truth of Johnny's words.

"You saved our lives," Johnny busted out in tears. "You somehow managed to get us aboard Lander one and detached from the wreckage of Nova. You've been unconscious now for days. Joanna has a broken wrist and Christy and I had a few scrapes and bruises too but basically for the moment we're alright. The baby seems fine. We're dangerously low on supplies and nothing yet has been heard from the rescue ships. Fuel supply is down to a little over four percent. All our consumables are dangerously low also. We're way off course and it seems unless we hear from the rescue ship in twenty days, We'll all die out here in space."

Johnny paused, giving Eric a moment to take all the bad news in.

Tears ran down Eric's his cheeks now as he looked down at his right nub wrapped in a bandage.

The three gathered around Eric as Johnny began slowly again.

"Our total status is critical. The situation is like this," Johnny began. "It would seem that we have but two choices here. We have approximately twenty days of vital consumables left. We have just a little over four percent Hydrogen fuel left in Lander's tanks. One option is to take the remaining hydrogen and convert it into consumables and the other is to make one more course correction and hope those rescue ships find us before the consumables are depleted. The Lander's backup batteries are already dangerously low. There's barely enough power to run the radar or communications."

Johnny looked Eric in the eyes and continued. "We're in pretty bad shape here man. We've got to do something and make a decision fast. I know you're hurt bad. We've got work to do if we're going to get out of this situation and It requires a quick response. But heck," Johnny said as he now grinned at Eric and cracked a smile. "You and I fought the king beast of the Nemesis. We'll pull through all of this somehow."

Eric grinned back through the pain and reached down and unbuckled the restraint then floated free. "Let's get to work then Boy." He patted Johnny on the back and glided away toward the cockpit saying, "If we can kick a dinosaurs butt on the Nemesis, We're not going to let a little thing like being lost in space stop us. We've been too far to give up now."

Eric sailed into the co pilot chair and Johnny followed close behind.

"So, what do You think?" Johnny asked Eric.

"What should We do? We have twenty days air left now but if we transpose the fuel We'll have about thirty-nine days left."

Eric scratched his head and pondered before answering. "Shucks," Eric replied. "I say we have to turn this bucket towards home. If we change our vector the rescue ships stand a better chance of finding us.

We could possibly use three percent of the fuel for a correction burn and save the one percent for consumables giving us a few more than twenty days. At least we'd be drifting inward toward the sun in the right direction."

Their eyes met as they turned and asked the girls for their opinion. Christy and Joanna looked at each other a moment then Christy spoke first.

"I agree," she said. "Let's head for home."

"Me too," Joanna spoke up. "I'd rather we die trying to get home than die way out here past the asteroid belt." Johnny and Eric's eyes met again as they now realized it was unanimous. They all sat strapped into Nova's cockpit with one last attempt to turn the ship inward toward home.

"My best estimate is that we're about twenty million kilometers outside the asteroid belt," Eric reported. "If we focus our vector perfectly, we should be able to sail over the belt and make to a vicinity that the rescue ships should be searching for us."

"Ok then," Johnny agreed. "Then lets get the program configured."

Eric began his calculation into Nova Landers main c.p.u. "Ok," Eric reported. "I've got it figured down to the millisecond on the burn. I've checked my math six times now and the computer and I keep coming up with the exact same equation for the burn."

"That's a good deal," Johnny stated. "Lets get it programmed into the computer and get this show on the road."

Christy already had the final data entered.

"That should give us a three minute burn in 60 seconds after my mark. Mark," she injected.

The red digital counter activated and clicked backwards from sixty seconds.

"Here We go," Johnny held up his hand, and the others all grasped hands in salute. "Here's to Nova landers last burn," Johnny broke the shake and the timer clicked to zero.

Nova Landers engines spat fire and rumbled to life gradually pushing the ship inward toward the bright star Sol. The longest three minutes endured as the rumble vibrated and echoed through the ship. Twenty seconds to shut down Joanna reported. Slight gravity was felt on board as the engines continued their final feeble push.

Then suddenly silence engulfed the Lander as the engines fell silent.

"Fuel status one point three percent remaining," Joanna reported.

"That should allow us eight extra days of air to breath. In twenty-eight days if the rescue ship doesn't arrive we're dead." Christy stated in a small flat voice.

"Well," Eric said exhausted but trying to conceal his sickness. "At least now we're drifting toward Mars."

"Ok," Johnny ordered. "Joanna, You and Eric get down to the lower deck and get the hydrogen converter engaged. We'll convert one per cent and save the small balance for making emergency mini thruster burns."

Eric kissed Christy on the forehead as he floated free and blindly followed Joanna toward the back. The pain in his missing leg was something he was having to deal with. He tried not to show it but phantom pains were throbbing and hurting just as if the leg were still there.

Joanna began getting the hoses out and hooking them into the fuel tanks.

"You take it easy a minute she said. I'll get this hooked up."

"I'll be alright," Eric replied.

They concentrated on the task at hand and in a few minutes the pumps were pumping hydrogen into fuel cells to be converted to oxygen and water for consumables.

Suddenly sweat began popping from Eric's face as he watched the volatile fuel trickle through. The pain was throbbing so intensely in his missing leg as he closed his eyes and started to drift into unconsciousness.

He was alone now. In and out of a state of being like none he'd ever experienced. One moment He stood on top of a baseball mound in his youth and the next moment he was sailing swiftly across the galaxy to some unknown mysterious land. His consciousness in this state had brought him to a place of giant rushing waters. The tiny rock he stood on was surrounded on all sides by the falling thundering water and as he looked up to follow the source of falling liquid he saw the miracle of the black spectrum against a dark blue sky. He suddenly realized that the falling liquid was not water at all but was a much finer consistency and texture. The black violet rainbow got its power from the falling liquids source at the very top of the far away beginning of his dream. Eric slowly ascended the column toward the source of all power.

Eric had died. He'd never get to know his little boy or return to Earth. But something told his spiritual existence that the power of the light would make everything alright. So he crossed over to begin a new even more fascinating journey.

It had been three days since the correction burn and Nova lander glided slowly but gracefully over the asteroid belt.

The three gathered on the flight deck to hold the last rights and say a final good-bye to Eric.

"He was an explorer." Johnny tearfully said as he saluted the body of his friend.

Christy's tears were streaming out of her eyes as Johnny closed the sarcophagus and glided it into the narrow escape chamber.

"Good-bye ole friend," he said. Rest in peace now. You go and explore my friend.

The hatch unsealed and the outside door slid open as the sarcophagus floated slowly out of the bay and ever so gradually moved away from the drifting Lander. The crew watched still in shock and disbelief as the tiny box sailed into the darkness and disappeared above the asteroid belt. "We'll never forget him," Johnny said as Christy wept openly.

"But I'll miss him so much," her cry's echoed. "I'll always love him."

"We all will Christy. He was one hell of a Man." Joanna said with tearful eyes.

Christy felt so numb and alone now. Here inside the edge of the asteroid belt she felt the baby inside her move and kick as if to remind her there was hope. She was less than three weeks away from giving birth. The ship's oxygen would run out in three weeks unless the rescue ship found them. If they conserved they had twenty-five days of consumables left. Nova Lander coasted silently like a ghost ship through the dark void powered down to conserve life support. The lander looked cold and dark as it rolled aimlessly away from the chunks of icy rocks that orbit between Jupiter and Mars.

Johnny awoke from a dream sitting in his command chair aboard the Nova Lander.

"This is all that was left of the Nova Pluto expedition,"

Johnny thought to himself.

The stars ahead just didn't seem to shine as bright as they once had. He'd lost his longtime buddy and the psychological effect was beginning to take hold of his being. Alone He sat thinking and reminiscing the times they'd spent together since their early friendship days.

Johnny thought back to the first time they'd met in physics class. There Eric stood, running his mouth and laughing to some college girls and joking about the position of Mars having to do with conception.

Eric was twenty seven then and Johnny was only seventeen years old. It was the first time He'd laid eyes on this man who was to become such a great friend and important part of his life.

Johnny stepped forward seeing the older man there talking and laughing with the two girls. He remembered Eric's first words as he looked away from the pretty girls and saw him for the first time.

"What's Up Dude?" He then remembered his reply. "Lots of space dude." Their very first laugh and the beginning of a long true friendship began.

Johnny chuckled to himself remembering the older man that at first had been like a father he'd never had.

"You're the reason we're still here my friend." He whispered the words out softly alone. "If you hadn't gotten us into the Lander, none of us would be alive. I'm gonna miss you so much my ole friend."

Nova Lander drifted on slowly through the void. It's consumables dangerously low. The crippled Lander was down to three days life support and awoke to the crackle of static and a far away voice calling the names of U.S.S. Nova crew. Johnny awoke and floated forward adjusting the frequency as he floated down in his chair. He heard broken words fade in and out catching only parts of an urgent transmission. He fine-tuned the receiver and listen close to the far away message that was now barely audible.

"U.S.S. Nova Lander we have located you on long range radar. This is Rescue Command ship Exodus. Do You read us? Can You reply?"

The distant voice faded out as the crackle returned to the speakers. Johnny responded.

"Yes We hear You. Our situation is desperate and consumables are dangerously low. We lost second Commander Eric Alley over three weeks ago. Our remaining oxygen supply is a little over seventy hours. What is your present status? Do You have an exact fix on our position? Please respond." Johnny released the mike button and listened intensely. Static filled his headphones as he sat waiting patiently for the reply knowing full well that the longer it took for them to reply meant the farther away they were.

It seemed like an eternity before the voice finally returned to his headphones.

"Yes U.S.S. Nova Lander, We read you and understand the urgency of your situation. U.S.S. Exodus is proceeding at full throttle toward your drifting location. We should arrive your location in about sixty-nine hours. We will be there. Remain calm and conserve consumables as much as possible. Help is on the way. Admiral Decker of the U.S.S. Exodus over and out."

A cheer broke out among the three. Help was almost here and all they had to do now was move slowly and conserve oxygen until Exodus arrived.

Johnny knew that the girls had been frightened up until this point. The look of hope now came back to their eyes as the three embraced in celebration.

Suddenly Christy doubled over with pain almost screaming. "I think it's time she cried. Little Eric doesn't seem to want to wait for the rescue ship. He's coming now."

She yelled out a cry as the second pain hit her way harder than the first. Christy strapped now to the medical table aboard Nova Lander bit down on the object Joanna inserted in her mouth.

"Push Honey Push!" she encouraged as beads of perspiration flowed from Christy's body.

Christy remembered the pain being so intense and the presence of Johnny and Joanna in the cubicle with her was far from her mind now as she thought about Eric.

"This one's for you Baby."

She reached down to the depths of her soul and drew from all the strength she ever had and gave one final surge of power to her abdomen pushing with all her might. She momentarily passed out with the relief of the passage of the baby through her birth canal.

She was exhausted and the slap of bare skin startled her back as there was a pause and then the cries of a baby filled the smaller ship.

"He's absolutely adorable," Joanna exclaimed.

Johnny grinned from ear to ear at the resemblance of the little child to his deceased friend.

"Wow!" He said. "Look at little Eric. He sure is something alright."

He made little baby noises as the baby trembled from the warm sponge bath Joanna was giving it.

Joanna gently wrapped the baby in a warm blanket and cautiously floated the baby toward the mothers outstretched arms. She clutched the tiny newborn gently to her breast and it immediately began to suckle his first meal.

"Your Father Eric Paul Alley named You, Eric Armstrong Alley," she told the newborn. "He was a great explorer indeed. I concur."

She kissed him softly on his head as he suckled his first meal.

"Yep! That's little Eric alright," Johnny's voice said with forced smile tear in his eye. Joanna kissed the baby's head.

Christy's exhausted smile was evident as she softly closed her eyes saying. I know Eric can see him. She slept soundly with baby safely in her arms.

EPILOGUE

A thud and a clank awakened her as the rescue ship latched onto the Lander and began the depressurizing between the hatches. They were home free. They'd been rescued with just barely enough consumables left to survive. Christy and the crew of four again breathed the fresh oxygen being pumped into Nova Lander. With the swinging open of the hatch rescue had arrived and the remaining three and little Eric Armstrong Alley were now in the capable hands of the U.S.S. Exodus rescue crew.

They'd somehow survived. They'd been the first humans to make contact with an extraterestal race since ancient times. Not one scientist would have admitted that aliens had once lived on Mars and now resided on what use to be the fifth planet in this system of worlds. They'd been to the edge of the solar system and discovered the mini dark Nemesis that now sustained the Plutonians.

Communication with the Plutonians society was totally silent. Not even a hint of an intelligent radio signal was heard from the Plutonians again. They had the Trioxis stone. Whatever reason they had for breaking a treaty of trust was not known. Until this very day no one knows whether Nova's sabotage was done by the Plutonians as a whole or whether it had been done by a rebellious individual or group. But for now the Plutonians were covering up the truth with silence. Hidden by the black light of their companion star.

Possibly as the atomic clocked ticked, Earth and Mars base were contemplating the possibility of a surprise attack from them. Whatever reason they had for their actions a determined response was now in the hands of politicians to decide.

They were almost home. A good ship and a good crew had combined their efforts to go to the edge of the unknown system and explore. Somehow like the steadiness and sureness of the passage of time. Johnny felt sure now looking down at the child's innocent face, that possible Little Eric Armstrong Alley just might be the one to make a return trip some day to Pluto and it's black small Nemesis Star.

They, the Ancient Cydonian civilization, that built the pyramids. Not for tombs, as the world had always been led to believe, but as fall out shelters to protect their ancient ancestors and earth dwellers of the day, eons ago when the passing Nemesis caused extreme havoc and catastrophe in this very solar system.

Eons later in our present day the planets of our system still wobble on their axis in an ancient memory dance of this dark mysterious Nemesis.

ABOUT THE AUTHOR

Full Name, Donald Eric Wilkins But ! I have always gone by Eric Wilkins my entire life and I always will.

Born, 1157 pm December 24, 1950

Henderson N. C.

Loved Astronomy from early age.

Lived many years on this Fantastic Spaceship Earth.

My Bucket List is almost full and I will soon go on to explore the Universe.

The Earth is moving toward Leo at the dizzying speed of 390 kilometers a second. That's a little over 242 miles per second.

You're on it too. God speed !

www.ingramcontent.com/pod-product-compliance
Lightning Source LLC
Chambersburg PA
CBHW031215260626
47169CB00007B/2071